The Leftover Woman

ALSO BY JEAN KWOK

Searching for Sylvie Lee

Mambo in Chinatown

Girl in Translation

The Leftover Woman

A Novel

Jean Kwok

wm

WILLIAM MORROW
An Imprint of HarperCollins*Publishers*

THE LEFTOVER WOMAN. Copyright © 2023 by Jean Kwok. All rights reserved. Printed in the United States of America. No part of this book may be used or reproduced in any manner whatsoever without written permission except in the case of brief quotations embodied in critical articles and reviews. For information, address HarperCollins Publishers, 195 Broadway, New York, NY 10007.

HarperCollins books may be purchased for educational, business, or sales promotional use. For information, please email the Special Markets Department at SPsales@harpercollins.com.

FIRST EDITION

Designed by Kyle O'Brien

Library of Congress Cataloging-in-Publication Data

Names: Kwok, Jean, author.
Title: The leftover woman : a novel / Jean Kwok.
Description: First edition. | New York : William Morrow, an imprint of HarperCollins Publishers, [2023] | Summary: "An evocative family drama and a riveting mystery about the ferocious pull of motherhood for two very different women in New York City"— Provided by publisher.
Identifiers: LCCN 2023004444 | ISBN 9780063031463 (hardcover)
Subjects: LCSH: Motherhood—Fiction. | Family secrets—Fiction. | LCGFT: Novels.
Classification: LCC PS3611.W65 L44 2023 | DDC 813/.6—dc23/eng/20230206
LC record available at https://lccn.loc.gov/2023004444

ISBN 978-0-06-303146-3 (hardcover)
ISBN 978-0-06-334698-7 (international edition)

23 24 25 26 27 LBC 5 4 3 2 1

For Stefan and Milan

Part One

May 6, 2022

My beloved, I understand that forgiveness may not be possible. Some deeds cannot be undone. I took someone essential from you that last tragic evening—the blood, so much blood. My hands will never be clean again no matter how hard I scrub. What I was capable of then was only limited by my desire, and my desire could consume the world.

Yet now, so many years later, I write to you because we are both ink and paper to each other. I have marked you as you have marked me, and you are written into the language of my soul. When you think of me, you must only remember glimpses, snapshots taken from a speeding train that you then try to piece into a cohesive narrative. Please, let me construct my truth for you, flawed though it must be. My only hope is your understanding, not in the sense of compassion but simple comprehension.

There is a question that I'm sure you've asked yourself again and again, lying alone in your bed, thinking of me. This is my answer. And after you have heard it, I hope that, perhaps, you will come to me.

I confess I have a daydream of you.

One day, there is a knock on my door. It is raining. My head snaps up, my heart flutters. I close my eyes, afraid of the hope that rushes through my body like wine. I make myself take a careful step to the door, and then another. I am dizzy but I must not fall.

Through the glass, I make out a dark figure outside, carrying an umbrella, because in your thoughtful way, you are always prepared. A halo of light illuminates the rain cascading over you. Your jaw is clenched as you peer through the windowpane. You too are apprehensive. You don't know if you should have come.

I hurry to unlock the door before you can flee. My hands fumble with the knob and finally, I cast it open. We stare at one another a long moment. Despite all our sorrows, despite the days that have passed, we recognize each other. I think you're the most wondrous thing I've ever seen. I restrain myself, though. I must not frighten you more than I already have. A few hot tears escape. I dash them away.

Your breath catches. A smile touches your eyes; a miracle.

You step across my threshold.

ONE

Jasmine

Fifteen years earlier

I stood outside the Manhattan Chinatown teahouse and laid my palm against the windowpane. It was littered with advertisements. I cupped my hands around my eyes and peered in between a colorful flyer for a self-defense class and a Help Wanted ad. I ignored my reflection. I had always longed to be invisible. The Chinese believe our fortunes are written in the physiology of our faces, that the breadth of a forehead, the droop of a lip can seal our fates. For me, this was true. My visage had determined my path in life. Ever since I was a small girl in our village in China, I'd hated my face.

The customers inside were warm and laughing, pouring steaming oolong tea into small porcelain cups, scooping up fish balls with their chopsticks. Waiters and waitresses pushed loaded dim sum carts between the round tables as patrons picked out their favorite delicacies. There, a young father bounced his daughter on his knee as he blew on a wonton to cool it down for her. When the mother smoothed back the child's wispy hair with a gentle hand, I was homesick for a past I'd never experienced.

A man pushed past me to enter the restaurant. I hurried in behind him before the door shut. A burst of warmth greeted me, along with the luscious smells of soy sauce chicken, orange-scented beef, and scallion pancakes. The chatter was all in Chinese and for a moment, I could pretend I was back home.

My jacket was too thin, and I realized how cold I was, even though it was already the beginning of March. I only had five more months before I'd have to repay the snakeheads who'd arranged my passage to New York. I pressed a hand to my icy ear. My plastic-framed glasses fogged so badly I had to remove them. The moment I wiped them clean, they clouded up again. I dropped them into my large, weather-beaten canvas bag next to my sketchbook. I'd clipped my thick hair into a bun. Messy strands had escaped. I could feel them plastered to my face and neck.

"Can I help you?" There was an edge of impatience to the plump, middle-aged hostess's voice. This might have been the second time she'd addressed me. She'd spoken Chinese instead of trying English first like she should have with someone my age. It must have been clear that I was fresh off the boat. She ran her eyes over my threadbare coat, and I could sense her inaudible sigh.

I spoke over the pulse tripping in my throat. "Can I please see the manager?"

"What?" she said, impatiently. "Speak up."

"I'm looking for a job."

She gestured for me to follow her to the back, where the kitchen was located. This restaurant must have been four times the size of the one back home. Would I ever get used to the extravagance and wastefulness here? Plates shoved to the side, filled with discarded leftovers: partly bitten pieces of lotus root, cilantro and radish garnishes, a salt-baked chicken leg, much of the meat still on the bone.

Weaving through carts and customers, I saw friends and relatives using their chopsticks to drop delicacies like spicy tripe into each other's rice bowls. We stopped next to a table with two beautiful women around my age. What were they—twenty-four, twenty-five?

They were impossible to miss in this room filled with families. It was like there was a spotlight focused on them and they knew it, preening and giggling over their tall red bean ices.

I took in the way they held their shoulders back to accentuate their graceful necks, the slender fingers that posed and enticed. They were both wearing too much makeup but instead of diminishing them, the colors seemed a signifier of power, like the way poisonous creatures clad themselves in bright hues instead of camouflage. I was envious. Not of their pulchritude but of their fearlessness, the way they'd seized their genetic peculiarities—because that's what beauty really is, when you think about it—and decided to wield them.

A small man wearing a wrinkled gray suit much too big for him exited the kitchen and approached me. He looked as tired as his faded eyes. "You're looking for work? What's your name?"

I started to push my glasses up my nose, then realized I'd taken them off. I felt exposed without them, especially with the two women watching us. How many times had I already had this conversation? Could I trust him not to report me? I stared at his shoes. "Umm, I'm . . . I'm a very hard worker—"

He barked out a laugh. "Let me guess, you don't have the right paperwork and you want me to give you a job even though you're too scared to even tell me your real name. Forget it." He waved a dismissive hand and turned to leave.

"I can clean tables, waitress, serve dim sum. I'm dexterous and have a good memory." My heart was racing. I was talking too quickly. I couldn't return to China and my disastrous life there. I closed my eyes. I had passed the menu board on the way in—what had it said? "Your specials today are braised pork in gravy, shrimp with vermicelli and garlic, and vegetarian crystal dumplings."

He paused. "Can you come in full-time?"

"A few nights a week."

He shrugged. "I have people lining up to work twenty-four hours a day, especially if they're in your situation."

In my peripheral vision, I noticed both women perk up as a young man stepped past us on his way to the kitchen. He was hunched over, his head averted, as if trying to make himself less conspicuous. He wore a navy jacket with an elaborate emblem on the sleeve. A worn guitar case was slung over his back, an incongruous sight for a person heading into the depths of a restaurant where there were vats of boiling oil and flustered cooks, not to mention live lobsters.

The manager spotted him and erupted like a bulldog confronting a Doberman in the street. "What do you think this is, a storage area?"

The beleaguered man took a deep breath but didn't stop. "I'm so sorry, I'll stash the guitar. You won't notice—"

There was something familiar about his warm tenor that called to me. I didn't recognize the voice, rather the inflection of his Chinese, the rhythm of his words. I tended to avoid young men, with their grabby hands and clinging eyes, but I was riveted to this one. His hair was dark and silky, the gleam of amber highlights visible even in the fluorescent lighting.

"Come here." The manager actually stomped his foot.

The man slowly turned toward us and when he caught sight of me, he froze.

My heart lurched. I stared into a face that I both knew and didn't know at all. Two thick slashes of eyebrows, dusky skin, a square, masculine face with eyes like melted chocolate. Anthony. He was etched into my soul and yet entirely new to me. I remembered gangly shoulders, a broad open grin, his thin fingers plucking on guitar strings while perched on the steps of his house, one of the largest in our village. Then his family moved away and it stood empty, with me staring into the blank windows day after day. How many times had we shared a package of uncooked ramen noodles before he left, sprinkling the seasoning on top so we could munch them like chips? My eyes rested upon the man, but my soul recognized a boy I hadn't seen in ten years, my best friend when I was fourteen years old.

He was gaping at me. Then he whispered, "It's you."

A smile started on my face. To see him again so unexpectedly in this strange country made me feel like the sun had burst forth from my skin and I could barely contain it.

For a moment, wild emotion gathered in his eyes, joy and something else. In two steps, he crossed over to me. He reached out his hands. Before he could make contact, though, I flinched. Images of another man's fingers, the pain of his grip, arose between us. My mind whispered, *I need to stay hidden.* Sensing my fear, he froze. As I watched, his face shifted. The happiness drained from his eyes, leaving them as cold as the bitter air outside.

The manager was scolding him in one endless stream as we stared at each other. "Now they are taking musical instruments to work. We are not a karaoke club. What will be next? Why don't you bring your cats and dogs too?"

The women, who had already stood up to leave, fiddled with their bags. They were observing us intently, loath to leave our little soap opera. Really, they were watching Anthony. Now that he'd appeared, I was incidental.

He set down his guitar case and seemed to be straining away from me, as far as possible without moving his feet.

I wanted to embrace him and to flee but most of all, I didn't want him to leave. To cover my confusion, I said, "You have nothing to say to an old friend?"

His lip curled. "I didn't realize we were still friends."

The manager's monologue petered out. He fell silent and watched us along with the two women.

Anthony continued to regard me with his challenging gaze. My heart was full. I hadn't allowed myself to think about how much I'd missed him during the many long, unhappy years since he'd moved away. But the last thing I needed right now was to be discovered by anyone from my past. That thought was almost immediately drowned out by my emotions—clearly, I was the dumbest melon in the history of dumb melons. This was Anthony, once the person I trusted most in the world. And my affection-starved heart couldn't let him leave, not now when he was standing right here before me, not even with the anger darkening his face.

"I'm sorry—" I stammered. "I had no choice. I know I hurt you." Even as I said this, I understood it was the worst possible thing I could have uttered.

His entire body stiffened for a second before he laughed, and that laugh struck me like a hammer. "Jasmine, right? It's a wonder I remember your name."

I curled my hands into fists as indignation and hurt burned through me. Others had treated me like this, but never Anthony. "We were inseparable. And now you're pretending you can't even recall my name? How old are you, two?"

The manager said, "Okay, let's forget the whole thing. Get to work."

Anthony ignored him. "We were children." He enunciated each word to make sure I understood. "I've done many things since I last saw you and you pretended not to see me." He caught himself, flushed a bit. "Not that I cared. You never had the ability to hurt me. You were only a silly little girl who followed me around."

How dare he? He was only a year older than me. I deposited as much disdain into my eyes as I could. "Fine. I forgot you were always too good for the rest of us because your family had the foreign road open to you. You must be happy with your American name now that you can finally use it." I was so heated I needed to unzip my coat, which I did with an angry flourish.

He stared down his nose at me and said with finality, "Goodbye, Jasmine."

He bent to grab the strap of his guitar case again but as he stretched out his arm, the sleeve of his jacket pulled up slightly and I caught a glimpse of a faded red string bracelet.

My mouth fell open. It couldn't be. The bracelet appeared to be made of Chinese knotting cord, woven thickly in an intricate braid. He saw me staring and clasped his other hand over it. When he straightened, it was hidden underneath his sleeve again. He slung the guitar over his back as my gaze snagged on the logo on his jacket. It seemed familiar. He then ignored all of us, including the manager, who had fallen into a stunned silence, and stalked off toward the kitchen.

At the doorway, he turned back for a moment to stare at me. Was that regret in his eyes? Before I could react, he was gone.

I turned to the manager, my thoughts whirring. "I'm so sorry. But about that job, I can cook too and—"

He snorted. I'd lost him. "Our cooks are all men. And you're too much trouble." He flicked me a quick look, then hurried after Anthony.

I closed my eyes in disbelief. There went another work opportunity. Had I really seen Anthony again? How could he have said those things to me? He couldn't have made it any clearer how much he disliked me. But that bracelet . . . and then I remembered where I'd seen the emblem on his jacket.

Tears welled up in my eyes. I turned to leave before they could shame me further. My hair was falling out of my big barrette, and I yanked it free, the long mass unraveling down my back. I stumbled into something furry and perfumed and realized it was one of the young women who had been watching our entire pathetic exchange.

"Sorry," I mumbled.

To my surprise, she didn't move even though her petite companion was already at the door, tapping her glittery shoes. She peered intently into my face. As I focused on the woman up close, I saw that she was a few years older than I'd thought, possibly in her late twenties. In any case, she was lovely enough to sink the fish and make geese fall from the sky, with an expressive mouth and silky hair. She was all cream and pink and curves, a delicious surface masking the cool intelligence gazing out of those dark, luminous eyes.

She pursed her lips and seemed to make a decision. "I overheard you. You're looking for a job, right?"

When I nodded, she searched her large gold tote, burrowing through skeins of yarn and knitting needles—the last things I'd expect to find in her purse—while muttering, "Let me give you a name. Do you have something to write on?"

I wasn't sure I could trust her, but I desperately needed a job. I pulled my sketchbook out of my handbag right as she found her pen. "Here."

"Ooh," she said, and started to flip open my book. "You draw?"

I reached out and held it closed. "P-please stop that. Just put it on the back."

She pouted, then jotted down a name and address on the back cover. "Come to Opium. They're always looking for new cocktail waitresses. Ask for Aunt Glory and tell her Dawn sent you." She stopped, looked at me from underneath her lashes. "No papers necessary."

"Really?"

Dawn nodded, ran her eyes over me one more time, then leaned in to whisper, "But remember, appearances are everything."

TWO

Jasmine

I told myself I was only here out of curiosity. I was standing in front of the martial arts studio door with the same insignia as Anthony's jacket: a black circle edged in yellow with red hands in the center. I'd recognized it from the flyer stuck to the door of his restaurant. He'd probably hung it there himself. FREE WALK-IN SELF-DEFENSE CLASSES FOR WOMEN. After our scene yesterday, I'd taken one of the little tags with the address as I left, even though I swore I never wanted to see him again.

I certainly wasn't here because I wanted to be close to him. *You were only a silly little girl who followed me around.* I cringed at the memory, my cheeks stung from the embarrassment. It wasn't even the insult, though that also throbbed like a bruise, more that he knew better than anyone how the other kids had excluded me and used this knowledge to hurt me. Kind, thoughtful Anthony who had once spent hours trying to return a baby rosefinch to its nest.

I wanted to forget this present-day version, his hard, closed face and averted eyes, but I couldn't stop thinking about that red bracelet on his wrist. Even though many Chinese wound up in Chinatown, seeing him again still felt like some sort of cosmic coincidence, like fate allowed us to meet from a thousand miles away.

I'd made him a bracelet like that for his fourteenth birthday. I had no money, and I was too shy to give him one of my drawings. Perhaps I'd already sensed that change was coming. My parents were entertaining visitors in our home, men who laughed too loudly and looked at me out of the corners of their eyes as they drank their rice liquor. Pa's friends had never done that before.

Anthony and I had been sent to the stream to catch crabs for his birthday celebration that evening. I was giddy to be released from my chores and swung my legs as I balanced on the luggage rack of his rickety bicycle, twirling my woven basket with one hand.

"Stop that," he called, pedaling hard on the dusty, narrow road that ran through the fields. His bony back was warm against the tanned skin of my arm. "You're going to make us crash. We're almost there."

"You're such an old man," I retorted.

The moment we arrived, I leapt off the bike and took off. "Race you!"

I heard his footsteps pounding behind me. I'd always been faster. He'd recently grown a couple of inches, though, and shot past me. We were both laughing and panting by the time we reached the base of the waterfall. Smooth sheets of iridescent stone glimmered in the sunlight. I loved the rushing music of the falling stream, the smell of mud and grass, the spray cool and damp against my cheeks. The water had eroded the plunge pool. On the periphery, where the waves were calm and sediment collected, we rolled up our simple cotton pants and waded. The sand tickled my toes.

"There's one!" I cried, pointing to a flash of motion I'd seen beneath the surface.

Anthony bent down at once. He expertly pushed with his thumb on the crab's back and flipped it into the basket I held. The river crab scrabbled futilely to clamber up the smooth bamboo sides. Soon we had the basket mostly filled and climbed the outcropping that hung over the swirling plunge pool. We settled into the small, dry indentation in the rock where we always sat, warm from the sun.

We were trying to count the crabs we'd caught, all scrambling and swarming, when he said, as I'd known he would, "I think some of these are too small. They won't be good eating."

I let him drop about a third of them back into the water before I laid my hand on his arm, right above the mole in the crook of his elbow. "You're too softhearted, Anthony. We can't free them all."

He hunched his shoulders and stared at the ledge. "My folks won't mind."

I stared into the distance. The words were thick and stuck in my throat. "Ma will be angry with me. She'll say our family lost face by not contributing enough."

His eyes flew to my profile, his gaze stricken. I would be beaten if we didn't bring enough. My parents weren't like his, who could afford to buy any meat or fish they wanted. "Let's go catch some more then."

I shook my head and smiled at him. His eyebrows were furrowed, the moon-shaped scar on his forehead from when he'd fallen on a protruding nail as a toddler lighter than the rest of his skin. "We still have enough. Hey, I made something for you." I pulled my gift from my pocket and held it out to him.

"Two people connected by the red thread will always be tied together," I said, as he stared at it. Ma never told me stories, but I always listened when she put my twin brother, Hong, to bed. I would turn to the wall, so I didn't have to see her pet his cheek or tussle his hair. "The magical cord might stretch or tangle, but it'll never break, no matter how far away they might be from each other."

Anthony's cheekbones turned bright pink. "This is for . . ."

"What?"

"Boyfriend girlfriend."

I gasped and snatched my hand away, still clutching the bracelet. "No!" Had I not heard the whole tale? I started babbling, the waterfall roaring in my ears. "That's not what it is for us. It only means we're best friends and always will be. This was a stupid idea. I can give you something else."

His coloring settled back into its usual tawny hues. He reached out and loosened my fist to uncover the bracelet. "I like it. Will you put it on me?"

Still embarrassed, I avoided his eyes as I tied it around his skinny wrist. "I wanted to decorate it with beads, but I didn't have any."

He looked at the colorful knots of string—green, yellow, turquoise, and orange—neatly set off from the rest of the bracelet by a dark gold thread I'd taken from my mother's sewing basket. "These bracelets are supposed to be a pair. You should have a matching one."

I shook my head. I had wanted to make myself one, but I was afraid of being discovered, though technically I was allowed to use the sewing basket materials for mending. "I don't need one."

"I'll make it for you," he promised.

For months after that I caught him with little ragged bits of red thread in his pocket, all knotted and twisted. He never succeeded in making anything that didn't look like something the cat had thrown up, though. We didn't know it then, but we were already speeding through our final months together. My friendship with Anthony had formed the safe boundaries of my childhood, a buttress against the cold disdain of my mother and Hong's infuriating teasing. I'd found shelter within those walls without knowing it. Soon they started to crumble and there was nothing I could do to stop it, nothing at all. A year and a half later, Anthony was gone.

I hadn't expected him to resent me so much. This adult Anthony didn't want me in his life, and I respected that; I had never wanted him to be unhappy. If only I could see if those knotted beads were on his bracelet, then I'd know it was the same one I'd given him. I wouldn't pursue him beyond that. I couldn't have someone connected to my village in my life anyway. If he hadn't moved away years ago, I wouldn't even have considered following him here. This was pure curiosity. I'd leave as soon as I checked out the bracelet and we would never need to see each other again. It wasn't like I was lonely for a friend. A pang ran through me, and I ignored it—except for Grandma, who had passed on, I couldn't trust anyone, not even the people I loved most.

If I saw him here, I'd act surprised. No one could blame a woman living in New York City for taking a self-defense class. I steeled myself, then hauled open the heavy metal door. It took me a few tries. This must have been some kind of test, where only people strong enough to open the door were allowed to take their class.

A sturdy-looking young woman with a blunt-cut pyramid of hair sat behind a rickety table with the sign-up sheet in front of her. When she spoke, her voice was low and assured. To my relief, she addressed me in Chinese. "Hi, you must be new. I'm Yan. Please fill in your name with your phone number."

I hunched my shoulders. "I'm not sure I'll be staying."

Yan's voice was pragmatic and calm. "That's no problem. But for our records, everyone coming through must sign in. Otherwise, you can't enter."

I scribbled my name and contact information on the sheet.

"Go down the hallway. Changing room's to your right, studio's to the left."

I hesitated. "I don't have anything to change into." Why hadn't this occurred to me? Probably because I didn't have much other clothing aside from my usual plain pants and shirts.

She looked me up and down. There was no judgment in her gaze. "What you have on is fine and you can do the class barefoot. So you're all set."

As I took a step toward the dressing room, I felt light-headed, like I'd been spinning around at high speed. This was a terrible idea. No one from our village could know I was in the Beautiful Country.

I was turning to leave when I heard Anthony's voice behind me. "What are you doing here?"

I wrapped an arm around my stomach and tried to calm my racing pulse. My voice wavered. "I-I could ask you the same thing. You're the man at a women's self-defense class."

"I'm teaching with my uncle Nick." Of course, I remembered the uncle who lived in America and would bring him here one day. Anthony had changed into a black kung fu uniform that stretched over his muscular shoulders, belted at his narrow waist. Even barefoot, he was taller than I recalled. I stared at the long sleeves that covered his wrists and heaved a sigh.

He glanced at Yan, who was still behind the desk. She was watching us with avid curiosity and a hint of wariness. A slight flush crept up his jaw. "Can I talk to you for a moment?"

As I followed his stiff back down the hallway, I had a sudden urge to jump him from behind and wrap my arms and legs around him like a monkey. When we were younger, I would sneak up on him like that while he was practicing shooting marbles in the dirt outside his house. I used to cackle like a maniac when he jumped out of his skin. Anthony had always possessed an inherent faith in the goodness of everything. Maybe I could convince him not to be so upset with me anymore.

He led me into a small office. There were framed photos of students in kung fu uniforms winning prizes and a girl who seemed to have nothing to do with martial arts. There were countless shots of her from childhood on. Anthony's cousin, perhaps? His uncle obviously loved his daughter very much, I thought wistfully. The office was crammed with trophies that overflowed all the available shelf space, spilled onto the desk and floor. Anthony had always taken kung fu lessons back home but no matter how many times I'd asked, I'd never been allowed to join him. Ma thought it was a waste of money for a girl.

His guitar case and an animal carrier were stashed in a corner. A three-colored cat was prowling around and rubbed itself against my knee, purring outrageously. I leaned down to pet its thick, soft fur. I would have loved to sketch its white paws and stripy tail, the blaze of orange behind one ear, the gray pattern that descended over one eye like a pirate's patch.

When the cat ambled away, I looked up to find Anthony facing me with his arms crossed, his lips set in a determined line. "I'd like you to leave."

The words sliced into me. I flinched before I could hide my expression, and from the guilt that edged into his face, I knew he'd seen it. I ducked my head and took a step toward the door. "Fine. Goodbye, Anthony."

His voice behind me. "Why on earth do you want to take a self-defense course anyway?"

I shrugged but didn't turn around.

Before I could touch the doorknob, he said hurriedly, as if loath to see me go, "Do you really expect me to believe this was a coincidence?"

Now I'd had enough. All my tension condensed into fury and heat rushed to my face as I turned to him. "What should you think then?

That I followed you to this foreign country and I'm just hoping you'll fall to your knees and beg me for forgiveness for your rudeness, even though against all odds, after all these years, we've found each other again?"

The lines on his face hardened. "You don't need to make fun—"

"Don't I?" I said, walking toward him. "I apologized to you, Anthony. You didn't need to lash out at me."

"I—"

"No, you listen now. This is your studio but it's my turn to talk and if you feel the need to run away, be my guest." I waved at the door.

He clenched his jaw but didn't move. His eyes were bright with indignation underneath the crescent-shaped scar, faded now. He looked as stubborn as he ever did as a boy, and at the corner of his left eye were the same three little freckles that formed a triangle.

At these reminders of the Anthony I had loved, I sighed, the anger leaking out of me. "I shut you out of my life with no warning. It must have seemed like—"

He broke in, his voice harsh and furious. Suddenly he was looming over me with his fists clenched. "Like you were too good for the rest of us? With your new life and big house and *him*?"

I cowered but managed to squeeze out, low and urgent, "I had no choice."

He scoffed. "Of course you didn't. No choice but to treat me like trash on your shoe. Ignoring me even though I ran after you like an idiot, hoping at least to be your friend. Time and time again, I thought you hadn't seen me, that you were busy. The excuses I made for you in my head."

"I couldn't—"

"What?! Couldn't treat me with any type of decency?" He raised his voice, a muscle ticking in his jaw. "Couldn't what, Jasmine?! Couldn't have picked me instead? You were *my* girlfriend!"

At this, we both froze. We were breathing hard. I stared at him incredulously. "What? I was never your girlfriend."

He deflated and looked down, unable to meet my eyes. He stammered, "I-It was a secret."

I said, enunciating slowly, "So secret that even *I* didn't know about it?"

A hot flush crept up his chest and neck, and he nodded.

Now it was my turn to avoid his gaze. I stared at the floor as I said in a tiny voice, "I tried. Your parents refused."

"What?!" It was an explosion of air and disbelief.

I risked a glance upward and he was flabbergasted, his eyes wide, mouth gaping open. His lips moved though he seemed unable to speak. At his obvious surprise, something inside me loosened. He hadn't known. I'd spent years wondering.

I gave a short laugh. "They always had their eyes on the Beautiful Country for you, Anthony. Or did you never grasp the reason they gave you an American name from the day you were born? They understood that your uncle would bring you here and that your future would be abroad, not in our little village. I knew we weren't involved but I would rather have been with you than . . . I told my parents I would accept an arranged marriage if they asked your family first. Believe me, I had to fight to make my folks agree."

"Why didn't you ask me directly?" His voice caught, straining to contain some emotion I struggled to decipher. Frustration? Anger?

I was still staring at his uniform. "I was embarrassed. We'd never . . . I never saw you that way. I was sure they'd talk to you, and you'd find out. To be honest, when you tried to approach me after the wedding, I was still resentful and wounded. I thought you felt guilty for rejecting me when the matchmaker approached your family. Anyway, whether it was up to you or your parents, I wasn't good enough."

There was utter silence, then he took me by the chin and tilted my head up to meet his eyes. His expression was unreadable. I wrenched my face away as a hot tear overflowed. I dashed it away, angry at myself for displaying vulnerability while he remained so stoic.

"But fine, Anthony. I understand. I don't see any trace of the boy I was friends with anymore. That boy may have been hurt—and yes, you've made it very clear that you're anything but hurt by me—but he would have heard me out. He was kind to every living thing, thought the best of everyone. I'm sorry I intruded on your life here. I don't know why I came to see you again. I won't bother you anymore."

He was speechless as I backed away from him. I strode out of the office and toward the exit as quickly as I could. I could hear him coming after me. I wanted nothing more to do with him. Yan stared at me as I grabbed the handle, pushed the main metal door—and bounced off of it. What was that thing made of, lead?

I felt his hand on my arm. "Jasmine."

I stopped but I didn't turn around. We both stood there, silent. He squeezed me gently and said quietly, "I was—"

It was too much for me. I couldn't stand to be on the cusp of friendship. I couldn't bear the memories. There were so many emotions raging through me that I didn't know what I was feeling. I wrenched my arm from his grasp and rammed my whole weight against the door, running out of the studio and out of his life.

THREE

Jasmine

After I fled the studio, I was determined to forget about Anthony. I needed to get my own affairs in order. I shivered, remembered when my future was only a dark box, a room painted black with no window or door in sight. I had carved my own exit, walked through it, and now I had to pay the price. I shouldn't have let him derail me. I, of all people, knew how quickly kindness could turn to cruelty.

If I didn't find a job fast, I'd be at the mercy of the snakeheads. Back in China, getting in touch with the gangs who smuggled people into the United States had been easy enough. Everyone in my village knew who they were.

When I was told the astronomical sum I would owe them, I had swallowed hard. "What happens if I can't earn the money in time?" I'd heard stories about the sort of punishments inflicted on those who tried to escape their debts.

The snakehead licked his lips. "A young woman like you? You'd work for us, for as long as it took. There are a lot of men who'd appreciate your services."

I understood the type of employment he meant. I didn't know then that most of the legitimate restaurants and stores in Chinatown would reject me because I didn't have the right documentation. After Grandma passed on, I had to get away no matter the cost. When I first landed in New York last August, I went to sleep every night with the jade hairpin she gave me clutched in my hand, pretending I wasn't adrift in this vast ocean called the Beautiful Country. I prayed no one would ever find me here.

The alley loomed dark and threatening, dismal corners filled with shade. I passed a homeless man who sat propped against a building, forgotten by all who had ever loved him. I turned away and walked down the street to the pawnshop, clutching the red jewelry pouch in my pocket. I wasn't going to sell anything. Not really. I was only getting an appraisal. If the hairpin was worth anything like what I suspected, I'd have a significant part of the money I needed to repay my debt.

"When you're old enough to marry, you'll stop wearing braids," Grandma, her round face tender, had said when I was a little girl. "And we will coil your hair into a bun and fasten it with this."

The hairpin was my history, the accumulation of generations of women in my family who had starved and died rather than let it out of their hands. They cherished it as a powerful talisman, an amulet of love, healing, and protection. I could never sell it. Maybe I could put it up for collateral, though, and when I managed to earn enough, come back for it. I had already liquidated everything else Grandma had given me. I wouldn't let go of the hairpin. My chest was heaving as if I might break out in sobs. I told myself it was due to the chill in the air.

A bell chimed as I stepped inside the little pawnshop. It was empty except for the heavy, bearded man behind the register. I didn't like massive men. Why couldn't he have been a woman instead? I kept my gaze fixed to the glass counter, where a goldfish swam in circles inside its bowl. I took the silk pouch from my pocket and slid it over to him. My voice quavered. "How much is this worth?"

I watched as his thick fingers unzipped the material and pulled out the hairpin. The large piece of emerald-green Imperial jade had been meticulously carved to form translucent pomegranate seeds borne on intertwining branches of pure gold. A vivid long-tailed bird engrave expertly into the outer part of the stone seemed about to take flight. The striking colors reflected light like water. Smaller precious stones shimmered, bright leaves that sparkled against the ripe fruit. Even now, the sight of it took my breath away.

The man grunted in surprise. I looked around the store while he examined it. All these cabinets filled with other people's desperation. How many stories like mine could these objects tell?

He peered at the hairpin through his jeweler's loupe and inhaled sharply. "This is very old."

I nodded and forced myself to meet his eyes. "From the Qing dynasty."

He raised a scraggly eyebrow as he took a swallow from a large glass of water. "That's what they all say. You looking to sell?"

"No, I only want to know the value today in case I want to pawn it."

His heavy-lidded gaze turned crafty. "I can lend you seven hundred dollars for it. That's a very good offer, young lady."

I ran a sweaty hand down my pant leg. I had done my research. My throat felt tight as I said, "It's worth at least thirty thousand, probably more."

His eyes lingered on it. "Even if it was, and I'm not saying it is, I wouldn't give you more than seven hundred."

I shook my head and held out my trembling palm, relieved when he dropped the hairpin in it. "I'm sorry to have wasted your time."

The late afternoon sun almost blinded me when I stepped outside. The masses of people mountain, people sea streamed around me, threading through the fissures defined by the skyscrapers in crowded New York City, utterly uncaring. All that concrete and brilliant glass, the loud roar of traffic, the stench of gasoline and asphalt made me clutch my stomach as I staggered down the street. What was I going to do now? Grandma had passed away and the last little bit I had left of her seemed unable to protect me.

My phone vibrated. It was a text.

Jasmine, this is Anthony. I don't know what to say.

That was it? He wrote to tell me . . . nothing? I stared at the characters until they blurred before my eyes. How had he found my number anyway? The sign-up sheet for the class. He must have gotten it off that. What did this mean? My phone remained silent. It was apparent that nothing else was forthcoming, no invitation to see him again.

I thought I understood. This was a message in a bottle cast into the sea. He probably felt guilty for how we'd left things, and this was his attempt at a slightly friendlier closure. Well, I'd done enough chasing after him and the whole mess of emotions he represented. I didn't care if he was wearing the stupid bracelet I'd given him. He wasn't the boy I knew, and the girl he remembered was long gone. Plus, what kind of lame note was this? My life was complicated enough without a guy who couldn't even communicate clearly.

It used to be different with him. As a child, I often had to work on the farm. In addition to feeding and taking care of the animals, I transplanted rice by hand to the paddy fields in June, legs in the water, back aching. I harvested it and helped clear the fields in the fall. November was busy with the planting of wheat and reaping of soybeans, sweet potatoes, cabbages, and icicle radishes. But whenever I could get away, Anthony and I picked wild berries, stained our hands and mouths, sucked nectar out of the stems of honeysuckle, folded small paper boats to float in the stream. We'd understood each other perfectly then. And those picture cards that we had used as currency: brightly colored drawings of ancient gods and demons. We'd shoot rubber bands at each other's and if we hit them, the winner took that card. I'd always been a better shot than him and often won. Sometimes he gave me ones he knew I wanted to paste into my own collages.

I came to the corner and instead of the green mountains of my childhood, a taxi blared. Traffic rushed down the avenue. I sighed. We both needed to move on. He'd made plain his desire to get me out of his life. I put my phone away. I wouldn't write him back. This would be our goodbye. In my limited experience with men, it never ended well for me.

I had entrusted my heart to Wen after we married when I was only fourteen years old. He loved my skin and hair. He loved being seen with me. I'd been too young and stupid to understand that his adoration was for the things I could do for him, the sons I would bear him, the status I could bring him, and not for me. All he wanted was a wife to give him face.

I let so many injustices go over the years but I could never forgive him for his ultimate betrayal. I discovered the truth one day when I was nineteen years old. That evening, I didn't care if he was watching or not as I stepped into the round wooden bathtub, secured by three bands of metal. He had seen my naked body often. I wouldn't let his presence ruin my bath this time. I'd already become far more protective of that which lay beneath the surface: my mind, my spirit. I slid into the hot water, wrapped myself in warmth that seemed to sink deep into the cold at my core. I sighed as I leaned my head against the rim. The stone weighing down my soul eased a bit. As my eyes fluttered closed, I breathed in the scent of the peony soap.

I flinched as Wen moved closer and began to pour water over my hair from behind. "Jasmine, I was wrong. How can I make you feel better?"

I tried to steady my voice, stared up at the brown rafters supporting our tiled roof. "I want to stop trying to have a baby for a while. I'm still too young. My body isn't ready yet."

He hesitated, his hands resting on my hair. We both knew that plenty of women my age had children, and after several miscarriages, I'd finally carried to term last year, only to be devastated when the midwife told me the baby died right after birth. "Of course," he said after a moment. "I have only ever cared about your well-being. We have enough time, after all."

I felt the lies in his words like a pebble wedged in my shoe but I needed to play along, to pretend I was as charmed by him as I used to be. I allowed a corner of my lips to turn up in a small smile and looked over my shoulder at him. His handsome face was filled with concern. I noted the frustration hidden in the tightness of his mouth.

In the years when I had loved him, I had pored over every minute change in his expression. I had learned to read him like a language I adored. "Truly?"

"Absolutely," he said as he cupped my face in his hands. I bit back a hiss when his cold fingers brushed against the bruise beginning to darken my hairline. He was usually more careful. "I am so sorry for earlier."

I pressed my lips together. "You hurt me."

He leaned in, heedless of the water wetting his fine shirt, and rested his forehead against mine. "I know. My mind was clouded. Of course, the miscarriages aren't your fault, and you can't help the way the country potatoes on the street stare at you. You are as lovely as a crane among chickens. I only acted that way out of worry. And it'd already taken me so long to find you. I wish you wouldn't wander alone in the mountain."

"You said it was no wonder a whore couldn't conceive sons." His words had been the least of my pain. But I couldn't talk about the other things he did to me when he was enraged. I didn't dare.

He winced. "I was not myself." He rolled up his sleeves and lathered my hair. I closed my eyes. "Let me make it up to you. I want to plan a beautiful wedding for us."

My eyelids flew open and I forced myself to remain calm. I glanced at the ring weighing down my finger, diamonds sparkling in the hand-engraved band of yellow gold. "Whatever for? We're already married."

He coughed. "Well, not in the eye of the law. Of course, our wedding banquet was sufficient for everyone in this village, but you'll turn twenty soon and we'll be able to marry legally." His voice deepened. "I want you to be mine in every way, my beautiful Jasmine."

Once, I might have turned to him, flushed with pleasure and anticipation, leaned toward him like a flower to the sun. But now I would die before I allowed myself to be officially bound to this man. He had broken more than my heart. He'd shattered my will, my spirit, and my voice. Worst of all, I had let him. I would never again be led blindly into the darkness. If I had to walk, I would choose my own path with my eyes wide open.

How much money had he paid my parents for my bride price? There had been gasps and whispers, though I'd never seen a cent of it. With so few girls under the one-child policy, we were valuable commodities to be auctioned off as young as possible. However, even in our little village, it'd been unusual for me to be handed over to the matchmaker at fourteen. Most parents waited until the girls were sixteen at least, but from the moment I started developing curves, I'd attracted too much gossip. Wen was considered a real prize, with his government position and residence permit to live in Beijing, where he spent much of his time. He was also one of the tallest and strongest men in our village. It didn't matter that he was already twenty-six years old when we married, I told myself then. He would love and protect me.

Well, I was no longer that naïve girl. I wanted to slap his arrogant face. I wanted to run out of that house and never return. But I held myself back. If I wanted to be truly free of him, I couldn't be impulsive. I needed to plan. I had to be smart.

"Wouldn't you like that, my darling?" he asked. "I'll buy you the most gorgeous dresses, even a Western white one, if you want. More paints and pencils for your little hobby. Whatever you desire."

I ground my teeth. I needed my "little hobby" the way a fish needed water. Without a pencil in my hand, I wouldn't know how to engage with reality, how to make sense of the confusion of my life. But I had no allies except for Grandma, whose health was failing. I had to become strong so that no one could use me like Wen or my parents ever again. I had to play the game and win this time.

So, I made myself gasp with pleasure. "With lace and a veil?"

He chuckled, reassured. "Nothing is too fine for you. And we'll supplement your bridal jewelry as well. It will go to our son eventually anyway."

I clenched my jaw, knowing he couldn't see. I braced myself. "A wonderful investment in our future." I turned to him, half-rising out of the water so the droplets rolled down my breasts. At his intake of breath, I kept my eyes wide, lips soft. "But won't you give me some time to plan it properly? I want to savor the creation of such a joyous and important occasion."

Eyes roaming over my body, he nodded. "Of course."

I kissed him tenderly, then sank back into the water while he finished rinsing my hair. Who was I becoming? Whomever I needed to be. I knew he loved me in his own twisted way. It wasn't enough, though. In some ways, everyone I'd ever cared for had been taken from me, even Wen, even though he was right beside me. My own parents essentially sold me to him, Anthony moved away, and now Grandma was ill. I couldn't trust anyone to be there for me. My gaze blurred as I stared at the ceiling and Wen massaged my scalp. The haze of steam surrounding me felt as damp and pervasive as grief.

He went on and on about the glory of our wedding, how often he'd thought about me during the months he was in Beijing, his important work for the government, how wonderful it would be when I finally joined him there, how much his parents would miss having my help in their restaurant. I knew he'd never bring me to Beijing. His mistresses wouldn't be pleased with his young country wife. How it had hurt me when I'd first found out about them, but they were nothing compared to his greatest lie, which I'd just discovered. That was the worst thing he'd ever done to me.

I gasped as he lifted me out of the water like I didn't weigh a thing and set me on my feet on the rug, the water streaming down my body. He dried me tenderly before pulling a thin cotton nightgown over my head. It smelled of the same laundry soap Grandma used. I pressed my lips together to keep a sob from escaping.

My mind was as exhausted as my heart. All I wanted was to be rid of him. "I'd like to go to sleep now."

"Of course." He led me to our canopy bed, ducked under the upper wooden panels inlaid with gold leaf and mother-of-pearl, and held back the translucent curtain while I lay down.

When I slipped under the covers, he followed me despite my rigid spine. My heart sank as I felt his weight settle behind me. I stayed as stiff as a board until he started stroking my arm. "You're the only one I love, Jasmine."

Liar. It might be partly true or merely another manipulation to ensnare me further. It didn't matter. I had to acquiesce until I could make my move. Despite myself, I relaxed in his hold. I'd loved him for years. He was the only man I'd ever known intimately. I didn't want to be in his arms, even if it was all I had desired for so long. A storm of emotion rose within me: anger, sadness, regret. I kept them all inside. I needed to be numb. That way I'd be safe.

But as he kissed my hair, I let the girl inside who had lost the man she loved take this moment with him. I swept those bitter pieces of my broken spirit into that naïve girl who'd been willing to do anything to please her parents, even marry a stranger twelve years her senior. I was in mourning. This was my goodbye, to him and to me. My lashes were wet.

His caresses became more insistent. He turned me over to face him. He didn't notice my tears.

Afterward, he murmured, "I'll never let you go."

FOUR

Jasmine

"I'm afraid your English isn't good enough," the architect told me. Her expression was kind. "We have a number of Western clients, and we need to make the right impression. I truly am sorry."

I trudged down the narrow stairs until I emerged onto the street again. I'd known the receptionist job was a long shot, but I was becoming increasingly desperate. The sky was gray and white, verging on rain. A gust of air whipped through the avenue and an old newspaper rose from the sidewalk, swirled for a moment in the late afternoon shadows, then fluttered downward. How would I ever earn enough at this rate? What would the snakeheads make me do if I failed? Would they force me to stay in one of their houses? I'd heard about the stained mattresses crammed into those places, lined up across the vinyl floors, crawling with roaches.

My telephone buzzed and I jumped, startled. It was a second text from Anthony.

I'm sorry for my behavior. I spoke in anger. I understand why you acted the way you did.

A small smile lifted my lips as I read and reread his message, trying to decipher how he was feeling. I stuffed my phone in my bag, annoyed with myself. After all I'd done to escape my village, why in the world would I reconnect with someone linking me back to it? It was better this way. He had apologized. It had to be enough. He was only trying to make amends and surely hoping I wouldn't misinterpret it as an invitation to return to the studio.

I spent hours going in and out of stores in Chinatown, searching for a job without any success. I passed by his self-defense studio three times, though I made sure I was looking the other way. I gave myself a mental shake and made myself stop thinking about him. When would I ever learn? I had to protect my goals. Anthony had no place in that. Every large man on the street reminded me of Wen and I ducked my head in fear.

My resolve lasted the rest of that day and the next as I crossed off every Help Wanted ad in the Chinese newspaper. I remembered Opium, the place that woman in the restaurant—Dawn—had mentioned. It wasn't in Chinatown, though. They'd surely reject me for my bad English. I'd try that last, after I was sure there were no other options. I kept myself so busy that, thankfully, I had little time or energy to think about Anthony.

I sat in a quiet corner of Columbus Park to ease my tired legs. The day was sunny and slightly warmer than it had been but there was still a chill in the air. I pulled my coat tightly around me. A small girl wearing a red jacket skipped past, singing some English nursery rhyme.

I took out my sketchbook and started to draw her. As my colored pencils flew across the page, I forgot about the cold and soon realized I wasn't portraying that little girl at all. It was another self-portrait. I'd been doing this for years, iteration after iteration. Why I was so obsessed I did not know, especially since I hated the idea of being examined. But I had learned that through my hand on the page, I could reinvent myself, and that was something I felt compelled to do.

My phone hummed again in my bag. My breath caught but I stopped myself from looking. I didn't like to be interrupted when I was working, and I was sure it wasn't from Anthony anyway. I frowned at my sketchbook as the image appeared: a little girl in the faded red dress I used to wear. The round hands clutching each other, half-hidden in the cotton folds. Black slippers on the small pigeon-toed feet, a line of chrysanthemums around the neckline, knobby knees, and skinny calves.

I normally lost myself entirely when I drew. That was one of the reasons I loved it. But this time, even as I was shading in the square pocket on the skirt, my phone buzzed in my mind like a mosquito. Finally, I snatched up my bag and checked the screen.

It was another message from Anthony. I closed my eyes, waited a moment to open it. What if he took back the apology? What if he was angry I hadn't written back?

> I understand you might not want to see me again after our last interaction but I would appreciate another chance to speak to you.

Despite myself, my heart lifted. I touched my finger to the characters forming *last interaction* and *appreciate*. Such grown-up, formal phrases. What I saw was not indecision or distance on his behalf now. I saw a proud man protecting the vulnerable boy inside. He didn't know that Wen forbade me to see him. Wen had been bitterly jealous of him and anyone else I cared for, checking in constantly, calling almost immediately even when I was with Grandma. Anthony had taken a chance and if I didn't reply, I would likely never hear from him again.

I had my fingers poised over the keyboard, ready to type an eager answer, when I caught sight of my self-portrait. Where the head should have been, there was only a void. The perfectly realistic body cut off abruptly at the neck. There was no visible injury. Try as I might, I could never draw my face. I wondered if I could even call my work self-portraits. Sometimes there was a head, but it was floating away, severed from the body, a mass of faceless black hair. Or the head of an animal appeared in my stead, or a wilted flower that grew from the bloodless neck.

Anthony wasn't the boy I loved anymore. He was a man and my history with men had been tragic. Slowly, I put my phone away.

No one knew better than I that while your mind might disappear, the body must endure.

I stared at the little girl, who was now balancing on one leg as she played hopscotch. She was about the same age as my daughter, the one I'd been told died soon after birth.

The day before my bath with Wen, I had snooped through his computer. I only had to watch him enter his password once to memorize it, and thus I had access to all his accounts. I was searching for details about his mistresses and if any were a threat to me. I hated myself for this, but I couldn't stop. It was like picking a wound that never healed. Leaving him wasn't an option; I'd gathered this from everyone around me. After all, who else would want me? What else was I good for? Not even my family would take me back, especially since Grandma's influence had been muted by her illness. And most of all, I still loved him. He took care of me; he knew better than me. I clung to him, lost and afraid.

"Of course, there's no one else," he lied. That was when I was still innocent enough to confess my suspicions about the other women. Then he went on to say, "Men have different needs. But you are the only woman in my heart. You will always be the only one for me."

One of the subject lines made me pause: "With Gratitude." Perhaps some woman thanking him for a gift? At first, I exhaled in relief when I read:

We are so indebted to you for your help with our adoption of our beloved baby. As you can see from the attached photo, she is thriving and healthy. She is a joy to us in every way.

But then her picture loaded. The shock hit me, as startling as jumping into the icy river. In her tiny face, I met my own eyes, widely spaced, a rich brown flecked with gold. My entire body trembled as if struck by an electric current. This couldn't be. Of course not. It was a passing resemblance, that was all. A coincidence. I was making too much of it. I started searching for other emails. From his familiar tone and references to their past, the man writing these messages seemed to be an old friend of Wen's. He had an American name despite his excellent Chinese. The baby had been adopted by him and his wife, and they lived in New York City. The orphanage listed was close to my village. Then I found her birth date and my hands started to shake so much I could barely use the keyboard. It was the same as my daughter's.

I searched through Wen's correspondence. He'd arranged for a possible adoption when I was still pregnant, in case the baby turned out to be female. A tear dripped onto the table and I realized I was crying. Those days when he'd cherished me, running his hands over my belly, whispering songs to our unborn child. All that time, he'd been planning to get rid of our baby if it was the wrong gender. Most couples in the countryside were allowed to try again if the first was a girl, but as a high-ranking government official, Wen was held to a stricter standard. He would only be permitted one and he wanted it to be a son, someone to carry on the family name, to inherit and take care of us when we were old.

I'd held my baby in my arms for only a few precious moments. I was dazed from the birth and yet, when I gazed into her reddened face, I recognized that my life had changed. Her visage was indelibly imprinted upon my soul. Then the midwife took her away. I heard her cries growing fainter. I must have fallen asleep and when I woke, Wen broke the news gently, told me our daughter hadn't survived. I howled with grief as he held me. He'd sent our baby to the orphanage that very night.

Now, at his computer, I felt cold everywhere, like a lake frozen over, the ice killing everything in its wake. I heard a wild roaring in my ears. Wind swept through my internal landscape, sending leaves scuttling, trees uprooted and twisting any remaining light into shadows. I collapsed on that desk and wept—for my daughter and myself. How could he have taken her from the safety of my arms and sent her out into the world? My darling, tender baby, who had snuggled her cheek against my hand, was being raised by foreigners who ate with knives at the table instead of chopsticks. Who knew what had happened to her since? No one could be trusted, especially not with the care of my child.

I felt hollow. I didn't dare confide in Grandma because she'd grown absent-minded by then. I was afraid she would inadvertently reveal what I'd discovered. I had to escape Wen. After that, I was only a shell. The worst part was that no one seemed able to tell the difference. I knew how the innocent could be used. Look at the secrets surrounding my own birth. If only I could take my girl into my arms and create a safe reality for the two of us, some ephemeral bubble where we could love each other. If I could save her, maybe I'd be able to rescue myself as well.

That's when I started making plans to be reunited with my daughter, no matter the cost.

FIVE

Rebecca

"I gotta say, this doesn't look good for you."

Rebecca barely registers the gruff male voice drifting over the high supermarket shelves. Underneath the fluorescent light, she considers the jar labeled "Luxury Spanish Olives" in her hand. Mother wants Sicilian Castelvetrano but at this rate, Rebecca's lucky to find anything from the right continent. What type of caterer runs out of garnishes within the first hour anyway? How much are her colleagues drinking? It's so typical of Mother to send her on a lowly errand because Rebecca obviously has nothing more important to do. Her stomach is churning and a wave of pent-up energy sweeps over her. She feels like a bottle of champagne that's been shaken and not yet uncorked. She has to get out of this store. These olives, no matter how inferior, will have to do or else she'll wind up missing her own soirée for the sixtieth anniversary of B&W, the publishing house where she's the reigning editor in chief.

She's placing the jar in her shopping basket when she hears a high child's voice. "But it was already open."

Fifi. Rebecca freezes. Her head swivels, searching for the source of the confrontation. How dare this man speak to her daughter like that? Where in the world is Lucy? Their nanny is supposed to be taking care of Fifi. Rebecca left them only a few minutes ago while she went to find the olives.

"Sure it was. And what about your older sister here? I've had enough trouble with stealing . . ."

The voice becomes unintelligible as Rebecca walks as swiftly as her heels allow toward the end of the aisle. Where are they? All the tension in her starts to boil. She wants to kick off her shoes and run. She peers down the next one. Empty. One farther. An elderly couple staring at boxes of cereal blinks at her as she strides by. Why can't she find them? The bland elevator music taunts her with its relentless good cheer.

She pauses, chewing on a nail, a filthy habit she broke years ago. Her pulse is pounding the way it does after she's run a hard race. She's about to open her mouth and shout for Fifi—but what would people think?—when she hears a raised female voice with a heavy Chinese accent.

"We not do anything. You stay away from her." It's Lucy, trying to defend Fifi with her limited English.

They're in the opposite direction. She pivots and almost trips over herself as she heads as quickly as possible toward them. How should she handle this?

"Confrontation is so gauche," Mother always says. "A lady finds another way."

A young man wearing headphones and bobbing stares at her in surprise when she pushes past him, almost knocking him over.

"You people come to this country, and you can't even learn English right." The heavy voice breaks off as Rebecca rounds the corner. She can hardly focus on them because her vision has gone white. She realizes she is shaking with rage.

The grizzly white man in his late forties is wearing a bright blue apron. He stops as he takes in the sight of her. His features are rough and flattened, like someone hit him with a shovel, and he's raised one admonishing finger. She deliberately allows her light coat to swing open, revealing the Oscar de la Renta cocktail dress underneath: sheer black lace over a golden slip. She looks down her nose at him, head high with her pale coiffed hair swept into a French twist.

The man straightens from his threatening stance, looming over Fifi, and says to Rebecca, "Can I help you, ma'am?"

Rebecca places one hand on her hip and asks in a deceptively calm voice, "What is going on here?"

Fifi's face is waxen, her eyes terrified beneath her glossy black bangs. Her little pink glasses are about to fall off her nose. She's clutching Lucy's pants in a death grip. Lucy doesn't appear much better, hunched protectively over Fifi, the skin on her cheeks mottled and red. A bag of potato chips lies on the floor with the top gaping open.

The man smooths a few strands of his comb-over with his hand. "Nothing to concern you, ma'am. I've got this handled."

Rebecca fires each word like a bullet. "That is *my* daughter you're accusing of theft."

The man's jaw drops, and his eyes skitter from Fifi to Lucy, then back to Rebecca. "But I thought . . ." He points at Lucy. "She—"

Lucy speaks to Fifi in Chinese and at her words, Fifi releases her and rushes into Rebecca's arms.

"Mommy!" she bawls. "It was already open! I didn't know, I just picked it up. I didn't do it, I swear!" She's sobbing so hard, her narrow shoulders are heaving. Lucy's eyes are red-rimmed and miserable. She fishes a tissue from her lumpy bag and hands it to Rebecca.

Rebecca flicks her eyes over her nanny for a moment and represses a shudder: wide plaid pants, a large blue and red cowboy shirt with padded shoulders, some kind of kerchief knotted over her messy hair. With the way that girl dressed, you could almost forgive the man for thinking they were a bunch of thieves. She wraps her arms around Fifi and takes off her daughter's glasses to wipe her eyes.

She kisses the top of Fifi's head, which is hot and sweaty. "Darling, it's all right."

The man has recovered some of his defiance. "Someone's got to pay for those chips."

The injustice of it burns Rebecca. She opens her mouth, and nothing comes out. This type of direct hostility is so uncomfortable. She hates dealing with people like this.

Before she can compose a careful reply, Lucy steps in front of her and places her hands on her hips. "You make Fiona *cry*. You a bad man. You a racist."

At Lucy's vehemence, the man takes a step back, raising both hands. Rebecca takes the opportunity to join forces with her nanny and says, "I'd like to speak with your supervisor about this situation."

The man seems to shrink with every passing word. He becomes as pale as wax and starts muttering about a misunderstanding. His eyes dart from Fifi to Rebecca, as if he still can't believe they belong together.

"I apologize." He hastily retreats, almost running.

"I try explain," says Lucy, wrapping an arm around Fifi.

Rebecca shakes her head. "It's all right. It wasn't your fault. Come on, we're already late for the party."

Right as the housekeeper is removing Rebecca's coat, her mother swoops in to give her a delicate kiss on the cheek, smelling of irises. "Darling, couldn't you get here earlier? I've had to entertain your friends."

Rebecca swallows at the thought of her mother interacting with her colleagues. She glances through the arched doorway of the foyer at the mass of people sipping champagne in the majestic living room underneath sparkling chandeliers. Lucy is busy hanging up Fifi's thin jacket, which is hardly needed now that the weather's getting warmer. Deciding to hold the party at her mother's penthouse was an act of desperation. After considering the many possibilities for disaster, Rebecca had decided to bite the bullet and go through with it anyway. Where else could she host such a large event without exceeding her publisher's budget? The Carey Madison scandal had hit like a train wreck only a few months ago and it was essential to boost morale at B&W, not to mention keep up appearances for the rest of the publishing world.

The walls are covered with the artifacts of her father's life: newspaper clippings, portraits, and awards interspersed with the Degas paintings he'd collected. Theodore Whitney Jr., legendary publisher at B&W. He's gone now. She feels a familiar burn at the back of her eyes. She swallows and pushes away her grief, still so fresh after two years. "My colleagues look like they're entertaining themselves. I got tangled up at work and had to stop at home to change. Then you needed those olives." She takes her mother's hand in her own and smiles. "But thank you for opening up your home for this."

Her mother sighs and frees her hand, runs it over her tastefully highlighted hair. Her diamond tennis bracelet glitters against her Chanel tweed dress with matching suit jacket. For a moment, Rebecca admires the fine bone structure that made her a renowned beauty in her youth, until her mother speaks again. "It was the least I could do, especially given your current circumstances. Though honestly, I don't know what the fuss is about. It's not like you need to *work*."

"Mother!" The strong scent of freesias from the towering flower arrangement against the wall is making Rebecca dizzy.

Her mother sniffs. "I always told you it's not easy to be a woman in a man's world."

Rebecca is struggling not to spontaneously combust when she feels Fifi tug on the hem of her skirt. Fifi says, "Do you want to see my new magic trick?"

Gently, she pries Fifi's fingers off her delicate dress. "Sweetie, why don't you go with Lucy and Grandma now and you can show me your trick later tonight? Mommy has to talk to her colleagues." This was why she brought Fifi, so her daughter and mother could entertain each other and hopefully keep her mother from making any indiscreet comments to Rebecca's coworkers. Despite Mother's disappointment in Rebecca's infertility, as if it were a failure of will rather than biology, she knows that her mother delights in her adopted grandchild.

Fifi's face crumples. It must be all the emotion from that scene in the supermarket. Rebecca feels a flash of renewed anger. "Can we borrow your phone so me and Lucy can look at pictures of me as a baby?" Fifi asks.

Lucy steps in and says, "Your mommy need her phone, but you should show your trick. It is very good magic."

Her mother gives Fifi a warm smile. Had she ever looked at Rebecca like that? She bends down and kisses her granddaughter on the cheek. "What can you do this time?"

"I can bend a spoon! A real metal spoon. You want to see it?" Fifi gives a little skip.

"Of course. Let's go see if the cook can find us one." Her mother walks away hand in hand with Fifi, completely ignoring Lucy, who is left standing alone in her oversize shirt, staring at her industrial shoes. Her nanny looks so out of place that Rebecca realizes she should have offered her an outfit to wear for the party, but her own clothing probably wouldn't fit her bulky nanny anyway.

She fights down the urge to apologize for her mother and says, "Will you please follow them and make sure Fifi stays out of trouble?"

Lucy nods and hurries after them.

That grocery store incident plus Mother has made Rebecca late. Who knows what's happening in there without her? Normally she'd fix her makeup in the bathroom but there's no time and no one's around anyway. Rebecca is quickly swiping on a bit of lipstick in the gilt mirror underneath a portrait of a group of stretching ballerinas when a pair of marketing interns step out of the private elevator and gawk at the spacious wood-paneled foyer. They don't wipe their feet on the welcome mat before stepping onto the antique cream Persian carpet.

"Check this place out!" one of them, a tall redhead, hisses to the other. "Can you believe that people actually live like this?"

The brunette with a head full of curls says, "Of course Rebecca volunteered to host this bash after her royal fuc—" She breaks off as she catches sight of Rebecca's cool stare.

Rebecca raises an eyebrow in disdain, while inside she is huddled in a ball of shame. To have sunk so low that even interns are gossiping about her.

The redhead rushes in to save her friend. "What a gorgeous place this is!" They both have turned bright pink, Rebecca notes with a trace of satisfaction. And she hadn't needed to say a word.

Fortunately for them, Rebecca's stocky assistant, Oswald, comes barreling out of the living room so fast, she's almost afraid he'll run her over. "Rebecca—"

She interrupts him with a raised finger as the two women quickly make their escape. "What on earth are you wearing? I told you to dress up!"

Oswald stares at her, holding his arms out to the side, revealing a black T-shirt underneath his ill-fitting jacket that reads, "Ceiling Cat Is Watching You," complete with illustration. "I totally did! I bought this blazer just for you."

"From the clothing-by-the-pound place?" She peers at him more closely. "And why are your eyes so red?"

He says with a break in his voice, "We had to give Petunia back. It turns out miniature pigs activate my allergies almost as badly as any other pets, plus they're illegal in New York. And my partner kept complaining every time we had to put sunscreen on her. Said it was like marinating a pork chop."

She pats him on the shoulder. "I'm sorry. I know how much you loved her."

"Pigs have very sensitive skin. They get sunburned like that." He snaps his fingers. "Anyway, you have to get inside—Gina Park's already here! And she's got Isabel Navarro with her."

Rebecca stills. "What?! Didn't Isabel move to Argentina?"

He nods. "Gina says Isabel's new book is finished."

"Oh my gosh, I heard that rumor, but I didn't believe it. That's fast," Rebecca says, thinking aloud. "She just won the Pulitzer last year. She must have had this novel on the back burner. Where are they?"

She turns toward the living room. Oswald grabs her arm. "Wait! They're not alone."

"What do you mean?"

"Mason Grady is with them."

Rebecca gasps. "What the hell is he doing here? I didn't invite him. This is a B&W event."

He shrugs his beefy shoulders. "He said he ran into them at Gina's agency and decided to tag along, since you and he go back such a long way."

"Ran into them, my foot! I bet he was hanging around because he wants to get in good with Gina before the auction and now he's had all this time at the party with her. I knew I should have gotten here sooner."

"What auction?"

"Isabel's!" Rebecca says over her shoulder as she heads into the living room at full speed. "Every publisher in town is going to jump on that novel the moment Gina decides to sell it."

Oswald tries to keep up as she threads her way through the crowd. Here, so high up, it feels possible to escape the dirt and noise of New York. An enormous antique German oak apothecary cabinet from the 1880s is filled with books both modern and old that have not only clearly been read, but well loved. The spines are creased, the pages affectionately and respectfully handled. The small square drawers contain cards covered in her father's impatient scrawl, notes about each title and where it may be found in the penthouse. The antique furnishings have been in their family for generations. They're stuffed with memories. Dad leaning forward in the Louis XV armchairs with padded wings, giving some silly elementary school essay of hers his full attention, the lamplight illuminating the delicate patterns in the silver blue upholstery behind him like a halo. Mother looking on with amused impatience as he pretended to try to squeeze underneath the oval Ottomane sofa during their many games of hide-and-seek. In the end, it had always been about her father, glowing and as seemingly eternal as the sun.

Now Rebecca nods at her colleagues and exchanges quick greetings as she squeezes past them. She knows they don't see any of this. It's still inconceivable to her that Dad passed away due to something as mundane as a heart attack while all these physical items outlasted him, unchanged. And today, there's a tangible exuberance in the air fueled by the lush surroundings and expensive alcohol. Everything seems possible when surrounded by this much money.

"Wow, great digs, Rebecca."

"Like a scene from *Gatsby*."

Who knows? This party might bolster her faltering reputation after all, if not her popularity. She has never been able to master her father's knack of seeming accessible while maintaining a professional distance. She's accepted that she comes across as aloof, if not downright cold.

The French doors to the terrace have been opened to the warmer weather, and beyond, Rebecca can see the breathtaking view of

Central Park, the city she grew up with. The air is balmy. A spectacular sunset streaks the sky with orange and gold, filling the inside space with a warm glow. Her father's custom-crafted Steinway grand piano sits in the middle of the living area, dwarfed by the soaring ceilings and Corinthian columns. Rebecca had been so bad at every type of music lesson that even her taskmaster mother had told her to stop. She'd been placed in ballet instead, a blessedly silent activity, after which her father quietly started accumulating Degas paintings with their tranquil ballerinas.

She pauses to chat with the soft-spoken head of their sales team even as she scans the crowd for Gina and her entourage. Isabel Navarro is exactly the type of award-winning, bestselling author that the new, reinvigorated B&W under Rebecca's guidance needs to cultivate—vibrant, daring, and beyond reproach. She remembers an interview on NPR where she'd heard Isabel speak passionately about the need for integrity and truth in art.

Excusing herself with a little smile, Rebecca climbs a few steps of the black marble staircase that spirals up to the master level so she can see over the crowd. She says to Oswald, "Is Brandon here yet?"

He's huffing a bit from scrambling behind her. "I haven't seen your husband. This place is so enormous, he might be tucked behind a pillar somewhere."

"Ah, I found Gina." There she is, Gina Park with her soft black hair and wide brown eyes is standing with a small group in the sunken library adjacent to the living room. Gina is the sort of person who listens more than she speaks and is calm and gracious to all. Who can imagine that she's one of the toughest, most powerful agents in publishing? "Let's go get them."

As Rebecca steps into their circle, Gina says, "What a wonderful celebration. Those lamb meatballs with tzatziki are to die for." She gives her a hug, then says to Oswald, "I like your T-shirt."

Rebecca ignores Oswald's I-told-you-so look and checks out Isabel Navarro in the flesh. Those cheekbones would look fabulous on the *Today* show. Isabel is in all black: a daring sheer blouse with billowing sleeves strategically covered by an embroidered Cavalli vest. A shimmering scarf tied around her waist cinches wide capri pants above pointed toe heels. What an outfit—provocative, unconventional, and utterly brilliant, like Isabel herself.

"Isabel, this is Rebecca Whitney, editor in chief of B&W," Gina says. "Rebecca, this is—"

"Oh, Isabel Navarro needs no introduction," she says, breaking into a warm smile. Isabel gives her a long look, languid and penetrating. "I've been a fan of yours since your debut. And I hear you have a new book."

Gina tucks Isabel's arm under hers. "We are going to find a wonderful home for both Isabel and her latest novel, which she's just completed. It's extraordinary."

Isabel delicately takes a flute of champagne from a passing server with her free hand. "This is my magnum opus. I've been working on this book for years."

"Well, I'm sure you'll have your pick of publishing houses. Hope you don't mind my crashing your party, Rebecca." And there he is, Mason Grady, executive editor, and her former colleague at Horace Press, sauntering over to join their conversation. He's so irritating, with that southern good-old-boy drawl, the unkempt dark hair that looks like he hacked it himself, the crinkles in the skin around his eyes. Acting like he's some innocent farmer who's just fallen off the back of a pickup truck when Rebecca knows he graduated magna cum laude from Harvard only a few years ahead of her. Even his shirt is wrinkled, a subtle reminder that he's a self-made man. He does that I'm-a-poor-guy-from-the-wrong-side-of-the-tracks facade well, she has to give him that, even if she doesn't buy it for a second. He's a straight, good-looking man in publishing: "privileged" doesn't even begin to describe his circumstances. The only concession he's made to the formality of the occasion is slicking back his hair.

Rebecca forces herself to sound gracious. "Of course not."

"Nice place you've got here. And to think I imagined you were a scholarship student like me back in college."

She gives a harsh little laugh. He never thought that. The many comments he's made over the years about how *he* worked his way up the ladder, how some people had to earn a living, unlike others who were given everything. He's only saying this now to drive that point home to Isabel, who is indeed eyeing him with interest. To change the subject, Rebecca asks tartly, "Where have you been?"

"Needed to call an author. Might even be one of the ones I inherited from you after you left Horace Press." He gives her a wink.

"Well, I really couldn't pass up the promotion at B&W," she says. "After all, who would?"

She's feeling triumphant at the flash of jealousy in Mason's eyes when Oswald blurts out the question everyone is wondering. "Isabel, why aren't you staying at your current publishing house? I'm Oswald, by the way." He waves his fingers at her.

Gina says, "There are always a number of factors—"

Isabel interrupts her. "Oswald, do you know what it's like to be an author?"

He flushes a little. "Umm, not really?"

"It's like being a duck in a Peking duck restaurant."

Everyone laughs awkwardly.

Ever-tactful Gina nibbles on her crostini piled with goat cheese, walnuts, and honey. "My dear, no one would ever compare you to a duck."

Isabel arches her eyebrows. "There is no restaurant without the duck, but no one consults the duck on policy either. And when the book doesn't sell, the duck is the one on the chopping block."

A rich female voice chimes from behind Rebecca. "We at B&W understand that not every book can be a runaway success and we're willing to nurture our authors through both prosperous and lean times in their careers. I'm Simone, by the way, the publisher."

Rebecca pulls herself up straighter as her boss and Isabel shake hands. Impeccably dressed in a double-breasted blazer with tonal lace sleeves and wide peak lapels, Simone is tall and imposing, one of only a handful of Black top executives in the extremely white field of publishing. Her unerring instinct in reading people, combined with razor-sharp business acumen, has brought her to the height of the industry. Simone's charming smile has lured many into a false sense of security. Rebecca will never forget the uncomfortable discussions they had when it became clear that Rebecca's author, Carey Madison, had lied about some of the more self-sacrificing and virtuous events in that memoir. She has no desire to incur Simone's displeasure ever again.

Isabel inclines her head. "Anyway, to answer your question, Oswald, the reason I'm not staying is that my editor left, and I was assigned to someone else. I've heard certain rumors about her fickle nature. I want to be somewhere that if one of my books were to be less successful in any way, my team would continue to support me. I need an editor I can count on."

Both Mason and Rebecca leap in.

"We—"

"But—"

Mason graciously gestures at Rebecca for her to proceed.

She takes a deep breath. "Believe me, Isabel, we at B&W are not only excellent at selling books but we are in it for the long haul."

Mason smoothly says, "As are we at Horace Press. We pride ourselves on building trust, which is the basis for every real relationship."

They glare at each other. When is she ever going to be free of him? At Horace, they were the two prominent literary editors, competing for the same authors, time and again. It didn't help that their tastes were so similar. And it doesn't help that he's male, she thinks bitterly. In this day and age, why do so many still believe a man is always better?

Mason then says, "Isabel, it's really so great to see you again. Last time was what—the National Book Award ceremony last November? Did your wife travel to New York with you this time?"

"Yes. In fact, she's the reason we'll be in town for a few months. She's booked for a number of photo shoots."

Mason takes a sip of his beer—of course, he's drinking beer, even though Rebecca knows he can drink most people under the table. "Such a talented photographer. Loved meeting her. Gina, you probably hardly had the chance to chat with her 'cause you were so busy table-hopping."

The agent laughs. "I know, Isabel wasn't the only one of my authors who was nominated. It was quite an honor to have two authors at the award ceremony. But we managed."

Mason turns to Rebecca, who is quietly fuming. "Did you get to meet Isabel's wife there?"

She flushes dark red. How dare he. Everyone knows about Carey's disqualification. She stares him in the face, and he has the grace to look slightly ashamed of himself. "I didn't end up attending. Won't you excuse us a moment?"

Gina gives a little cough as Rebecca drags Oswald away with her. "Simone, what a lovely blazer."

For Mason to bring up the last-minute National Book Award disqualification . . . and in front of Isabel and Gina, no less. Rebecca's pulse is pounding so hard behind her eyes she almost collides with Fifi.

"Mommy, may I show you my trick now?" Fifi's lips are stained with chocolate, as are her hands and her Stella McCartney butterflies dress. Lucy hovers a step behind. There's no sign of Rebecca's mother, who clearly has more important things to do. Rebecca takes a step back but it's too late. Fifi's dirty fingers are clutching her dress.

Rebecca gasps, then shrieks, "Lucy!"

Her nanny's mouth falls open and she springs forward to pull Fifi away. "So sorry!"

Rebecca scrubs frantically at the chocolate stains. Why had they decided to hire a nanny straight from China? Improving Fifi's Chinese isn't worth this. Couldn't they have found someone more thoughtful, less frumpy, who understands better the value of appearances? Someone more attentive to Rebecca and her needs?

Oswald squints. "If you don't look too closely, you can hardly see the smudges. Much." He hesitates. "Or maybe just close your eyes altogether."

Rebecca says to Lucy through gritted teeth, "Can you please keep her entertained? And clean? Why don't you two find Grandma?" Where is her mother? Wasn't the whole point of bringing Fifi to keep her mother out of trouble?

Lucy nods and takes Fifi's chocolate-covered hand in hers without even a wince. She doesn't seem to mind the grubbiness at all. She speaks to her in rapid Chinese. Fifi beams and chatters back.

Rebecca rubs her forehead. What a disastrous evening. As the two head toward the terrace, she is left looking after them, feeling bereft even though she's the one who sent her daughter away. Failure has never been tolerated in the Whitney household and yet here she stands, a disappointment as an editor in chief and a mother.

SIX

Rebecca

After Fifi and Lucy disappear into the crowd, Rebecca turns to Oswald. Desperate times call for desperate measures. She cranes her neck and stands on tiptoe, scans the crowd. "I need help. Where the hell is Brandon?"

He raises an unkempt eyebrow. "Oh, your delightful and delicious husband?" He jerks his head.

Rebecca looks over and heaves a sigh of relief when she spots Brandon, surrounded by what looks like half the female population. She can't really blame them. It's not just the rich blue Ralph Lauren shawl-lapel dinner jacket that brings out his eyes. Their friends teasingly call them "Beauty and the Brains," with her being the brains part. But it's more than that. He's sophisticated and appealing, having traveled the world and accumulated a host of amusing anecdotes, including from when they met while she was backpacking through China and he was doing field research. It was quite an un-Rebecca-like thing to do, but that was when she wasn't quite sure of her place in the world. It's really about Brandon's intensity, she decides, the way he's completely devoted to whomever he's speaking to—even now, tawny head bent, listening attentively to some young and fluttery editorial assistant while he sips from a Scotch.

She squeezes through the crowd and taps him on the shoulder.

He smiles when he sees her. "Darling, you're a vision."

Even though she's never sure when Brandon truly means a compliment or if he's only uttering one of the many phrases he's stored in his memory, she can't help a little smirk as she says to the group clustered around him, "May I borrow my husband?" All those disappointed faces are so satisfying.

As they step away, he says, "What's wrong?" Looks, magnetism, and perceptiveness too: she won the jackpot with Brandon, as her mother never fails to remind her.

Aware of Oswald following close behind, she hisses, "I need you to charm someone for me."

He arches an eyebrow. "Sounds more like you're asking me to take out a hit on someone. Who is it?"

Rebecca loops her arm through his as she drags them through the crowd. "Isabel Navarro. You remember me talking about her? International bestseller, Pulitzer winner, and National Book Award finalist, that rave review in the *New York Times*? She's looking for a new publisher."

His voice rumbles in her ear. "And you need to be the one to bring her into B&W's welcoming arms."

Rebecca nods. He knows better than anyone how much her career needs a boost. She's deep in a downward spiral and if she doesn't pull herself out soon, everything she's worked for will be lost. She'll be an embarrassment to the Whitney name. She smiles affably at the colleagues who greet her as they pass, preening a bit at the admiring glances Brandon attracts.

Isabel, Gina, Mason, and Simone are still standing together, perusing a collection of framed photos on the bookshelves. Gina is peering at a recent one of Rebecca in front of the Colosseum in Rome, underneath cloudy skies. She's just finished a marathon and is wearing a black Nike cap and shorts, wrapped in a silver space blanket, grinning proudly at the camera, golden medallion in her hand.

"I need to get more exercise." Gina sighs. "I've always wanted to take up running but I don't have the time to join a club."

Before Rebecca can offer to show Gina the ropes, which would absolutely be her pleasure, Mason gives a low whistle. He sets down a picture of a teenage Rebecca aiming an air pistol at a target. Her extended arm is straight and strong while banners fly behind the crowd watching her. "National Junior Olympics, huh? I bet you could give me a run for my money."

Rebecca purses her lips. "Do you shoot?"

"I'm from Texas. What do you think?"

Before she can answer, Brandon steps between them and extends his hand. "I'm Brandon, the sharpshooter's husband. If I were you, I wouldn't make her angry, that's for sure."

Mason gives him an assessing look. "Mason. Pleasure." His tone suggests it's anything but that.

As they shake hands, each clearly squeezing harder than necessary, Rebecca says, "Brandon, my publisher, Simone. And this is the wonderful author I've told you so much about, Isabel Navarro, and her agent, Gina."

When Brandon takes Isabel's hand, he says a phrase in Spanish and Isabel's eyebrows shoot up. Rebecca has seen this before. His pronunciation is so impeccable that Isabel recognizes a fellow Spanish-speaker with those few words and, indeed, responds to him in that language instead of English.

They are chatting amiably for a few moments before Mason says, trying to join the intimate conversation, "Brandon, are you from Spain?"

His face reflecting only mild surprise, he answers, "Why, no."

Gina asks, "Surely, you've lived there then? Or perhaps for your work? What do you do?"

"Actually, I'm a professor of East Asian languages at Columbia, specializing in contemporary Chinese culture and society."

A small murmur of admiration travels around the group although Mason's smile is stiff. Rebecca feels warmth spread through her chest.

"So, you must know Chinese too." Simone takes a skewer with prosciutto and melon from a passing server. "How in the world did you come to learn such a difficult language?"

"Brandon was a child prodigy," Rebecca interjects, beaming. "Didn't you already speak four languages fluently by the time you started elementary school?"

"Five." At the exclamations of surprise and awe, he gives a modest little cough. "But it was all a matter of having multilingual parents who cared about giving their only child access to different languages from a young age. And I came by the Chinese quite easily because I was born and raised in Beijing. My folks are diplomats. They're still there, in fact."

"What is the secret to your success?" Isabel asks.

He shrugs. "I think I have a good ear. For example, I would say that you're from the Patagonian region."

Her eyes widen. "How did you know?"

"I can hear it, just the slightest hint." Then he launches into Spanish again and makes Isabel smile. Rebecca's spine loses a bit of its rigidity. What would she do without him?

As they're chatting away, Gina pretends to fan herself. Turning to Rebecca, she says, "Oh my, what a talented husband you have."

"So charming too," Mason says with a bite in his voice, closely observing the conversation he won't be able to join.

Now that Isabel's attention is occupied, both Rebecca and Mason turn to Gina, the one who will decide who gets to bid on Isabel's new book. At Horace Press, Gina always sent her books to Mason, much to Rebecca's chagrin. Mason went into publishing right after Harvard, unlike Rebecca, who took a year off to travel, and he was a bit older too. He'd been ahead of her in their careers, until Simone, her father's replacement, decided to take a chance and hired her away. Mason wasn't pleased about that.

Simone gestures at a framed cartoon of Rebecca's father, originally published in the *Atlantic*. "Teddy was a remarkable publisher and an absolutely brilliant editor. We had authors begging to move to B&W just so they could work with him, even though he hardly took on anyone new."

Gina sighs. "Truly a legend. He is sorely missed."

Rebecca swallows at the sardonic glint in Mason's eyes. Of course everyone thinks her success is due to her father's legacy, even though she refused every offer from B&W until after he was gone. Turning to Gina, she says, "Speaking of authors, when will we have the chance to read Isabel's new novel?" In her peripheral vision, she sees Mason lean forward.

Isabel interrupts her conversation with Brandon. "I do not wish to feel like I am on the meat market, so we are going to be very selective."

Gina nods. "We will only be offering the manuscript to a small number of publishers."

Simone says with a hint of steel in her voice, "Well, you know Rebecca is one of our very best."

Gina smiles but remains silent, and Rebecca understands that Mason's earlier allusion to her absence at the National Book Award has hit its mark. She slides him a furious look, which he pretends not to notice. Not that Gina hadn't known. All of publishing knew. That memoir by Carey Madison, one of Rebecca's stars and her very first acquisition for B&W: hitting multiple bestseller lists, chosen by a celebrity book club, shortlisted for any number of awards, and then the exposé in the *New Yorker* accusing the author of both plagiarism and inaccuracies.

She draws her hand across her face. It's been a nightmare. Disqualified from the National Book Award, accusations that the editor—Rebecca—and publishing house hadn't vetted the manuscript thoroughly before publication. Why doesn't anyone understand she was lied to as well? She glances at Isabel, engaged in animated conversation with Brandon. This isn't only about Isabel Navarro but Gina herself. Whatever the top agent does, others will follow. Rebecca might be able to get Isabel on her side with Brandon's help but Gina is a far harder nut to crack. Being cut out of a prestigious auction like this would be a great blow for Rebecca and B&W.

Since they lost Teddy, B&W has been struggling to attract and retain their top talent. That was a part of the reason she was hired, to bring fresh blood to the house. It had nothing to do with her being related to him, not at all. It was the culmination of her dreams to be at B&W, where she belonged, and perhaps one day to become publisher like her father, but to have done it by herself. Her father would have been so proud and then, perhaps, finally, Rebecca would be allowed to be proud of herself.

It often ends badly with the children of very successful people. At Harvard, she saw her wealthy classmates twisted by the pressure of their legacies, overly confident, spoiled and defiant, attempting to pretend that being born to tremendous privilege didn't matter. Most of them failed to equal, let alone exceed, their parents. Well, it matters to Rebecca. Why had she been so lucky? What did she ever do to deserve it? Nothing at all. It's been an uphill, Sisyphean climb to earn her good fortune, if not entirely, then at least in part, but it's a necessary one. Her father taught her that.

"Being born with beauty or talent or wealth, that's pure dumb luck," he said once. "What you do with it, that's what distinguishes a great man."

He'd stared at her a moment, slightly flushing, perhaps realizing that his daughter was not, indeed, a man. She didn't mind, though. She would be great, no matter what it cost her. And of course, he'd wanted a son. Men like him and of that generation usually did, to carry on the legacy and preserve their wealth, yet he'd never breathed a word of that to her. She simply did her best to fill those invisible oxford shoes. She became the son he never had.

Mason is talking to Simone when Rebecca spots Oswald leading a distinguished Asian man dressed in a three-piece suit over to them. A little girl is holding his hand, possibly a year or two older than Fifi. Rebecca narrows her eyes. When the man comes up to Gina and kisses her, she wants to smack herself in the forehead. Why had she never realized Gina had a daughter?

After introducing her husband, John, Gina gestures to the girl. "This is Emilia. We only live a few blocks away, so I thought it'd be easier for John and Emmy to meet me here. We're heading to a family event after this."

The wires connect in her mind and Rebecca knows exactly what she needs to do. She draws Oswald slightly aside and whispers, "Quick, go get Fifi *now*."

Oswald darts off. As Brandon switches to English and deftly draws John into his conversation with Isabel, Rebecca considers Emmy. Taller than Fifi, more confident too with her shoulders thrust back and head held high, dark hair twisted into a low bun.

"Do you take ballet?" Rebecca asks.

Emmy blinks, a deliberate sweep of her long llama-like lashes. There's something disconcerting about a child so young being this poised. "How did you know?"

"Well, I took ballet for many years myself and I can tell from the way you stand."

Gina laughs. "Those lessons are certainly good for their posture."

Oswald returns with Fifi and Lucy, who join their circle next to Gina. It's clear that a clumsy and mostly ineffective attempt to clean Rebecca's daughter has been made. Rebecca presses her lips together to stop herself from criticizing Lucy. What have those two been doing, rolling in the mud? Fifi looks like a street urchin next to polished Emmy.

Gina visibly thaws as she catches sight of Fifi. "Why, hello! What's your name?"

When Fifi only presses back against Lucy's legs, too shy to answer, Rebecca says, "This is Fifi. She takes ballet too." Fifi's lessons have not been good for her posture, as evidenced by her hunched shoulders and bowed head. She pushes up her glasses with her grubby little hand.

"Where do you go? Emmy's at Quill Ballet Academy."

Rebecca beams. "Fifi too. One of the best dance schools in the city and nearby as well."

There's more warmth in Gina's dark eyes as she nods. "Exactly." Watching their conversation, Mason glowers.

Emmy speaks up. "I'm in the pre-professional level."

Now Fifi straightens. "Well, I'm *going* to be in the pre-prof-f-fess level. Right, Daddy?" She tugs on Brandon's crisp pants.

Taking a deep sip of her Pinot Noir, Rebecca resolves to get Fifi into that class as soon as possible, no matter what that irritatingly too-thin ballet teacher of hers says. Brandon sees his daughter and bends to cup her chocolate-streaked cheeks in his hands. He says something in Chinese that makes her giggle before he kisses her on the nose. Rebecca can practically feel everyone in their group sigh. She ignores Emmy sticking out her tongue at Fifi and Fifi's swift reciprocation.

Fifi continues. "And I can do magic. I can bend a spoon! You wanna see?"

Her high voice penetrates the crowd, and at this, everyone stops to gather around. Lucy is just standing there and Rebecca can see the shadows under her eyes, even through the large, tinted glasses she wears. Rebecca worries people might think she's mistreating the staff. Lucy registers Rebecca's regard and straightens her clothing, runs a hand through her unruly hair. It's always such a mess, with her bangs escaping from their pins. Why doesn't she fix that?

Everyone is waiting for the magic to begin. Rebecca raises her eyebrows and makes a little impatient gesture with her hand to indicate that Lucy should produce the spoon. After all, Fifi has performed this trick for her mother and presumably anyone else who would watch. Her nanny jumps a bit as she realizes what Rebecca's asking for and looks around wildly.

Lucy spots a server holding a tray loaded with tasting spoons filled with scallop ceviche. "Excuse me."

The server doesn't deign to notice her. He is bending forward to offer the hors d'oeuvres to Gina. Lucy taps him on the shoulder and the entire tray slides forward. Rebecca's mouth gapes open as she watches the disaster unfold, as if in slow motion. A cascade of spoons, scallops, avocado, and mango pieces tumble over Gina's silver-tiled Armani jacket.

"Holy sh—" Oswald moans.

There is a moment of horrified silence, then everyone rushes to help Gina, who is gasping in shock. The server is apologizing as he attempts to clear the floor of the debris. Lucy stands unmoving while Mason smothers a laugh. Simone already has a bracing arm on Gina's shoulder. Over the agent's head, Simone's eyes are closed, and she has a resigned expression on her face that says, *Please give me patience*. Then her large eyes open and flash at Rebecca with another clear message: *Fix this*.

Rebecca dabs frantically at Gina's jacket with a cocktail napkin. "Oh no, I am so sorry! I can't believe this happened. Your beautiful blazer. I am so——" She's so flustered that she splashes a bit of the red wine she's holding onto poor Gina as well.

"It's really fine." Gina lays a hand over Rebecca's to still it. Her face is flushed, though her voice remains calm.

"No," Rebecca says, "it's ruined. Please let me pay for the dry cl——" Her mouth is racing a million miles a minute. How can this happen to cool, polished Rebecca? This is the result when you don't surround yourself with the right people. She can only blame herself. Herself and Lucy.

"There's no harm done. Although we will need to be leaving now because it looks like I'll need to stop at home after all." Gina's blazer is a spattered mess. Tiny pieces of red onion and cilantro cling to the metallic fabric. How will that ever come out? And every time Gina looks at it, she'll be reminded of this catastrophe.

As Gina, John, and Emmy head off, Isabel pauses to say to Rebecca in a low voice, "Do not be angry at your babysitter. It is the catering staff's fault for ignoring her, as indeed they have been doing all evening. You may notice that she has neither food nor drink." Then she glides after the group with Mason trailing behind.

Simone shoots an exasperated look at Rebecca before she strides off to catch up with Gina, undoubtedly to smooth everything over as best she can. When Rebecca starts to follow, her boss stops her with a quelling gesture. Her presence would only make things worse. What an embarrassment in front of Simone. And that smug Mason too.

She turns to glare at Lucy, who is red-faced, clutching a sniffling Fifi in her arms. So many recriminations are running through Rebecca's mind that she sputters, unable to get any of them out.

Before she can speak, Brandon places himself in between them. "Darling, you're upset. And rightly so." He takes her into his arms. She inhales his comforting scent of cedar and can barely stop herself from sobbing. "Let me take care of this for you."

Her mother's voice comes from behind her. She must have seen the commotion. "Yes, no need to make a scene. Come with me and we'll get you cleaned up."

As Rebecca, her mother, and Fifi head toward the bathroom, she glances back to find her husband speaking to Lucy in a calm, disapproving voice in Chinese. Her nanny hangs her head. Thank goodness Rebecca doesn't have to handle this herself right now.

"I don't know what I'd do without him," Rebecca says, taking a shaky breath.

Her mother nods. "Brandon's a treasure."

SEVEN

Jasmine

The wind gusted against my chest as I headed down the sidewalk. I stared at the name written on the back of my sketchbook. Opium. I'd have to speak English. But Dawn had said no documents were needed. The shadows were growing long and painted the billboards in darkness. I was moving through my life like a spirit trying to recover something I'd never had, some dream of an ideal existence whispered in an innocent ear. I took a deep breath and descended into the mouth of the subway, that massive beast that lay in wait underneath the city.

No one made eye contact on the train as we swayed through the pitch-black tunnels, streaks of light flying by like fallen stars. I became increasingly nervous as we left Chinatown. How could I create a future with Fiona? My daughter, Fiona Whitney, nicknamed Fifi, so close to me here in New York and yet so far away. Was there anything I could trade for our life together, enacting an ancient bargain like in the old myths? The underground air was warm and suffocating, clogging my lungs. It didn't matter that she might be the flame and I the moth. I had to keep following, regardless of what might happen to me. Or else she'd truly be lost to me forever and I'd be lost as well.

I couldn't think too much about her now or how far I was from achieving my dreams. Like so many others, I had to carve myself into different roles so I could function and survive—immigrant, artist, worker, mother, woman.

I wandered through a dark jungle of skyscrapers before spotting a neon sign that read OPIUM. I felt a tiny shift in the air around me; a prickle in my spine, that primitive warning mechanism telling me to beware of crossroads where demons and witches lurked. Something moved in the shadows. Despite the icy wind, it was a woman dressed in a red lace bra and tight leather shorts, most of her breasts and thighs exposed: a prostitute. As I watched, she called out to a passing man. This could be my future if I didn't repay my debt. First, I had to take care of the snakeheads; then I could worry about Fiona.

There was a garrisoned area outside the main entrance, guarded by a trio of Chinese lion dogs. It looked like the club had just opened for the evening and was expecting a crowd, though no one was in line. What was this place? I'd thought it would be a restaurant.

After a few minutes of consideration, I stepped up to the bouncer at the door. He checked out my plain clothing, gave me an incredulous look, like he had no idea what I was doing here. At least he was Asian.

I braced myself. "I'm here to see Aunt Glory."

He blinked at me. "Sorry, my talking not work." He said "sorry" in English and his tones in Chinese were so incorrect I barely understood what he was saying. Appearances were deceptive. He must have been an ABC, American-Born Chinese. I repeated slowly, "Aunt Glory."

He muttered into his radio, then handed it to me.

I listened to the male voice, which said in crisp Chinese, "Come in. Walk by the cashier and friskers. They know to let you in. She will meet you past the curtains."

I could do this. I'd applied for a lot of waitressing positions, and someone here spoke my language at least. Inside I could already hear the music blaring. There were a few men waiting to pay the cashier, who looked up and waved me on. There was another bouncer frisking people. He gestured for me to pass as well. I went through a pair of dark curtains and was hit by a wave of air-conditioning. They had the temperature set to freezing in here.

I stopped abruptly. A shrill, keening alarm went off in my head, signaling that some boundary had been breached. This was no restaurant. Moving neon lights cut through the dark to flicker off writhing bodies like flames. Spotlights illuminated the strippers working the poles on the stage, which ran through the massive room like a giant bar. Small groups of men clustered around the raised podium. Almost everyone was Asian, including the blonde undulating on the floor on top of a blanket of money, with more bills tucked into her underwear, garter belts, and shoes. The air pulsed with the sound of male whooping, as eerie as flesh-eating spirits falling upon their prey. It was mostly empty except for the staff, though it was clear the small number of patrons were determined to party. Bouncers dressed in black lined the walls, arms crossed.

I felt a blush heating my cheeks. Breasts covered by pasties, naked curves, and nudity everywhere, though the effect was false. True nudity didn't look this exaggerated, all large chests and tiny waists. This was a cartoon rather than a charcoal sketch, the flesh airbrushed. The women's clothing was cut to reveal as much as possible, though the operative areas were still hidden, creating the illusion of nudity just as sex could create the illusion of intimacy.

The cocktail waitresses carried little black trays with drinks balanced on top and wore a bizarre mutation of the traditional Chinese wedding dress: red embroidered silk leotards with a Mandarin collar, slit down low in front and cut high on the thigh. It was as if a flock of brides had decided to make bathing suits of their gowns. The little cuffs on their wrists simply hung there with no sleeves attached. Evidently, the air-conditioning had been set for the fully dressed male patrons.

Was this what fallen women looked like? My mother would have said, *They are ruined*. But as I moved closer, I wasn't sure I could distinguish predator from prey. It was unclear who was inside the cage and who was out, though it was very apparent who would be footing the bill. I noted the hapless gaze of one of the men, the way the dancer took his money with a smile. It seemed to me these women were like skydivers without parachutes, leaping into the air, hurtling toward the ground, eyes wide open even as they faced destruction. *Fallen* implied an accident. Whatever this was, it was no accident.

There weren't any tacky paintings of Chinese dragons wound around naked Asian women or the like, which told me this place wasn't catering to the Western crowd. This was Asians exploiting Asians. Some of the men leered at me like motion detectors fixating on anything that moved. However, once they took in my form, wrapped in layers of clothing, they blinked and looked away, embarrassed. Their desire was empty, like that of hungry ghosts, devouring for all eternity and yet never satisfied. Some of the women eyed me as well, wondering if I might be a client, even if I was too poorly dressed, and I probably didn't look titillated enough.

I wanted to flee. Why had Dawn sent me here? Did I look like I belonged? This was what I'd always been accused of back home and it seemed that no matter how much clothing I piled on, my intrinsic lack of decency shone through. That was the reason for all the looks and whispers, the reason my own family disliked me. But then I took in the cash littering the stage and thought about what the snakeheads would force me to do if I didn't earn enough to repay them in the next five months. Fiona would be out of my reach, maybe for good. Could this place be exactly what I needed? Even if it was a strip club, I'd be in control of the money I earned.

A woman approached. This had to be Aunt Glory. My heart rate sped up. I could tell she was in charge because she didn't look like anyone else here. She was large and moved like a tank, low to the ground, solid and unstoppable. She wore a black suit, the matching black shirt buttoned to her neck. She had a thick jaw, jowls hanging around her throat, and not a speck of makeup on her face. Her hair was swept back, short, straight, and dyed pitch black above her shrewd eyes. She had an entirely different type of power than sexiness. She was a reminder that flesh was dangerous.

I wanted to head for the exit. She held me frozen in her intense gaze and before I knew it, she loomed over me.

She looked me up and down. "Is this a joke?"

At her immediate dismissal, all thoughts of escape drained away. That familiar feeling of rejection returned yet again. "I-I was hoping for a—"

"We already have enough cleaning staff." She jerked her head toward a woman I hadn't noticed in an alcove against the wall. The cleaner appeared to be a shapeless mass but as she turned partly toward us, I saw she was young, probably around my own age. I could make out dull features, possibly some sort of scarring on her skin.

Aunt Glory leaned in so close to my ear I was afraid she'd bite me. "Were you hoping for a more lucrative cocktail waitress job? Or perhaps you had some fantasy of becoming an exotic dancer? We're not looking for girls like you, dear. And you should be grateful. Now get out of here before you scare off my clients."

My cheeks were burning, my fists clenched, but for a moment, I felt validated by her rejection. Maybe I wasn't so indecent after all. I opened my mouth to tell her I was leaving anyway but then the cleaning woman moved.

I had thought she was blocking some sort of cage. Now I saw she was dusting a small red lacquered shrine. The sight of the altar holding cups of wine, an incense burner, and several oranges unleashed a flood of memories. We'd always had shrines in our house even though this sort of "superstition" was frowned upon by the government. Grandma had whispered the gods' stories to me. Indeed, inside was a large idol of Guan Yu, the red-faced god of martial arts and war, brandishing his sword. He faced the door to guard against trouble and violence. Whatever this place might be, they hadn't lost all respect for the gods. And if I could get hired, I'd have a chance to earn the money I needed.

I made a decision right then. I straightened up and pulled back my shoulders. "Dawn told me to come. I'd like to be considered for a cocktail waitress position."

Aunt Glory looked me over once more, carefully this time. I hesitated, then reached back and felt my hair. It was a tangled mess against my cheeks. A part of me screamed at myself to stop. Once you shot the arrow, there was no getting it back. But I had too much to lose. Closing my eyes, I unclipped my hair and shook it out, the long mass unraveling down my back, loose waves framing my face. Remembering that

I wasn't wearing any makeup, I bit my lips to give them some color. I was trembling but placed one hand on my hip to delineate my body and thought of how I'd smiled at Wen when I still loved him. I was looking at him, not Aunt Glory, as I filled my eyes with desire.

She stared at me. A wave of surprise flowed from her creased forehead to her slackened mouth. "Why do you hide yourself like this?"

I had no answer ready and so I said nothing.

She thought for a moment, then sighed. "I don't have time to play Cinderella."

She was about to go when I reached out and touched her on the sleeve. She stopped and stared disdainfully at my hand until I removed it.

"I hide myself because beauty is but an illusion like flowers reflected in a mirror and the moon in water."

I'd piqued her interest because she turned back to me. She raised an eyebrow. "Too good to reveal yourself here?"

I shook my head. "That isn't it. I understand that if the water is too pure, you cannot raise fish. It's only that unwanted attention has brought me trouble in the past." I paused, then blurted out what I really wanted to know. "Do the men touch you?"

She ran her eyes over my face again. "Not the cocktail waitresses. Not unless you want them to. There's no sex here anyway. It's against the law. That's why we have all these bouncers."

"Is documentation a problem?"

Now Aunt Glory laughed, a short little hiss. "We don't need that stuff from you. The way you look now, you're useless to me, but if we ever were to hire you, we wouldn't want your phone number, your address, nothing. We don't even need your real name. You don't show up one evening when you're booked, you're fired, and I don't ever want to see you again. Cash payout, every night. You know what we do need, though? We need your body, and we need your looks. I don't know what the hell is going on with you and I don't care. But let me tell you one thing, sweetie: no flower blooms for a hundred days. If you don't use what you've got, someone else is going to use it for you." Her voice was low and every word dropped like a brick. "You need to weaponize your beauty."

EIGHT

Rebecca

Rebecca narrows her eyes and shoots her target in the heart. She grips her .38 revolver with both hands, aims, and fires again. A neat grouping of bullet holes appears in the chest of her paper victim. Accuracy and precision: the terms aren't interchangeable. Teddy had drummed this into her during their frequent father-daughter sessions at the gun range when she was growing up. Accuracy refers to how close the shots are to the intended target; precision to how close the hits are to each other.

The past few days have been awful. Rebecca needs to remind herself she's tough and competent. No one questions their editor in chief when she decides to go in late to work on Monday morning, though as always, she let Oswald know where to contact her, just in case. She refuses to be intimidated by the hypothetical mass of possible outcomes that is the future; she believes in being prepared for any eventuality.

She also loves the grunginess of this place. At this time of day, it's practically empty. The hallway is a hideous green, the lights fluorescent, the ceiling panels bulge and sag. It's so ugly it allows her to feel polished in contrast. She's wearing golden La Perla lingerie that matches the highlights in her hair under a white collared shirt tucked into tight denim jeans. She wouldn't be caught dead in this outfit at work, and it makes her feel powerful—the lingerie, the gun, the buttons she's left undone. She's added rubber soles to the bottoms of her Jimmy Choo point-toe flats to keep her firmly braced against the recoil. The danger every time she handles a weapon has her alert and cautious, knowing she's holding death in her hands. After the first few shots, her mind recedes until there's nothing except her and the target.

This is where she goes to unwind, to be the Rebecca no one knows now that her father's gone. Not her mother, not Simone, not Brandon, though he used to love her in these types of outfits. He still does; of course he does. They're both so busy, that's all. She makes a mental note to plan a date night for them soon.

She forced him to learn how to handle a gun years ago, since she keeps hers in the small jewelry safe in their bedroom. He needed to know how to use it, just in case.

"In case of what?" he'd asked at the time.

She rolled her eyes. "You're all academic ivory tower and no reality."

Wrapping her in his arms, he murmured, "Let me show you some reality."

The effortless intimacy of the memory makes her chest cavity feel raw. Rebecca admonishes herself to stop being overly dramatic. That's what marriage teaches: when to ride the waves, recognize the difference between a ripple and a tsunami, understand the times to fight against the tide. They've been through so much together, but the greatest blow was the news of Rebecca's infertility.

"We can have a million cats. They're much better than children anyway," she had said, trying to be brave. They were in the car, on the way home from the latest specialist who'd told them it was hopeless: her uterus was that messed up. "Or we can travel the world and be free forever."

He had been sitting in the passenger seat next to her. He often became lost in his own thoughts, so they'd both tacitly agreed that it was usually best for her to drive. He laid a hand on her arm. "Or we could adopt."

Her breath caught in her throat. "Really? Even though you could—"

"*We're* unable to get pregnant," he said. "My sperm will not be doing anything without you."

She laughed and dashed away the tears welling in her eyes. All of the tests had confirmed that the problem lay with her, not Brandon, and he'd never made her feel guilty, not even through the stress of the attempted fertility treatments. Not once has he alluded to the fact that if he were with another woman, he'd have had no trouble conceiving at all.

Then Fifi came into their lives, making Rebecca happier than she's ever been—and there's a part of her that's glad she never had to give birth: the pain and the awkwardness of it all, the large swollen belly. She likes being in control, being fit and lean, going to the gym to swim her laps. She secretly believes that babies should be grown in a nice tank in a lab or at least in a discreet corner of the bedroom; we've surely progressed past the blood and gore and danger and discomfort by now. Avoiding pregnancy also allowed her to concentrate her energies on her career, this glorious rocket that had shot off into the stratosphere with much celebration and anticipated glory, and is now careening downward: a falling star, a brief flash in the darkness that soon could be gone forever, forgotten even by the few who'd witnessed it.

Suddenly, movement in her peripheral vision. Rebecca jumps. She can't believe her eyes but there is Mason Grady standing in the booth next to hers: five-o'clock shadow at this hour of the morning, dark leather jacket over a tan button-down shirt tucked into faded jeans. How dare he grin at her after his behavior at her party last Friday.

She removes her protective eyewear and earmuffs to hear him say, "Fancy running into you."

She eyes his long, lean form. Her tone is cool. "What are you doing here?"

"Not a whole lot of gun ranges in New York City." He jerks his head at her gun. "Wasn't sure what a former Junior Olympic sharpshooter would be using. I figured you'd have some fancy Fabbri or Holland & Holland custom-made number, not a Smith & Wesson 642."

"When it comes to guns, I'm all-American. And I shot a lot of regular ones before I ever started competing with air pistols." She checks out his weapon. "That's some firepower you have there. Overcompensate much?"

He pats his Colt 1911 with its .45 ACP cartridges. "A big man needs a big gun."

She scoffs. "I prefer reliability over size."

"That long heavy trigger pull of yours can impact your beloved reliability."

"At least mine won't jam at a crucial moment."

His face tightens and, for a moment, she glimpses the hard, predatory gleam in his seemingly lazy eyes. "I always come through, Rebecca. Or don't you remember Frankfurt?" Before she can answer, he turns and puts on his protective gear, loads up the Colt, and shoots. Watching him, she grudgingly admits to herself that his hands and body are steady in absorbing the heavy recoil of the 1911. A number of holes appear in the chest of his target, all within the outer rings of the bull's-eye.

He lays down the gun and turns back to her, pulling off his ear-muffs. "Bigger is better and don't let anyone tell you no different."

Rebecca snaps, "I don't need to be big to get the job done." She pivots to the range and quickly takes aim. Without hesitation, she executes a self-defense drill, sending two shots through the heart and one into the head of her target. She pumps two more bullets point-blank into the T-box kill zone between the target's eyes for good measure. She's always been good under pressure. That's part of what makes her an excellent editor.

When she looks at him again, his eyebrows are raised, and his lips pursed. "That's some beautiful shooting."

Not appeased, she says, "We promised never to bring up Frankfurt again."

"Is that the reason?" He sounds unexpectedly wistful.

"For what?"

"That after you were hired as the new star editor in chief of B&W Group last year, you poached top editors from everywhere, except for me."

She sputters, "Wh-What?! I would never poach . . . and that has nothing . . ."

He lays a gentle hand on her arm as her voice trails off, and she looks into his face, notes his tight lips, the sheen in his eyes. Could he truly be hurt? Before the international book fair in Frankfurt, they hadn't been close, and after, well, no one could blame her for keeping her distance.

In the sudden silence that falls, he says, "Look, the truth is I got Oswald to tell me where you were."

For a moment, she feels betrayed. "Why would my assistant do that?"

"I told him I wanted to apologize to you. I acted badly at your party. A man knows when he's crossed the line and I did. I'm sorry."

She blinks. Her throat is suddenly dry and scratchy. This is why he's dangerous, sneaking under her skin before she can arm herself against him. She forces herself to say, "A phone call would have sufficed."

His voice is soft. "No, it wouldn't have."

She keeps her intonation flippant. "Now I suppose I'll have to stop thinking of you as the enemy."

"Oh, don't be silly." He leans in so close she can smell the leather of his jacket. He bares his teeth in what a lesser opponent would read as a smile. "We're thick as thieves."

NINE

Rebecca

That evening, Rebecca lets herself into her brownstone with a sigh of relief. Mason's words are still ringing in her ears. He offset his thinly veiled threat with a wink. She knows better, though. In Frankfurt, she'd been foolish enough to jeopardize both her career and her marriage in one fell swoop, and now that she's in direct competition with him for Isabel Navarro, she's at Mason's mercy.

She's weighed down with the groceries she picked up after work and her tote bag feels like lead, stuffed with a manuscript that needs to be edited and another submitted by a hot new agent that day. That doesn't even include her most important task that evening: putting together a comprehensive plan so she can coordinate with the publicity and marketing departments to woo Isabel and Gina.

Her home isn't ostentatious but there's a sense of prosperity and comfort, from the fresh white flowers on the polished console table to the deep ruby carpet runner that curves around the staircase. The wooden stairs tilt slightly to the right from decades of footsteps running up and down them. They chose not to fix that when they moved in because they wanted to preserve the history of the house. The accumulation of time is something Rebecca believes in—time having been kind to the Whitneys in their long history. As she neatly hangs her keys in the wooden cabinet next to their alarm panel, she notes that Fifi's little pink sneakers are sitting underneath the small bench and coat rack, alongside Brandon's wingtips and Lucy's sturdy shoes.

Brandon's fine coat with its silk paisley lining is draped carelessly over the bench. She restrains herself from hanging it up properly. How else will he ever learn? Such a smart man and yet always misplacing his things. The air smells like roses and wood smoke and strawberry rhubarb pie, which he probably brought home. Oh good, that means she won't need to attempt to make dessert. She's decided that tonight will be an intimate family evening before she settles down to her reading and editing. Publishing demands all of her free hours and, mostly, she doesn't mind but she does need to carve out time for her child and husband.

She pauses at the arched entry to the living room, staying out of sight for a moment as she listens to the murmur of voices punctuated by the crackling of the fire in the marble fireplace. The temperatures tend to fall during these spring evenings, but it's really too warm for one. Brandon just loves the smell. He's reading in the welcoming green velvet armchair next to the fire with a crystal whisky glass in his hand. There's a pile of magazines and newspapers on the coffee table in front of him: the *New Yorker*, the *Atlantic*, the *New York Times* with the book review section set apart; there's a mention of one of her authors in it. A shaft of late afternoon sunlight slants through the tall window and lights up his hair, coloring it gold. She notices with satisfaction the bookshelves behind him, crammed with titles in English, Chinese, Spanish, Italian, French, Korean, Japanese, and Russian, a symbol of the cultured and intellectual life she was born to and always wanted to improve upon for herself.

Next to him, with their backs to her, Lucy and Fifi are snuggled up together on thick pillows in front of the fire. Fifi is absent-mindedly petting a sleeping Calypso, the funny little calico cat that they found meowing at their garden door a few weeks ago. Her toys along with what looks like half of the contents of Lucy's open bag are strewn across the thick sheepskin rug.

Lucy is trying to read some fairy tale in English aloud. She speaks slowly and haltingly. "It is not wit nor beauty that brings happiness but love and kindness, and Beast has these qual—quali—"

"Qualities," Fifi chimes in. Then she says something to Lucy in Chinese that makes her nanny's face brighten.

Watching those two dark heads silhouetted by the flickering light, so close to each other, whispering in a language she doesn't understand, Rebecca begins to feel an emotion that, if she were less well-bred, she might call jealousy. They look as if they belong together, just like the man in the grocery store had thought. Her daughter had many babysitters in the past, but Rebecca hadn't realized how much it would change things to have someone living in their home. She'd always been against hiring a full-time nanny.

"I can do it," she said. "I'm her mother."

But it soon became clear that there were deadlines and author crises and emergency meetings, and she couldn't do it all. Brandon helped as much as he could but then progress on his book stalled and he was lecturing at Columbia with bloodshot eyes. So, they'd improvised with a patchwork of babysitters, an exhausting weekly struggle to keep their quilt intact, making sure there was never a sudden catastrophic hole when someone was sick.

Finally, Brandon sat her down one evening and said, "We need full-time help, perhaps even a live-in nanny. The entire attic is empty."

"What?" she said. "It'd be such an intrusion on our privacy."

"But think about what it would mean. We'd be able to go out to dinner, just the two of us, like we used to, without all the arrangements. Fifi would have someone she could count on. And look, we've taken her away from her family and country. I'd like to hire a Chinese-speaking nanny."

"We *saved* her," Rebecca retorted. "Her family didn't want her. She would have languished in that orphanage."

His eyes were intent. "It'd be educational. An investment in her future. Think of it as a language-immersion program. Fifi's picked up some Chinese from me but not nearly enough."

This gave her pause. She knew it was her fault she was so ignorant of her daughter's culture. The truth was, her husband knew so much about China, it felt like she didn't need to learn. Rebecca hated being second-best and it seemed futile to compete with Brandon, so she left it to him. He could more than compensate for any lack on her part. And maybe she didn't like thinking about China as far as her child was concerned. Fifi was theirs and no one else's.

When she stayed silent, he threw up his hands and gave her a look. "This is for Fifi. So she doesn't grow up and feel like she lost a piece of herself by being ignorant of her own culture and language."

Fifi flashed into Rebecca's mind: her bright voice; her round, sweet arms around Rebecca's neck. "Okay, okay." Though privately, a tiny uncharitable part of Rebecca thought, *We gave America to Fifi, isn't that enough?*

Brandon conducted most of the interviews alone and it took him a long time to find the right person. He'd brought Lucy home to meet Rebecca and Fifi at the same time. When Rebecca saw her, awkward and unsophisticated in her ill-fitting blazer and too-short pants, she'd wondered why in the world he'd picked this woman as his top candidate, but when she saw Lucy approach Fifi, she understood.

Lucy bent down and stretched out her palm to Fifi, who shrank back against Rebecca's legs, gnawing on one of her stuffed octopus's tentacles. Lucy spoke so gently, with so much love, Rebecca felt like she could understand her even though she didn't speak a word of Chinese.

Hi, I'm Lucy, she imagined her saying. *I'll be your friend and ally and protector, forever and ever. Would you like that?*

When Fifi smiled and stepped forward to take Lucy's hand, Rebecca felt tears prick her eyes.

But now, she sometimes wishes that Brandon, Fifi, and Lucy wouldn't form quite so much of a unit, one that very much excludes her. It's hard enough to keep romance alive in a marriage. He has joined in their conversation in Chinese, laughing as he hands Lucy another book. Rebecca shakes her head. She needs to get a grip. She's just feeling the toll of the sequence of difficult days, crowned by Mason at the gun range this morning, of all things.

At her movement, Brandon catches sight of her. "Darling, you're home early."

She crosses the room and bends down to give Fifi a kiss on the forehead. "How are my two lovelies today? And what were you laughing about?"

Brandon opens his mouth, then closes it with a chuckle. "It's hard to explain. It's a Chinese joke."

Suddenly, a sharp pain strikes her, like a red-hot iron pressed against her flesh. She resents Lucy, she realizes, this usurper of her place in her daughter's affections, this woman who gets to experience all the tiny joyous moments that she must miss. That feeling, like a worm, buries itself further in her chest. It's like she's a stranger in her own home, as if she's the foreigner, which is ridiculous. Suddenly she wants, so hard and passionately that it almost takes her breath away, to grab Brandon and Fifi and sweep them away, cuddle with them in their bedroom the way they used to.

Fifi opens her mouth wide, pointing at one of her bottom teeth. "Mommy, my tooth is loose. It's 'cause I'm so good at biting."

She laughs as she admires the little tooth. Lucy is still clutching the book Brandon gave her. Rebecca announces, "I'm going to make dinner tonight."

But instead of seeming glad, both Brandon and Fifi appear appalled. "Surely that's not necessary," he says.

"I want to," she declares, ignoring the twinge of hurt. "I bought a jar of tomato sauce, your favorite kind. We'll have spaghetti. It'll be fun." At Fifi's downcast look, she pats her on the cheek. "Don't worry, it won't burn like the last time."

"I already make dinner," Lucy says.

At the looks of relief on Brandon's and Fifi's faces, Rebecca tries to suppress her disappointment. "I always tell you it's not necessary for you to cook for us. I just thought . . ."

But Lucy is not listening. She quickly sweeps her things into her bag and hurries into the kitchen, probably to finish preparing dinner. Rebecca frowns. Well, she does have a lot of work to do anyway.

"You don't need to feel guilty," Brandon says. "Lucy leaves earlier on the days when she has her English classes and I think she appreciates it that she can sleep at her sister's apartment in Chinatown those nights. I really don't believe she minds." It's true that their nanny only returns at daybreak on those occasions to get Fifi ready for school. He pulls Rebecca down for a lingering kiss on the lips. He tastes like Scotch, delicious.

She peers up at him. "Anything interesting happen today?"

"Same old, same old. Sucking up to my betters in my eternal attempt to attain that most coveted and elusive of prizes: tenure. Come on, let me make you a drink." He gets up and moves toward the wet bar next to the open kitchen.

"That would be divine." Rebecca takes Fifi by the hand. When Fifi stands, Calypso wakes up, blinking at them with her light green eyes, before giving them an affronted look and settling down by the fire again. That cat does look much better now, with her soft coat and big nose, even if she's not Timoto, the blond Siberian of Rebecca's childhood. She glances at the studio portrait of herself at age ten, all pink cheeks and honey hair, holding Timoto, who was as calm and noble as you'd expect from his long pedigree of international champions. Now they own this cat brought in from the streets. What have they become? Rebecca thinks to herself, amused, even as she reaches down to pet the little furball, who erupts into a frenzy of purring.

"I'll be right back to play with you after dinner, Calypso," Fifi promises before they follow Brandon into the dining area.

The air is already filling with the mouthwatering scents of salmon, dill, lemon, and garlic. Lucy has turned out to be an excellent cook, even though she didn't know much about Western cooking when she arrived. She only needs to watch how to make a dish once to be able to replicate it, and often improves upon it as well. With some surprise, Rebecca notes that her nanny is also, in fact, startlingly good with a knife. Lucy's cutting peeled potatoes into thin, exact slices, moving so quickly the blade blurs in her hands.

Brandon asks Rebecca, "What would you like?"

"How about a Grey Goose martini? Stirred—"

"Up, with a twist," he finishes for her. He's already pulling the chilled vodka, vermouth, and lemon out of the beverage center.

Rebecca looks on as he fills the large mixing glass with ice, then adds two dashes of orange bitters. As he's measuring out the vermouth, she realizes that she's not the only one observing her husband. Lucy's motions have slowed, her eyes following Brandon, or rather Brandon's hands, intently. She's staring at his long, elegant fingers, the way he pours in the vodka, the slow stirring of the liquid blend. Strange, especially since Rebecca has never seen her drink any alcohol at all. But then Lucy realizes Rebecca has noticed her and jumps a bit, catching herself, and returns to slicing the potatoes with keen, lethal precision. Rebecca shivers. The quick, furtive way Lucy glanced at her was unsettling, the light glinting off her knife, her expert movements.

Brandon finishes straining the martini into a glass, adds a twist of lemon garnish, and offers it to her with a flourish. He then turns to Fifi and says, "And an Apple Special for the little lady?"

"Yes, please," says Fifi happily, settling on a barstool at the large kitchen island.

Rebecca takes a slow, grateful sip of her drink as she watches him make their daughter an Apple Special, the name he'd invented for apple juice shaken with ice and served in a fancy coupe glass, complete with a colorful little paper umbrella. She, Rebecca, is so fortunate, despite the mess at work right now. She looks over the souvenirs that punctuate their classic décor, all memories from the traveling they did before they had Fifi. Indonesian shadow puppets framed on the wall, the Turkish tea set in their cabinet, a Balinese sarong draped over a footstool, the Venetian Murano glass chandelier that sparkles above their heads. Those had been wonderful times and yet, Fifi coming into their lives was so bright and vivid that everything that happened before seems faded, like a dream where upon waking, she's no longer sure it occurred at all. She smiles at the framed photo montage on the wall of her and Fifi playing with chopsticks and making funny faces at the camera. That had been a happy day, one of many.

Lucy serves them a delicious meal of bright green pea and coconut soup, filet of salmon baked with lemon and dill in foil, accompanied by spinach and feta salad and roasted asparagus.

"Won't you join us?" Rebecca asks even as she knows her nanny will shake her head.

Lucy never sits with them at the table. Instead, she's already preparing a classic French gratin dauphinois for them to simply pop in the oven tomorrow. As Rebecca watches her sprinkle Gruyère cheese over the potatoes, she thinks how extraordinary it is, really, that their Chinese nanny has mastered these dishes so quickly. There are bits of crunchy ciabatta in the zesty salad and the salmon is covered in a sweet and tangy honey glaze that makes her close her eyes in delight. In a burst of generosity, she wonders what she would do if she didn't have Lucy to pick up Fifi and bring her to school and entertain her and bathe her, not to mention making these marvelous dinners. There's even a meringue lemon tart that combines the fresh creaminess of the topping with a rich, nutty brown butter cookie crust so that Brandon's strawberry rhubarb pie may be saved for tomorrow. After the last delectable bite, Rebecca declines when he offers her another drink at the table. She has to keep her head clear for an evening of work.

"This has been so lovely. Thank you, Lucy." She places her linen napkin on the table. "I'm afraid I can't linger, much as I'd love to. Brandon, would you please do the honors tonight?"

"Of course," he answers with a smile. "Fifi, ready for your bath?"

"Can Octie Lee Squiddy come this time? He loves the water," Fifi says breathlessly, hands clasped together.

He considers, then says, "Although he is an octopus, he's not actually waterproof, being made of cotton and stuffing. It'd be extremely unfortunate if he were to rot away."

"Not the recycling bin!" Fifi says, eyes wide, having seen other toys disappear that way. "Octie Lee Squiddy is *family*. You don't recycle family."

"Very right you are," Brandon says. "How about he sits and watches?"

Fifi nods vigorously and the two of them leave, Fifi scooping Calypso up along the way and hauling the cat upstairs in her arms.

"I'll join you two in a minute," Rebecca calls.

She quickly answers a few emails while Lucy puts away the food and clears the kitchen. Before she knows it, she's been dragged into a dispute between an author who hates her latest cover and the head of marketing, who loves it. By the time she goes upstairs, Fifi is tucked in wearing her freshly ironed pajamas, teeth brushed, and Brandon is sitting on her bed. He's performing some kind of play with a few of her

stuffed animals and Rebecca's antique porcelain doll. Henrietta is large
and lifelike, blue-eyed, with rosy cheeks, an uptilted nose, and long
brown plaits made of real human hair. She was created by a legendary
French doll maker and is extremely valuable, although what truly matters, Rebecca thinks to herself, is her sentimental value.

But Fifi doesn't appreciate Henrietta the same way. Last week, on one
of the nights Lucy stayed over at her sister's, Rebecca was awoken by a
high-pitched scream. At first she didn't know why her heart was racing
so frantically she could hardly breathe. Brandon, a heavy sleeper, was
snoring gently by her side. She lay still a moment, disoriented and dizzy,
grabbing a fistful of the bedsheet, trying to understand why she was
terrified, then the scream came again, wailing like a ghost over the
floor. Fifi.

She flew down the hallway to find her daughter sitting bolt upright
in her bed, gasping like a fish out of water.

"Sweetheart, it's okay," she whispered, gathering Fifi in her arms.
"What is it?"

Fifi couldn't speak at first. She was trembling so hard her teeth were
chattering. By now, Brandon had emerged and was leaning against the
doorjamb, sleepy and disheveled. Rebecca ran her hands up and down
Fifi's arms.

"You're so cold and no wonder, it's freezing in here." She tucked Fifi
underneath her comforter. "It's all right, Mommy and Daddy are here.
Nothing can hurt you." She waved at Brandon to go back to bed, which
he did after mouthing, "Are you sure?"

Fifi choked out a few words in such a low voice that Rebecca couldn't
understand her. "What did you say? Please, tell me."

Finally, Fifi whispered in her ear, "She's watching me."

The hairs on the back of Rebecca's neck rose. "Who?"

Fifi raised a trembling finger and pointed at Henrietta, who was sitting across from the bed as usual, her glassy eyes staring right at them.
"I heard her fall off the shelf. She was trying to get me." At this, she
burst into tears again.

After her sobs subsided, Rebecca said, "But you can see that she's
where she always is. It was only a bad dream. And dolls can't hurt you,
ever."

Muffled in Rebecca's shoulder, Fifi said, "She's not a doll. She's a ghost woman. She was wronged and she's come back." She lowered her voice. "These types of ghosts don't just scare you, they can *kill* you."

"Well, I love ghosts," said Rebecca firmly. What in the world was a ghost woman? Had Lucy been scaring Fifi with her foreign stories? She would be sure to have a word with her nanny.

"Why?"

"Because ghosts are a part of our history, and I love history. Neither ghosts nor dolls can hurt you, so go back to sleep, darling."

Fifi sniffed. "Will you stay?"

And Rebecca held her daughter's hand until she fell asleep again.

But Fifi has been afraid of Henrietta ever since. This is devastating to Rebecca, who has always dreamed of having a daughter who would play with that doll, just as she and her mother had. Fifi's rejection of Henrietta feels like a rejection of Rebecca herself, and indeed, the entire Whitney lineage. So despite Fifi's insistence, Henrietta stays in her room. This is surely just some phase her daughter is going through.

"How can she possibly be afraid of her?" Rebecca asked Brandon. "It's not like she looks like a deformed adult. She's lovely."

"It's the effect of the uncanny valley," Brandon replied. "You know, the unsettling place inhabited by dolls and robots. It's been proven that humans react positively to humanoid figures until said figures become too human. At that point, the little differences—like the inability to make appropriate eye contact or unusual speech patterns—create feelings of discomfort and disgust, sometimes even leading to terror."

"Well, what can we do about it?"

"I'll just tip Henrietta over into being more fully human. Leave it to me."

And he is doing it. Rebecca leans against the doorway and watches as Henrietta expresses contempt in a snooty French accent for those plebeians like Octie Lee Squiddy who get jam on their tentacles. Fifi manages a small giggle, though she still seems quite wary of Henrietta. In the soft light from the table lamp on her glossy hair, Fifi looks as perfect as a doll herself, all dark eyes and mischievous pink mouth.

Fifi's eyelids are drooping but she stirs and turns toward the doorway, little arms outstretched. "I love you."

Rebecca beams and pushes herself off the doorjamb, then gasps as someone rushes past her to gather Fifi in a hug. It's Lucy. How long has she been standing there? Rebecca waits for her daughter to push her away, to tell her that she wanted a kiss from her mother, of course she did, but Fifi does no such thing. Instead she clings to her nanny. As Lucy smooths back her hair and gives her a final kiss on her forehead, it becomes clear that Fifi was indeed addressing Lucy all along. Rebecca throws an exasperated look at Brandon but when he turns to her, his face is wearing an expression that veers dangerously close to pity.

As Lucy passes Rebecca on her way out, Rebecca expects her to flush and stumble in embarrassment, possibly to apologize as she realizes she's overstepped. Her nanny does no such thing.

Lucy brushes past her with a tiny smirk, triumphant.

TEN

Jasmine

The dress and shoes were on my bed. I hesitated and then unbuttoned my baggy shirt. I had to try for the position at Opium even if there would be no turning back once I started down this path.

I looked in the three-way mirror and saw a dizzying number of re-flections. All the angles of my face proliferated into infinity, and yet, every one of them seemed distorted to me. I bent closer so I could perceive only my forehead, the angle of a cheek. I'd been spun through my life like a leaf in the wind, cast here and there in accordance with other people's desires. I closed my eyes. I had no desire to see myself too clearly.

A little girl had once run up to me in the market and said, "Your face is like a flower." I'd never found myself to be beautiful, though. I'd always felt like a bull's-eye had been painted on my face. Beauty without power was a curse. A commodity even if I'd never reaped its benefits. It never even brought me love. I remember when I was about six years old, tucked into a corner in our neighbor's kitchen while Ma and the other women dyed boiled eggs red. Like the others, Ma was pink-cheeked and giddy with laughter, small and solid in her apron. It was the full moon party. The baby had survived to be one month old, and it was a boy, which everyone spoke about in hushed terms, as if the baby was exceptionally clever to have been born male.

"Oh, this one has cracked in the hot water," Ma said, fishing out a broken egg.

"Give it to your two kids. They're surely hungry by now," one of the other women said, a slight emphasis on *two*. Even I knew that Ma had been extremely fortunate to have borne twins, and one of them a boy, when only one child per family was allowed.

"You are always kind and generous," Ma said, giving face.

She glanced at me and then carefully placed the egg in a bowl for Hong. She offered it to him tenderly, smoothing back the cowlick on his head. He was cheerful and thoughtless, with a face like a moon-cake and brains to match. Mouth full, he shot a look at me, guilty and triumphant. I didn't even get a nibble. I sniffed a bit to myself, not for the egg, which I loved dearly, but because of the ache in my throat that grew more painful each time this type of thing happened. I assumed then that it was because Ma felt bad about her good fortune for the sake of the neighbors. It wasn't until years later that I understood the true reason for her dislike.

Over time, I became exceptionally gifted at hiding. I knew how to fade into the background, to allow people to forget I was in the room. The thought of leaving that comforting cocoon of invisibility now terrified me. I stared at the shiny black leather dress I'd borrowed. In my mind, a new woman sauntered over to the mirror, one who had always been hovering, waiting: a new me. I felt the impending change soaking its way through my skin, into my cells. The winds of fate were whirling around me and I was hanging on to trees and bushes by my fingertips, trying to retain some iota of who I was before being swept away.

I still hadn't replied to Anthony's texts from a few days ago. I'd picked up my phone a dozen times and yet I hadn't done it. I looked around my small room. It was utilitarian and clean, unencumbered by any personal touches. Light streamed in through the window. The tree outside was barren but during the summer months, it made my room dance with dappled sunshine. The box containing my old sketchbooks sat next to the desk, my art supplies neatly bundled on top. There was a corner devoted to cooking: a hot plate, a water cooker, a mini fridge. This finally belonged to me.

I was in the Beautiful Country. I needed to let my past go if I were to have any hope of walking into the future I longed for, a future with my daughter in it.

I'd do my makeup first. Though I'd almost never worn any cosmetics, I painted on eye shadow and blush with a steady hand. I was, after all, an artist. I understood the borrowed colors were wrong for me, too pale and light, too pink, made for white skin not like my own, which was tan with a golden tint. The lipstick was heavily perfumed and overly sweet, and I was surprised to find that I enjoyed painting on myself. If I got this job, I would buy some makeup of my own, perhaps some plums and browns, a deeper red for my lips. I checked out my features with a professional eye. For once, I didn't wince or look away. I was seeking to enhance instead.

Not good enough. I remembered the iridescent, hypnotic quality Dawn and her friend had exuded, the overblown sexuality of the other women at Opium. I went into the bathroom and opened the cabinet. I took out a small pair of scissors. I carefully combed a precise section of hair into my face. Then, holding the wastebasket underneath to catch the severed locks, I snipped bangs just long enough to brush my eyebrows. I could always clip them back when I didn't need them.

After sweeping away the hairs that stuck to my cheeks and nose, I examined myself again. I looked different. The bangs gave my face a deceptive, childlike artlessness while the makeup highlighted my eyes and lips. The combination was seductive and innocent at once. I loosened the rest of my hair. Now that my face was ready, I took a deep breath and stripped off my clothing. I examined the body that Wen had once believed belonged to him.

When my parents accepted his bride price for me, Grandma had performed the hairpin ceremony in private. Ordinarily, it took place when a girl reached the age of fifteen or after she was engaged to be married. But Ma had decided that since I wasn't officially old enough when betrothed, it wasn't necessary.

Grandma disagreed. She and I walked for over an hour to reach the little temple at the top of a hill. I knew Grandma's knees hurt her, even with the walking stick, so I went as slow as possible, one arm linked through her elbow.

"My daughter-in-law might run the house but I'm still your grand-mother," she huffed. Even though Grandma was owed a certain amount of respect due to her age and status as Pa's mother, Pa was away working at the factory most of the time.

I picked a leaf out of her halo of white hair. It was disheveled as usual. "You need to take better care of yourself." I eyed her frail frame. "A bowl of rice with a few scraps of preserved cabbage and a tiny square of stinky tofu isn't enough."

She sniffed. "We don't eat our friends." She loved our farm animals. I often overheard her chatting with them. She wept every time one was butchered, and yet her spirit remained open. She and Anthony were two of a kind. "But you must take my share. You need your strength."

I said nothing. I was the first to go without when our harvest was bad. Ma sold any surplus and kept only enough for us to survive. "So many mouths to feed in this house," she grumbled.

When we finally arrived at the small temple, barely large enough for the two of us, I skipped with joy. I loved the cool interior, the smell of incense, the golden idols of the goddess of compassion, Guan Yin, and the Buddha. I ran a finger over the walls, made of intersecting red wood panels carved with an intricate latticework.

Grandma needed to sit on the stone bench outside for a while before going in. "You are such a good girl. Always the first up in the morning, boiling water for everyone, taking care of us like a servant."

"I don't mind," I said, though deep inside, I did. I wished I could take lessons in music and martial arts like Anthony. Most of all, I wanted to have more time to draw in my sketchbooks.

In the temple, we both lit incense and placed it in the holder in front of the shrine. Grandma closed her eyes, prayed to the gods, then gestured for me to kneel on the cushion on the ground.

I felt her gnarled hands gently untangle my braids, then comb through my hair stroke by stroke while the sunlight threw saffron lace patterns across the floor. Dust motes hung in the air as the incense smoke curled around us. She coiled my thick hair into a bun, then held up the bright jade hairpin.

I shivered a little, dazzled. The pomegranate hairpin seemed to glow like unearthly fruit from another world. I closed my eyes as she slid it into the depths of my hair.

"You are a woman now. You are a pearl in the palm of my hand." She brought me to an upright position and unexpected tears clouded her old eyes. She turned over my fingers to expose the blisters formed by the hours I'd spent washing, peeling, and cutting sacks of potatoes to be made into pancakes for the market.

"Don't cry," I whispered. "I hardly feel them, Grandma."

She pulled my forehead to hers. "My dear, unwanted grand-daughter. May your future husband treat you better than your own family."

They had indeed been glad to be rid of me. Wen offered himself as my protector and in a way, he was. My fingers were no longer reddened and numb. But I hadn't stopped to consider the new prison I was entering. Once I became a wife, my appearance went from an asset to a liability. Could I be trusted? Was I flirting? He was proud of my looks but at the same time, no one else had better glance my way and if they did, it was my fault. Over the years, he'd often flown into rages. The worst part of it was, I never could predict exactly when it would happen.

Any time I was out of his sight, he had to know who I was with and liked to invent reasons I needed to go home: he couldn't find his slippers, it was time for me to prepare dinner, the bathroom had to be cleaned. When he was traveling, his parents made me help in their restaurant. It was clear they'd been asked to keep an eye on me. I learned to avoid any male attention. Why was it that women had to pay the price for men's desires?

A car alarm ululated outside, wailing like a lost babe, and I jumped, startled and shaking in my bra and underwear. I picked up the dress. The stitching on the leather was exquisite and fine, and when I pulled it over my body, it shaped to every curve. I cinched the wide black belt with a hanging golden pendant around my waist, strapped the high black heels—a size too large—around my ankles, and wobbled over to the full-length mirror on the bathroom door.

This dress was an exercise in negative space. What you saw was not the sweetheart neckline but the round breasts underneath; not the thick straps across the shoulders but the delicate collarbones they touched; not the hemline that stopped high on my thighs but the long, bare legs below it. I'd always been tall for my age and once I hit puberty, I became curvy as well, which made heads turn. I learned that if I draped clothing over myself and covered my waist, I could blur my figure. That was now undone.

I was breathing so quickly, I was almost hyperventilating. Panic gripped me like a giant, inexorable fist. I couldn't go out like this, completely exposed, a magnet for lustful thoughts and actions. But then I thought of my daughter and how much I still had to earn before August, and I was filled with the determination born of despair. Grandma had given me everything she had before she died so that I could leave. I exhaled, long and hard. I had no other choice. I couldn't sell the hairpin for what it was worth. And I needed money for more than simply repaying my debt.

I had managed to escape Wen for now. I had to disappear with Fiona before he found me.

ELEVEN

Jasmine

This time, I waited until well past dark, when I thought Opium would be in full swing. How could I keep from freezing before I got there? I also didn't want to draw undue attention to myself. In the end, I pulled on thin pants underneath the leather dress so that my legs didn't show, tugged my hood over my made-up face, and slipped on my usual plain shoes. With my coat closed, I looked the way I normally did.

I clutched the subway pole and shut my eyes as the car swayed. I was in a wind tunnel, hurtling into my future, leaving my past self behind at such high speed that I barely had time to touch my reaching fingers before I was whipped away. Fear blazed through me, heated and cruel as fire. All at once, I wanted to cry out like a little girl, *I just want to go home*. But there was no one to hear me and nowhere to go.

A block away from the club, I stripped off the pants and stuffed them along with my regular shoes into my bag. As I stood on the street, balanced on one spiky heel, a man passed by, and his head swiveled like a wolf in a cartoon. I stopped myself from flinching. This was what I wanted.

Nonetheless, I was relieved when the lion dogs guarding the club came into view. The wet concrete glistened in the dark from the recent rain, and I shivered. The row of clients waiting to be admitted wound down the block. I held myself erect and walked past everyone waiting, aware of the looks my bare legs were attracting beneath my coat. I would need to get past the bouncer. I squared my shoulders and unzipped my jacket so the dress was visible. A few men catcalled.

The bouncer was a different guy from last time but as soon as he saw me in my outfit, he jerked his head for me to pass. The same thing happened with the staff inside. I was relieved at first but then I stepped into a scene from the underworld.

Men were surrounded by undulating female flesh. Women were streaming all around me, breasts and hips swinging to the throbbing music that pulsed like a fanatical, overexcited heart. The club smelled of anticipation and perfume and cold, hard cash. The air felt rich and glossy, high, shot through with strobe lights and neon. Colors spun through the room, tumbling and falling, flickering off the swirling bills the men threw at the women like flames. Everyone was acting like they were having an incredible time, loud and high-pitched, screaming with laughter at nothing, faces taut with desire and frustration. The whole thing was feral and brutal and plastic, all at once.

I searched for Aunt Glory even as I sensed men zeroing in on me, a provocatively dressed, unattended woman in a strip club. I dodged a trio of muscle-bound slick guys and sighed with relief when I spotted her seated at an elevated table in a dark corner. She was wearing a jewel-toned emerald suit this time, with a matching shirt and tie. The bright color didn't soften her black helmet of hair or merciless eyes; it only made her seem harder, like a cruel goddess unmoved by prayer or sacrifice. As I approached, I realized there was a short line of sexily dressed women waiting to see her. Each one stepped forward, Aunt Glory examined them, spoke briefly, then nodded or shook her head.

Of course, I wasn't the only one trying to get a job here. Somehow the emptiness of the club last time had led me to assume I was the only desperate woman in New York City. What a country potato I was. This was why no one had been surprised to see me, the reason I'd been let through so easily.

I got in line behind a woman wearing a schoolgirl outfit, a tiny blue-and-white plaid skirt and Mary Janes. I peered around the two pigtails high on her head to focus on Aunt Glory, who wasn't alone on her throne. A bulky young woman with glasses sat next to her. Their shoulders were touching, heads inclined toward each other. It was the cleaning woman I'd noticed on my last visit. Dressed in a shapeless flowered blouse, she was cracking red watermelon seeds and spitting them into a small ceramic bowl. Why in the world was she involved in the selection process? As the line moved forward, I noticed that Aunt Glory glanced at the cleaner before she made each decision. Not just a servant then.

I checked out the competition. One woman had a mohawk, muscles for days, clad in a formfitting jacket and cropped leather top; another was as flat as a preteen, complete with wide, frightened eyes; two had the plastic-surgery duck lips and inflated breasts; the others ranged from pretty to distinctive to traffic-stoppers. They were the embodiments of every cliché of male desire: siren, whore, slave, schoolgirl, dominatrix. I watched as Aunt Glory gave the mohawk woman a nod, then turned away the preteen and a striking beauty queen. She was rejecting most of the candidates. I was keenly aware of the overly pale makeup I'd applied far too sparingly. There was no room for subtlety in a strip club.

There must have been some sort of system that Aunt Glory and the cleaning woman used in the quick exchange of looks that ricocheted back and forth. Then it struck me. They were scanning the reactions of the men. They were looking to see which women could entice some of the clients' attention away from the eager professionals already working the floor. I watched one of the dancers as she slowly stripped off her slinky top, the mass of men around her howling. This was power, I realized. The exotic dancer was directing the flow of desire, feeding their fantasies, making them lose their heads. In contrast, I was standing here with my back as rigid as a soldier's, gawking like an awkward virgin. That was not going to get me this job.

As my turn approached, I prepared. I forced myself to make eye contact with the men checking us out. A quick look, a small smile. I didn't have to fake the blush that rose in my cheeks, the way I shyly averted my eyes. My skin was clammy with sweat, and I made myself repeat this man after man. By the time I stood in front of Aunt Glory and the cleaning woman, several men in our vicinity were fixated on me with their fevered eyes. Despite the professionals around us, I was fresh meat. I saw their regard register in Aunt Glory's roving assessment.

"Dancer or waitress?" she asked.

"Waitress."

There was a faint smile on her face as she took me in, then she stopped short. "You were here last week, the one dressed like a slob." At my nod, she continued. "This is quite a difference." She glanced at my shoes, then reached to pull the golden pendant hanging on my belt, forcing me to take a reluctant step toward her. "Very nice. From a rich boyfriend?"

I shook my head. "I don't have a boyfriend."

"Oh, pretty girl like you." Now Aunt Glory smiled at me, surely the fake smile she reserved for the clients. "Don't you like men?"

"No."

"Women? Ever been in love?"

I was not prepared for this line of questioning, and I said honestly, "I'm not interested in sex at all. I only want to make money. There's no room for romance in my life."

"Now, that I can work with. Girls who think this is about finding their wealthy Prince Charming are gone after a week or two. This is a business."

"That's why I'm here."

I held my breath. She was about to nod when the cleaner placed a hand on her arm. As both of our gazes darted to her in surprise, I realized that I had unwittingly interrupted the usual flow between them. Aunt Glory had been about to approve me without consulting her and from the barely banked fury in the cleaning woman's eyes, this was unprecedented. But she was careful to hide her anger. She looked at Aunt Glory meekly, seemingly submissive.

Her voice was distinct: surprisingly melodic, despite the concealed vitriol of her words. "I'm not sure about her."

My eyebrows flew up beneath my new bangs while Aunt Glory said soothingly, "Why not, my dear daughter?"

So that's why the cleaning woman was involved in this process: she was the heir apparent.

She answered, "She might be the type who thinks she's too good for us. You know, those girls who are only playing at this, like a game. The ones who won't be able to follow through." She gave me a bland smile while her eyes blazed with contempt and jealousy.

Aunt Glory furrowed her brows. I understood she was right on the fence and the tiniest grain of sand could tip her in the other direction. She stared at me and made a little twirling gesture with her finger, so they could take a better look.

I was about to lose this opportunity. I glanced around at the men watching me, then closed my eyes. I thought back to when I was first discovering my sexuality, when I would have done anything to spark Wen's desire. I started swaying my hips to the music, shook my hair loose, and slowly lifted it off my neck, turning in a circle. Then I paused. Everyone could see the back of my dress: one long, thick zipper that clove the piece in two.

Heat ignited into fire. The men reacted. "Wooo hooo, baby!"

"Bend over, sugar."

"Can I get your phone number?"

When I opened my eyes again, Aunt Glory's daughter was fuming, knowing she had lost.

Aunt Glory patted her on the arm, then said, "Come back next Tuesday. You'll work from eight P.M. to four A.M. Wear your own shoes; the higher the heels, the better. We'll give you your uniform before your shift and you'll pay for it with your tips that night. Anytime you don't show up, you're out for good."

Her daughter spit out, "Don't forget we're a high-class club. Our dancers strip out of evening gowns, you got that?"

I was so astounded I almost burst into hysterical laughter. I gave a jerky nod and took one look back as I walked away. She was still glowering at me, her eyes two endless black pits. I hadn't even started and already I'd made an enemy.

A few of the men attempted to follow me but I made sure I was quickly swallowed by the crowd. Once I was certain I'd lost them, I leaned against a column to catch my breath. My pulse was racing, thin and high, at the top of my throat. For better or worse, I was in.

As I turned to leave, I caught sight of a flushed and wild-eyed woman, hair disheveled. I froze. She was raw, visceral, determined. She was a weapon and she frightened me. She raised a hand to her lips. Then I understood. I was looking at a mirrored wall.

That woman was me.

TWELVE

Rebecca

Rebecca is nestled deep in the velvet armchair by the fire, trying to concentrate on drafting a plan for Isabel and Gina, but her mind keeps wandering. Billie Holiday's bruised and languid voice winds through the darkened room, whispering of a man too lovely to last. To make things worse, Brandon has given up on reading and is watching her with a glint in his eyes. She's been so distracted by her problems at work, it's been weeks since they've had any real time for each other. The intervals between their moments of intimacy—and not just sex; sex is often less important than feeling connected and seen—are stretching longer and longer.

"Stop trying to distract me," she murmurs. "It won't work. I need to get this done tonight."

"Wouldn't dream of it," he says, a half smile tugging at his lips, "but you seem so tense. Let me help you."

He comes to sit on the thick, creamy sheepskin rug by her side and takes her slim, high-arched feet in his hands. When he starts massaging them, she closes her eyes. His hands are strong, firm, exerting the exact right amount of pressure.

"That isn't fair." She sighs.

After all this time, he knows her body. He moves up her legs, kneading her calves, stroking the back of her knee. She curls her legs up in her chair, pulling away.

She bends over to give him a gentle kiss. "I know I'm cold and unfeeling but I'm already in trouble with Simone. I really do have to work."

He heaves a sigh and leans back on his hands. The firelight plays over his hair and the proud bones of his face. "All right, I give up." With a rueful smile, he grabs a thick book in Chinese and begins to read again, settling himself into the pillows in front of the fire.

"I'll make it up to you, I promise," she says, irrationally disappointed despite having been the one to stop.

Already absorbed in his work, he grunts as he flips a page from right to left. She will never understand how he keeps all those languages straight. For a moment, she watches the light playing on his profile and sees him as he was when she first met him, in that karaoke bar in a small town in China. Fresh out of college, she wasn't sure if she wanted to go work for her father at B&W. She hoped to forge her own path, even if she loved books the same way her dad did. One of her roommates had been Chinese and they had decided to backpack through China together. At the last minute, her roommate had a family emergency, so Rebecca went alone.

She loved having all her possessions in her backpack: *The Lonely Planet*, five shirts, two pairs of pants, underwear, and a few toiletries. The crowded buses, filthy toilets, cold-water showers, and barefoot children when she ventured into more rural areas had been a shock at first, but any discomfort was softened by the cool breeze of freedom beneath her Birkenstocks. No one noticed how she looked, no one cared who she was. She didn't need to be perfect. She felt light and unburdened, with no need to worry about anything more than finding a place to eat and sleep each day.

The night she met Brandon, she was in a small family-run restaurant in a town so remote she hadn't seen another foreigner in days.

Not speaking a word of Chinese, she had two fingers behind her ears and was trying to moo like a cow to indicate she wanted a beef dish. Clearly, cows made different noises in China because the waiter looked baffled by the strange American lady.

He asked the English-speaking son of the owner to help translate. She later discovered that that son was Brandon's friend Wen. He took her order and suggested she visit the local KTV, the karaoke bar, after dinner. She wasn't surprised when he added, "You must meet our other foreigner." Everywhere she went, she was inevitably set up with any other non-Chinese in the area.

At the karaoke bar, Rebecca downed a couple of beers. She was unable to master any musical instrument, but she had inherited a good ear from her father and loved to sing. She had her eyes closed and was belting out the lyrics to "Sailing," one of the few English songs available, when she was joined by a glorious male voice. That resplendent, tender baritone seemed to have come from the silver screen, the prince serenading some lucky girl, evoking fields of wheat and endless summer days. And there he was, Brandon, stunning in that dimly lit place with his sun-streaked hair and dark blue eyes. He kept his gaze on her the entire time, harmonizing effortlessly, their melodies intertwined.

After their song, they were crammed together on the red leather sofa while she nibbled on a thin haw flake that was sweet and tasted like plums. Of course, he was indisputably attractive, but she was world-wise enough, even then, to understand that he knew it. She had already been traveling for a few weeks and was tired of the foreign tourists who thought they had the right to hook up with her because she was a woman alone in a strange country. She'd had enough of saying *hello, who are you* and *goodbye forever* within a couple of days.

"When are you moving on?" she asked, careful to avoid leaning too close to him.

"Actually, I'm living in a nearby village this year," he answered. "I'm doing field research."

Intrigued despite herself, she was still chatting to him when a young woman squeezed in beside him. The girl had skin flushed like a ripe peach and limpid, inviting eyes, and she spoke to Brandon in Chinese.

To Rebecca's surprise, he replied in the same language, gently but firmly. Then the woman gave her an envious look and left them alone.

Rebecca couldn't help asking, "What did you say to her?"

"I told her I was already occupied." Then he took her hand in his and kissed her knuckles.

Years later, whenever she felt a bit insecure (and who wouldn't, with a man like Brandon?), she'd remind herself of that night. Out of all the languages he'd mastered, he specialized in Chinese. Of course, she'd wondered if he might have preferred Asian women, but in a country filled with them, he'd picked her. And especially comforting was that he fell for her when everything she had was the clothing in her backpack, which she washed in hostel sinks with a bar of soap. He had appeared stunned the first time she brought him home in New York. They've been inseparable ever since, with Fifi completing the arc of Rebecca and Brandon, a seamless circle.

Except now, there was that incident with Lucy in Fifi's bedroom.

Abruptly, she asks, "Do you think Lucy seems different these days?"

"What do you mean?" His eyes flash with some emotion—wariness? She bites the inside of her cheek.

"She just seems to be acting a bit out of character, that's all."

He closes his book and sets it aside. "I don't think this is truly about her. You've been wound up all evening. What's really going on?" He rests a hand on her knee. "Talk to me, my love."

She stares into the crackling fire for a long time. "All I ever wanted to do was read great books. And then in some fit of arrogance, I decided I wanted to help shape them as well. Place my mark upon the path of contemporary literature." She runs her fingers over her face, rubbing her aching temples. "I'm a fool. My reputation is shot, people are laughing at me behind my back. I'm surprised Simone hasn't fired me already."

He takes her hand and holds it between his own. "You're one of the smartest people I've ever met."

She sniffs, smiling a little. "Says the spectacular polyglot."

He raises an eyebrow. "It's not remarkable, you know, what I do."

"Of course it is, darling." But this is what's always captivated her about Brandon, his self-effacing humility despite his many talents. From the day she was born, she's been surrounded by enough people who thought they were God's gift.

"No, I'm just an exceptionally good parrot. I've always been able to take in and regurgitate information without much understanding. I can replicate sounds in the same way. I'm only the illusion of brilliance and at some point, the world will figure this out and I'll be done for." He kneels so he can look her in the eyes. "But you, you're the real thing. No matter what they say or do to you now, don't forget that. Scandal, no scandal, reputation, it's all ridiculous. Isabel Navarro would be the luckiest author in the world if she had you as her editor."

"What did I ever do to deserve you?" she whispers, close to his mouth.

His face, those eyes like deep pools. She pulls him to her and tastes salt and heat.

"*Te amo*," he says, punctuating each phrase with a kiss. "*Ti voglio bene. Ik hou van jou. Te quiero. Ich liebe dich.*"

"I love you too," murmurs Rebecca.

His breath is solid and warm against her ear, and they clutch at each other like kids, desperate and aflame. She knows the firm curves of his muscles, the sweep of his back, the indentation of his spine, the curve of his lips, and the hot urgent blue of his eyes. His ferocity tonight makes her gasp. He smells like cedar; he tastes like desire. The shape of him rises up to meet her, like echoes from a vast lake, the many ripples of the times they've touched each other, loved each other; the sweep of her hair across his chest, the roughness of his stubble against her neck, his thigh between her legs. It's been so long. It's been too long.

Much later, when she wakes after dozing for an hour or two, she is lying on his chest in front of the fire, his skin smooth beneath her fingertips, the rug prickly against her bare calves. She feels his even breathing against her ear. He's always been able to sleep deeply and well. It's one of the many skills he has that she envies. Her mind constantly races, fitful, like a computer; once it starts up, it's on, screen blazing. But now she is content, looking into the darkness of the living room. The fire has died down into low flames, the weight of his arm against her waist. She doesn't care that she didn't manage to do any of her work. This is more important.

Happiness bubbles inside her and she can't contain herself. It feels naughty and delightful to refuse to worry about Lucy coming across them for once. She gives him a kiss on his shoulder, then eases herself out of his embrace. She drapes a soft blanket over him, adds a log to the fire, then pulls his shirt over her head, which falls to her midthigh. She closes her eyes and smiles as she inhales his scent. She pads into the kitchen to make some hot chocolate. Everyone knows calories consumed in the middle of the night don't count.

She's humming softly to herself as she pours milk into a little saucepan on the stove when she hears a sound. She freezes. It's coming from the hallway. "Hello? Who's there? Brandon, is that you?"

She takes a step toward the hall. The space beyond the archway is black as night and she can hear it clearly: a low, harsh, grating noise like nails against metal. It's emanating from somewhere close to the ground. She feels like there's some dark, misshapen thing waiting for her and she wants to call for Brandon again but can't seem to make anything come out of her throat. She takes one step, and then another, until she reaches the doorway and flicks on the light.

Rebecca exhales in relief. It's only Calypso, batting a small foil-covered package around on the floor with her white paws, so big in proportion to her compact body. It's lying next to where Brandon's coat is sprawled on the bench, the large side pocket gaping open. It's probably the wrapper of some half-eaten fruit cookie of Fifi's that he stuffed in there and then forgot. Really, he must be more careful. They'll get ants in the house if they leave food everywhere.

But when she bends down to take it away from the cat, her breath hisses out of her lungs. It's not a cookie wrapper.

The hallway goes soundless and white. She feels numb all over and the blood leaches from her face until she's shivering, wondering if she'll ever be warm again. Everything hangs weightless, suspended in a vast silence, and she knows, with every cell in her body, that if she moves, some terrible and inexorable chain of events will be set in motion and nothing in her beloved familiar landscape will ever be the same again.

She's holding something she and Brandon haven't used since the discovery of her infertility: a condom.

Part Two

THIRTEEN

Rebecca

After a while, Rebecca notices that her knuckles are white from clenching the unopened condom package, her nails leaving half-moon indentations in the foil. *It's a condom*, she repeats to herself. She wants to knock herself on the head to get her broken brain working again but nothing makes sense, none of her logical processes are functioning, like a motor that's been smashed to smithereens.

She once read somewhere that everyone has a garden inside of them, an acre of land that's all their own. Rebecca immediately knew how hers appeared: orderly and trim, neat hedges, well maintained, beautiful and tasteful, blooming with classics like roses, lavender, and possibly a few hyacinths.

When she'd asked Brandon about his, she'd expected some sort of flourishing place, filled with sunlight and apple trees, similar to her own. He looked surprised, then gave an answer that puzzled her. "My acre is a dark place, filled with shadows and mist. A swamp, really."

Then he'd smiled in his self-deprecating way, implying that he was joking, and she had laughed too, delighted at his modesty. But now she wonders if he'd been telling the truth: What lies inside that groomed, handsome exterior? One of her oldest friends had said, after meeting him, "He's so perfect, it must make you wonder if you're dreaming." At the time, Rebecca had found it to be a compliment. Now she wonders, How much of Brandon is real and how much is simply a projection of her own fantasies?

She wants, so badly it almost chokes her, to go into the living room where he's sleeping and shake him awake, demand answers, pound at him until he tells her the truth. But that's not what a lady does. And anyway, will she succeed? He often calls himself an open book, with a humble chuckle, and that seems to be true but there's another side of him that she only catches in glimpses: someone starker, his mouth set into hard lines, eyes a cold slate blue. She's always wanted to know that version of him, to unbandage his heart and tend to his wounds. There are questions he slides away from, becoming as impossible to grasp and slippery as the wind, things he will only speak about in the abstract if she asks; try to corner him and in some sort of verbal judo trick, he'll turn it on her and before she knows it, he's gone, with a little wink that says there was nothing there to begin with.

"Did you mind leaving China for me?" she asked once. He had come to the U.S. to be with her as soon as his field research was completed. Since then, he'd refused any offers to return to China for an extended period of time.

"How could I ever regret being with the woman of my dreams?" he answered, but the muscles of his jaw were tight with tension.

"I'm serious," she chided.

"My darling," he said, "so am I. You'll be the death of me with all your somber talk."

But when her father died, it was Brandon who held her as she sobbed, when she was beyond caring about appearances or anything else.

Suddenly the air is filled by the piercing shriek of an alarm. Her head whips around, her heart pounding hard enough to leap out of her chest. An acrid smell pours out of the kitchen. She races back in to find the milk bubbling over, hissing and boiling. Unthinkingly, she grabs the handle and recoils, cursing. The smoke alarm is wailing high above her head. She grabs a tea towel and manages to turn off the gas. An ugly red stain marks her hand.

"Is everything all right?" Brandon appears in the doorway, hair disheveled, gloriously naked except for his boxers.

She has an instant, visceral reaction to his broad, muscled chest and long legs—he had been a serious competitive swimmer—and somehow that mixture of desire and betrayal renders her completely mute. The shelves seem to circle around her in a whirlwind like some crazed circus; it's pandemonium inside her skull. Instead of answering, she presses her lips together and jerks her head at the stove.

"Your cooking skills are unparalleled, my love," he says with a wink. He gets the stepladder from the pantry and deftly turns off the alarm.

In the silence, she calms and takes a deep breath. Thank goodness all the noise hasn't woken Fifi or Lucy. What is she going to do? What should she say to maximize her chances of getting the truth out of her husband, like placing bets on a game of roulette? Thankfully, he seems to assume her stricken expression is due to the cooking incident and not a complete upheaval of the axioms that form the basis of their marriage.

"What's that?" Ever observant, he spots her burn, which she's cradling with her other hand. "Come here." He holds it under cool running water, then kisses her on the forehead like a child.

She relaxes, closing her eyes. There must be an explanation. But somehow, she can't make herself demand it right now. If her life is a house of cards, for tonight, she's not willing to blow it all down. She's going to live in it for a bit longer.

"Is everything all right?" He's looking at her intently.

She relaxes her face through an effort of will as she pushes the enormous jumble of her tangled thoughts to the back of her mind. There's too much going on in her life. She can't deal with this now. "All fine now that you're here."

"Go on upstairs and get to bed. I'll clean up."

She goes into the hallway and picks up the condom from the floor where she'd dropped it. She takes it with her to bed and feigns sleep when he joins her. In the morning, she gets up early and leaves before he wakes up.

She has never realized before what a coward she is.

Unlike many publishing houses, B&W looks more like some chic, high-gloss, chrome advertising agency than the dusty corridors of a long-forgotten university. Rebecca's office is ringed by glass walls, lined with her authors' books on the shelves. Photos of Brandon and Fifi are propped on her polished wooden desk, next to printouts of manuscripts and sales figures. She normally loves being surrounded by papers and knowledge and authors. Not today, though. After last night, she would rather be anywhere else.

She throws herself into her work, but her voice is too sharp, her eyes too glazed, until finally Oswald asks, "Are you all right?" as he's showing her his neatly typed comments on the hot new manuscript she hasn't managed to read.

"Of course I am!" she snaps.

When her assistant turns and starts to tiptoe out the door, she says, "I'm sorry. I didn't sleep well. Didn't mean to bite your head off."

He gives her a big, forgiving grin. He says in his loud, carrying voice, "No problem. I hate being hungover too."

At that opportune moment, Simone pops her head in the doorway. She is standing as straight and elegant as ever in her tailored cream suit jacket. Rebecca notices the deepened lines of strain around her boss's mouth and eyes. "Do you have a minute?"

Oswald's face falls so fast he should be in a cartoon. He blushes bright red and sneaks away with such exaggerated stealth he couldn't have painted the word *guilty* over her head more clearly if he'd tried.

She has jumped to her feet. "I'm not—" At Simone's raised eyebrow, Rebecca closes her mouth again. "Never mind."

Simone leans against the edge of the desk. "You know I absolutely believe in you and your talent."

Rebecca nods, fighting the urge to chew on a nail. This is going to be bad.

Simone continues. "I hired you because you're a brilliant editor, with unerring instincts. You're an international tastemaker. You are exactly what we need to bring fresh life to B&W, to take us further than even Teddy dreamed. And I was right: the *Times* profile heralding you as a new star, the way you've helped our other editors choose the books and authors to get behind, your passion, and intelligence."

Rebecca says it before Simone can. She's proud that she manages to keep her voice steady. "But then the Carey Madison scandal hit."

Simone gives her a hard stare, as calm and deadly as deceptively still water. "That didn't only hurt you, it maligned the reputation of our entire house. You aren't just any editor, you're our editor in chief. You are the face of B&W and all the positive publicity you've gotten only fueled the backlash. Honestly, I'd hoped this would have blown over by now, but it hasn't. Submissions by top agents have been reduced to a trickle. Some of our authors are talking about moving. I barely managed to talk the last one down. The entire ecosystem can't be poisoned." She leans in close. "I'm counting on you to fix this. I don't care what it takes, get in on that auction with Isabel Navarro. Not only your career but our whole imprint is on the line."

Rebecca hears her warning loud and clear. Thank goodness she still has a group of bestselling and award-winning writers or she would have already been fired. She refuses to be the albatross that brings down her father's greatest pride and joy. The very thought makes her shudder, as if a thin, cold blade were sliding between her ribs. She twists her fingers together. "I am so sorry. As you know, I made a big mistake when I trusted Carey. It was naïve of me, and I won't do it again. I'll make this right, I promise."

"Have you finished drafting the preliminary plan for Isabel Navarro yet?"

She feels the heat rushing up her neck. Brandon had completely sidetracked her last night. "It's taking a bit longer than I'd anticipated. I just need to put the finishing touches on it."

Simone crosses her arms, annoyed. "I hope you're taking this seriously."

"I am," she promises.

"And how are you doing with joining her auction? Any word from Gina?"

"I'm on it."

"Have you called her?"

Rebecca hesitates. "I think every editor in town's going to be doing that. I'm trying a more personal approach."

Simone pauses and Rebecca clutches her hands together. When Simone finally speaks, she looks her directly in the eye. "As you know, the relationship between the author and editor is all-important. Although money and publicity are of course significant factors, it's that click, that frisson, that cements the pact. It might be better—"

"Please don't suggest someone else to Gina," Rebecca says quietly. "I understand we have many excellent editors who'd jump at this opportunity, but you know my work. I'd be perfect for Isabel. Give me until the end of this week, that's all I ask. If Gina hasn't agreed to send me the manuscript by then, I'll step aside."

Simone purses her lips, then sighs. "I'm placing my trust in you. Don't let me down."

After she leaves, Rebecca sits at her desk and closes her eyes for a few moments to stop her hands from shaking. The uncertainty of her marriage on top of the stress of her career is too much. What is she going to do?

Her phone buzzes with an incoming email.

At first, she dismisses it as a mistake. Their regular car service confirming a pickup at Columbia in a few hours. Brandon always takes the subway home, and she certainly hadn't asked for one. But then she reads the text again: the car was ordered by him. Her hands are trembling. He hadn't mentioned anything. She checks their digital agenda. He's giving an undergraduate lecture that afternoon and the car is scheduled after that. He's not planning to come home first. Where is he going and with whom? What is happening to him and Rebecca?

"Hell," she whispers to herself. She can't keep this up. There's the scandal at work, Lucy replacing her in Fifi's affections, and now her husband might be cheating on her. She can't move her plan for Gina forward until tomorrow, but she can act regarding Brandon. She must, for the sake of her own peace of mind. Her mother always looked the other way whenever anything uncomfortable happened. Rebecca can't live like that. This not-knowing is worse than anything, because if he has been unfaithful, then the entire fabric of her reality will ripple and change: not only her past and present, but also those long years into the future where she's pictured them teaching Fifi to ride a bicycle, to drive, their daughter's graduation from college and marriage to a man as wonderful as Brandon, Rebecca and Brandon retiring and traveling together, two fit and happy senior citizens.

"I have to go out," she says to Oswald as she passes his cubicle.

He nods and gives her a conspiratorial nod, then brings his fingers to his mouth and zips it. She rolls her eyes even as her lips tug up in an unwilling smile. But her stomach fills with dread as she strides into the elevator.

She needs to confront her husband.

FOURTEEN

Rebecca

Rebecca is too agitated to enjoy the beauty of Columbia's campus, though it normally makes her feel like she's entered another dimension, with its neoclassical buildings in gray and red stone, the large squares of green lawn, the old-world feeling enhanced by the names emblazoned on Butler Library: Homer, Plato, Aristotle, Cicero, and Virgil. She heads down College Walk, passing the colonnade of Low Memorial Library. Now that it's warmer, clusters of students sit on its steps and sip takeout cups of coffee from the Hungarian Pastry Shop. When she finally enters Kent Hall, home to the Department of East Asian Languages and Cultures, she decides to avoid the horrifyingly slow single elevator and climbs the stairs.

She steps into the large lecture hall from the back entrance, at the top row of the balcony, surrounded by dark wood tablet-armed chairs. The room is mostly filled with students typing away on their laptops, some of whom are looking at her curiously. There's Brandon, a figure in the distance, down at the front of the massive space, impeccably dressed in a soft light green button-down shirt. When his eyes flicker to her and he gives her that half smile she loves, the ache in her lungs intensifies. Has she already lost him? Is their marriage a lie? She knows how easy it is to cheat and they've both been so busy. She gives him a little robotic nod, then settles into a seat above the long brass railing that divides the balcony from the lower rows.

He continues to speak, turning to indicate the notes he's written at the front of the lecture hall. "Introduced in 1979, the one-child policy in China is one of the most severe family planning policies in the world. Some women have been subject to forced sterilization and abortion. There are stories of women who are given injections to induce a stillborn baby if they are caught exceeding the limit. Some are required to undergo regular blood tests for pregnancy and scans to check that IUDs, issued by the government, are still in place. Penalties for those found to have violated the policy include demotion, a drastic wage reduction, or being fired. Fines are sometimes two times a yearly salary."

A young man with round black glasses raises his hand. When Brandon acknowledges him, he says, "Even if these reports are true, the Chinese government was only attempting to guard the prosperity of its people. Some scholars believe that the one-child policy has contributed to China's dramatic economic rise since the 1980s, alleviating poverty through large portions of the country."

"Indeed, what is moral in this situation?" Brandon says. "Anyone?"

An Asian woman sitting in the front row raises her hand. "The one-child policy added to traditional Chinese values of male inheritance and is an absolute disaster, especially in the countryside, leading to the infanticide of hundreds of thousands of female babies, either aborted in the womb or abandoned to die."

This is how they'd gotten Fifi, Rebecca thinks. Fifi had been left at an orphanage, probably because she was a girl, and her parents wanted a son instead. Brandon had arranged the entire adoption with the help of his connections, and it had all been surprisingly easy. She'll never forget that moment when she first held Fifi in her arms. She'd thought she knew love but her world tilted that day. She looked into her baby's innocent eyes and felt the grip of her tiny fist. She inhaled Fifi's sweet smell of powder and milk. Brandon's smile was so tender, the two of them holding Fifi, the new center of their universe.

"Those numbers have not been confirmed and may be greatly exaggerated," the young man retorts.

As the debate rages on, Rebecca checks out the young woman more closely. She's muscular and fit, with sleek hair and torn jeans above her chunky black Dr. Martens. Is Brandon looking at her? Could he be having an affair with a student? It's a cliché, she knows this, and a part of her despises herself for becoming the stereotype of the betrayed wife, looking for clues everywhere. How can Rebecca's body hurt so much that even a touch would make her scream? She values reliability but hates being predictable, which she understands are two halves of the same coin. The story of his past loves is one she's never really gotten out of him, not that she'd tried that hard. What type of woman does he fall for? And isn't the wife always the last to know?

In any case, Brandon seems to be his usual calm, charming self. This is a problem. He'll probably deny the accusation, whether it's true or not, and how will she know the difference? She hates to admit it but he's so practiced, so talented with language, so glib, and she wants to believe him, of course she does. In fact, she craves it, for him to tell her some reasonable story that she can accept so she can tuck this incident and all accompanying doubts into the dark recesses of her mind.

"Always know your own weaknesses," her father told her. "Know them better than your worst enemy and no one will be able to pull the wool over your eyes."

Rebecca runs through different scenarios in her imagination until the class ends. Students are bustling around, pulling on jackets and hats, slinging knapsacks over their backs, chattering and laughing. Then they begin to line up with sheaves of paper in their hands. They're either dropping them off on Brandon's desk or handing them to him personally.

She waits her turn until she gets to the front of the lecture hall, where the young woman with the Dr. Martens is still arguing furiously with the guy with the round glasses. What is Brandon going to do when Rebecca reaches him? If he's sleeping with someone in the room, he'll likely be more hesitant, perhaps not want to make it clear that his wife is here.

But as soon as she's within reach, he slings an arm around her and gives her a kiss on the lips that makes a few of the students wolf-whistle. "Hello, darling. To what do I owe the pleasure?"

"Just wanted to surprise you." A part of her eases a bit. The other woman is watching them closely. Why? Or is Rebecca overly sensitive to every nuance now?

Rebecca steps aside so more students can submit their papers to him. She waits until the rush has slowed, then steps up to him again. He's got his hand extended, accepting assignment after assignment.

She braces herself, then drops the condom into his palm, ensuring her body hides it from the students still milling about.

He blinks, then squints to see what it is. Surprise crosses his face. He shoots her a puzzled look and quickly hides the condom in his pocket before anyone else can see. He gives her a roguish wink, then continues shuffling the papers he's been given, though color now stains his cheeks.

Rebecca exhales. That was the right reaction. He was startled and confused, possibly a bit turned on, but she saw no hint of anger or defensiveness. No recognition. She waits for the students to leave so they can talk but a small group seems to be waiting for him, including the young woman.

He gathers his things, then leans down to whisper in her ear. "I must admit I'm a bit confused. Enlighten me."

She murmurs, "Why are they all hanging around?"

"I have office hours now. They usually walk with me."

The doubt hits her again like a bolt of lightning. As she eyes the female student, she keeps her voice low. "Oh? Quite an attractive bunch, don't you think?"

His eyebrows shoot up before he recovers himself and chuckles. He's leaning a hip against the desk with lazy, careless ease but his shoulders are rigid. "I suppose. But my taste tends toward irascible and ambitious editors. What is this all about?"

She wonders if she should ask him to speak in private, but some instinct tells her to drop the bomb while he's off-balance and see what the explosion lays bare. "I found that last night in our house."

She watches as his eyes slowly harden and begin to smolder with anger. It's like he's being turned to stone. The stiffness spreads through his body until he shoves himself off the desk and says to the students in a harsh voice, "Get out now, all of you. I'll meet you in my office."

Startled, they stare at him then shuffle toward the door. The young woman is the last to go and keeps her clear gaze fixed upon them.

The door has barely shut before he grabs Rebecca by the shoulders so hard she gasps. "You think it's mine? You came here to try to trap me?"

She tries to pull away but he's too strong. She glares at him. "Take your hands off me."

He releases her so suddenly that she stumbles backward. His eyes are blazing.

"It's certainly not mine," Rebecca says with some asperity. "The cat was playing with it after it fell out of your coat pocket."

"No, it did not," he says, "because I've never seen this before. I'm assuming you found this in the hallway?"

She nods.

"And there's no other adult in the house who might want to use protection?" he asks through clenched teeth.

"No, of course—" Her hand flies to her cheek. "But . . . Lucy's so young. She couldn't . . . she wouldn't . . ." It had honestly never occurred to her. She's never thought of Lucy as having a life outside of the one they saw, in which she was their caretaker for Fifi, let alone as a sexually active young woman.

"Don't you remember? Her bag spilled all over the floor yesterday. Why didn't you ask me about this right away? Isn't that what two people who love and trust each other would do instead of concocting elaborate games like this?"

Relief and embarrassment flood through her. "I—I was in shock. Even if you had—I just didn't want to know." Suddenly her topsy-turvy world has been placed back on its feet. Although she's not a religious person, she sends a quick prayer to the heavens: *Thank you.* Brandon isn't cheating on her. She doesn't need to recalibrate everything she thought she knew about her marriage. He's still her dear, lovely husband who wouldn't dream of being unfaithful. "Please let me make it up to you. Let's go out to dinner tonight."

A muscle works in his jaw. "Is Lucy available?"

"No, but we can ask her to skip her English class this one time. Look, I'm so sorry." She takes his face in her hands, feels the faint stubble, the brush of his hair, and kisses him tenderly, trying to put some of her remorse and self-reproach in the kiss.

He relaxes a little but says, "Unfortunately, I have a group of Chinese visiting officials I'm supposed to take out on the town."

That would explain the car he'd ordered. The reminder awakens the cynical part of her. What are their plans? Could he be lying? No, it would be foolish for him to book a tryst via their shared car service account. He is many things, but he isn't stupid. And she is honestly disappointed. After having possibly lost him in her mind, she wants to spend time with him tonight, reassure herself this truly is her reality. "Why don't I come along?"

He looks faintly surprised. "I'm afraid that's not a good idea. It's a very macho group. I'm not quite sure I'm manly enough to be included, actually."

She doesn't like the sound of this gathering. She runs a hand along his sleeve and smiles through her disappointment. "I imagine you'll manage."

"I'm going to be home late. They're expecting the entire American experience, so dinner and drinks afterward, possibly a club." He pauses and she understands how much it costs him to squeeze out the following words. "They're thinking of funding part of our program so I need to wine and dine them. You know I'm up for tenure soon and I'm not finished with my next book yet."

"You will be." His vulnerability reassures her. This is the Brandon she knows and loves.

He gives her a rueful smile. "I'm not quite as young and sparkly as I used to be."

She sniffs. "No one would call you old, especially compared to the dinosaurs running around here."

"Well, we child prodigies have a shelf life, you know. The further we get from our childhood, the less extraordinary we are, until we're just like everyone else."

She wraps her arms around his waist. "Now you're being silly. But go ahead and have fun tonight. I'll make this up to you another time. How about tomorrow evening?"

When he hesitates, she understands that he still hasn't completely forgiven her. His gaze is hard; there are tight lines at the corners of his mouth. And he's right. She should have asked him about the condom immediately instead of this ruse. They can talk it all out at dinner, not here with his students waiting for him in his office. "It'll be perfect because Lucy's home anyway. Only I do need to speak to Fifi's ballet teacher after her class. We could go to that lovely French place near the dance studio."

His eyes fill with affection at the mention of their daughter. "Sure, I'll meet you at the studio at the end of Fifi's lesson. She's been after me to see her in her new leotard."

Relieved, she gives him a quick kiss on the cheek. She had almost messed things up. She hesitates, then says slowly, "About Lucy. There's no question that she loves Fifi and does her best for her, as well as she can, but . . ."

"But what?"

She shakes her head. Why *does* she resent her nanny? "I can't quite put my finger on it."

There's still a hard edge to his voice. "Perhaps you underestimate her and maybe you underestimate me too. Look, I have to go. Don't wait up." He collects his things. When her eyes fly to his in surprise, he strides toward the door. "I actually think Lucy's pretty wonderful."

FIFTEEN

Jasmine

Someone slammed into me from behind. A hot liquid splashed onto my coat and neck, and the smell of coffee, incongruously delicious, engulfed me. I whipped around to find an older white woman, one hand pinching a half-empty Styrofoam cup between her thumb and forefinger.

I quickly checked my bag. I couldn't afford to replace anything. Luckily, nothing seemed ruined.

In English, the woman automatically started to say, "Sor—" but then she caught sight of my cheap coat and I saw her decide that I wasn't worth the apology. She gave a little sniff and strode away.

The streetlamps were just flickering on, balancing in that moment between day and night, as I made my way toward Opium to work for the first time. Strangers crowded me with their faces closed and eyes averted. Soon the sky was dark and the artificial lights turned the sharp shadows on the sidewalk sinister and twisted. I heard only my ragged breathing and the shuffle of my shoes on the bare concrete. I was wearing my normal clothing with no makeup. There was no need to dress in anything sexy since I'd be changing into the waitress outfit at the club.

I had prepared by going to the drugstore and buying the least expensive cosmetics I could find, which were at any rate the right colors for my skin. I got a pair of cheap high heels that were low enough for me to survive a long shift in them. I purchased bandages for my feet, which were already sprouting blisters from the initial interview.

Out of the corner of my eye, I saw something small and dark race toward me from an alleyway. I gasped but when I jerked around to face it fully, it was gone. A rat, perhaps. There was a stain spread across the sidewalk beneath a child's abandoned slipper. I tensed at a rustling behind me: footsteps, or the wind riffling through the trash on the street?

Suddenly, fingers gripped my arm hard, and I gave a half-strangled scream.

"Hey, don't I know you?" It was the young woman, Dawn. I exhaled. Her face was as made up as the last time I saw her. She was wearing leggings and sneakers underneath her fluffy coat. "Sorry, didn't mean to scare you."

I smiled. "From the restaurant. Thanks for the tip. I got the job. My name's Jasmine, by the way."

She studied my bare face as she fell into step beside me. "I knew you would. Where's your friend?"

I stared at her blankly until I realized she meant Anthony. "He doesn't know I'm doing this."

"Of course not. Boyfriends never like it, unless they do, and then you'd better watch out."

"He's not my boyfriend."

She gave me a sidelong look. "You tell yourself whatever you want."

When I didn't answer, she linked her arm through mine and we headed toward Opium together. With her next to me, I straightened up and pulled my shoulders back. Her companionship made the crossing easier and with a pang, I realized that I'd missed this all my life without knowing what I was yearning for: a sister, not necessarily by blood but through belonging. This type of belonging was what I hoped to share with Fiona someday. I was tall and long-limbed in a family that was short and stocky. My hair was thick and unruly, not silky and dense. My eyes were a golden brown instead of their dark coffee. I'd grown up not being reflected in the faces of my relatives.

I hardly knew Dawn, but our footsteps were in sync as we walked. Men gazed at her as much as at me when we strode past. For that, I felt a rush of gratitude for her being a buffer. She ushered us inside and said she'd meet me in the changing room while I went to get my uniform. The outfit was even tinier than I remembered, made of some cheap, stretchy polyester material. The music was already pounding and when the lights started flashing in time to the beat, it seemed to me that the patrons turned into skulls with coins in their eye sockets. Opium was an ill-lit landscape, inhabited by souls clustered around the dancers working the poles, each customer desperate to drink from the river of oblivion and forgetfulness that was sex, all locusts tied to one rope.

I pulled open the door to what I thought was the changing room, only to find a closet filled with cleaning supplies and aprons. Cheeks flushed, I slammed it closed, then saw a group of dancers with brightly colored sequined costumes and some cocktail waitresses milling around the women's bathroom to my left. So, the ladies' room was the changing room. Clearly the club didn't attract many women customers and the management couldn't care less about the comfort and well-being of their female staff.

I spotted Dawn among the group and she waved for me to join her. A bouncer was sitting on a stool outside the room, monitoring everyone who went in or out. He had slicked-back hair and was covered with tattoos from what I could see of his exposed skin. He was dressed in a fine charcoal tailored shirt paired with black pants underneath a large blazer. Several gold chains hung around his thick neck.

"Why is he here?" I whispered to Dawn. She gave me a shushing look.

The woman in front of us fumbled with her bag, then pulled out a bill and put it in his hand before being allowed inside.

I shot Dawn an alarmed look, wondering if we would need to tip him every time we went in or out of the bathroom, but she only gave him a brilliant smile. "How are you, Lone Wolf Jack? Any luck finding the perfect balut egg yet?"

"Hello," he said, his voice neutral, almost expressionless. He had a well-proportioned face with fine features. He would have appeared handsome or good-natured if not for the arctic coldness of his eyes. He looked me over, lingered on my breasts beneath my coat. "New girl, huh? You know what a balut egg is?"

"Lone Wolf Jack loves food," Dawn interjected.

"It's a fertilized duck egg and when you eat it, it's part egg, part unhatched baby duck." He patted his flat stomach. "Delicious when it's done right but very hard to get perfect."

I shuddered, my guts churning.

There was a spark of interest in his close-set eyes but the overwhelming impression I had of him was that of impersonal ruthlessness. "You got a name?"

I kept my gaze averted and blurted, "No."

Dawn quickly pulled me into the bathroom before I could say anything else. She hissed, "Are you out of your mind? He's triad. Didn't you see the Guan Yu tattoo on his arm?"

For an instant, I didn't understand what she had said. The air turned dense and impenetrable, clogging my lungs like smoke. Triads, Chinese organized crime, were deeply connected to the snakeheads to whom I owed money. In fact, the triads were probably the enforcers for the snakeheads. "Wh-what? Guan Yu is worshipped by the police."

Her expression told me how stupid I was. "*And* the triads. They kill people like they're cutting grass. Last year, one of the dancers was found dead in her apartment—the cops called it an overdose, but people say she didn't repay her debts."

The music and voices combined into a low-pitched pounding against my skull. My heart was firing like a machine gun. I thought back to the altar of Guan Yu I'd seen in the club, the one that had convinced me to apply for this job. So what had appeared to represent honest business and family values was actually a declaration of support for the triads. I had used wood to put out a fire and now I was exactly where I'd most feared: in a nest of organized crime.

She must have read the horror on my face because she said, "Relax, just don't give him any reason to notice you and you'll be all right."

"Why did the woman in front of us need to pay?"

"Because she's doing meth in the bathroom stall, and he knows it. The bouncers are supposed to keep out the drugs but most take extra payment to look the other way. In any case, he's mainly there to stop the men from following us in here."

I finally took in the scene inside the ladies' room. Women were crowded in front of the mirrors, faces covered in heavy makeup. Glittery gowns, thongs, and bras were hanging out of bags while the scent of hairspray and perfume permeated the air. Half-naked women banged in and out of the toilet stalls, chattering to each other as they changed. I caught snatches of conversation.

"I have to lose five pounds or my agent's going to . . ."

"Feel my breasts, they're as hard as . . ."

"And my chihuahua's got to go to the vet again . . ."

Everyone ignored me, which was a relief. They must have new women come and go all the time. Dawn found an empty space against the wall and started stripping off her clothing. She gave me an amused look when I ducked into a stall to change. The uniform was basically cut like a skimpy one-piece swimsuit, an imitation of embroidered red silk, with a Mandarin collar. The little cuffs around my wrists were just as annoying as I'd thought they would be.

When I emerged, the tiny outfit somehow stretching to accommodate all my curves, Dawn gave me a long, intense look before she whistled. "Look at what you were hiding under those ugly clothes."

In a free corner of the mirror, I stared at myself. My body was voluptuous, blank, and voiceless, an open invitation. My face, still bare of makeup, appeared naked and scared. I picked up my cosmetics.

After I was done, Dawn said, "I'm so glad you're here. We're going to be great together. Did you see the looks we got walking in? And that was without the costume and makeup."

At my confused expression, she cocked her head toward our reflections in the mirror. Side by side, dressed in the same outfits, we could be matching bookends. We were about the same height, though she had a wide-eyed, gamine charm while I was darker and curvier, with longer hair. We looked great together. Somehow, we made each other even more alluring.

She smoothed her hair. "I hadn't found anyone who could work the floor with me."

That's when I realized, my heart sinking, that she had seen this in me from the very beginning. That was why she reeled me in. Of course it hadn't been altruism or friendship or anything like that.

"But we need to get you through your first night before we try anything." She was searching through her bag. "My treat. Vitamin E or C?"

What? I furrowed my brow. "I don't need any vitamins, thank you."

She stopped pawing through her stuff and stared at me incredulously. "Are you for real?"

Someone sniggered behind us. I heard one of the dancers mutter something about the "cocktail waitresses pretending to be so goddamn pure."

Dawn pulled out a little pouch of blue pills and a white bag of powder. Although I wasn't sure about the pills, I recognized the powder from television. I swallowed, then shook my head, feeling like the stupid egg that I was. I hadn't even started work yet and I was already so out of my depth I felt like I was drowning. I had a sudden urge to bolt for the door, hurtle out of the club, and keep running until I was a child watching Grandma make my rice congee for breakfast again.

Dawn tsked like a schoolteacher. "You have no idea what it's like on the floor. You're going to need this."

When I took a step backward, she shrugged and popped a piece of a pill in her mouth. She swallowed it with a bit of water from the sink.

"What is that?"

"Ecstasy. I have a great supplier. I'll give you his name and number when you're ready." She gave me an arch glance that said, *It's only a matter of time*. "Come on, let's set things straight with Lone Wolf Jack and get you something else to muffle the pain."

She gathered her things, then grabbed me by the hand and led me to the triad bouncer.

She fluttered her lashes at him as she said, "Please let me introduce my new friend, Jasmine. She didn't mean to be rude before. She's just shy and this is her first night."

I held very still as his eyes roved over my body at length. I attempted a smile that felt more like a grimace, but he didn't seem to notice. When Dawn nudged me, I said, "H-hello, Lone Wolf Jack."

Finally, he looked me in the face and went very still. His voice was so quiet, I could barely hear him over the music. "Those are some gorgeous eyes you have, Jasmine."

I gave him a jerky little nod as we walked away.

Dawn said, with some asperity, "What part of 'don't give him any reason to notice you' did you not understand?"

"I didn't do anything," I protested. "You were flirting much more with him."

She sighed. "That's the point. Everyone flirts with him. Being awkward and reluctant makes you stick out."

Indeed, I could feel Lone Wolf Jack's gaze burning into my back.

SIXTEEN

Jasmine

"Come here, I got a surprise for you."

"Why don't you ladies sit in my lap?"

Dawn and I dodged catcalling men and groping hands to reach a smaller bar set near the back of the club. It was obvious the customers believed we were all for sale. I had tried to brace myself against the assault that was Opium, but nothing could have prepared me for the brutality of all that flesh on display, and more than that, the raw desire and sweat-slicked sheen on some of the customers' faces, the shamelessness of it all. It was the deliberate merchandising of sex, complete with invisible price tags.

I slid onto a polished chrome and black leather barstool with a sigh of relief. There weren't many clients back here, though a bunch of the cocktail waitresses were gathered around the bar. The bartender was a petite woman dressed in the same outfit we were wearing. I peered over the counter and saw she seemed so short because she was in flats instead of heels. A halo of streaked black, bronze, and blond curls framed her oval face and full lips.

She glanced at me with her heavily lined Cleopatra eyes. "What can I get you?"

I suddenly realized why she seemed vaguely familiar. "You were with Dawn in the restaurant."

She gave me a blank look until Dawn said, "Phoenix, she's the one who was arguing with that cute guy."

"Oooooh," Phoenix breathed. "I remember you now." She checked me out. "But you look so different, I can hardly believe you're the same person. What can I get you?"

"I'll have a vodka tonic," Dawn said. "Jasmine, the first one's on the house so you don't have to worry about paying. Management encourages us to keep drinking during the night because the clients buy our cocktails as well."

"Just a glass of water," I said. Everyone in the vicinity turned to stare at me and there was some tittering.

"So, we have a virgin here," Phoenix said.

"I'm not—" I stopped myself from finishing.

"You have no idea, do you?" she said, shaking her head while Dawn gave me a look that said, *I told you so.* "Believe me, you're going to want alcohol by the end of this shift. The men . . . well, let's just say they become more bearable the more you drink."

I was saved from needing to answer by Aunt Glory's appearance. Everyone hushed and straightened up. She strolled toward us, massive and imperturbable, guardian of her domain. Her nude face was not defenseless; it proclaimed her invulnerable to attack, like a warrior too lethal to need any weapons.

She examined me and said, "Good."

Dawn linked her arm through mine. "I can show her the ropes."

I saw a flicker of approval in Aunt Glory's eyes as she looked at the two of us together. She nodded. "Take the tables next to Dawn's so she can settle you in. Make me proud, girls."

There was a chorus of agreement as she swept away. In my thin outfit, I was already shivering from the icy air. I scanned the floor and was relieved to find no sign of the young cleaning woman.

I bent toward Dawn and asked in a low voice, "You know her daughter?"

"Lily?" she said in a whisper. "She's not here all the time and our lives are easier when she's not. She looks meek but she can go on a real vendetta against anyone she doesn't like and then, they're fired before you know it. I think she resents that Aunt Glory makes her work here. She's got a load of influence, so you need to stay on her good side."

Too late for that.

Dawn passed Phoenix her stuff to stash behind the bar. As I handed my bag and coat over too, I asked quietly, "Can you please put water in my drinks instead of vodka?"

When the bartender said nothing and stared at me with no expression, I added, "I'll tip you extra."

Then she smiled and gave me a little nod.

I was learning how things worked at Opium. It was going to be hard for me to make it through this night without drinking, and even though I loved an easy way out as much as the next woman, I'd learned that the price for oblivion was too high.

Dawn passed me a small round tray and a notepad with a pen attached. "The work's super simple. It's just drinks, no food. The men are what you need to pay attention to." She led me to a section of tables as she talked. "Don't waste your time on some loser who's going to nurse a beer all night. If they don't throw down a bunch of bills or a credit card, move on. If they're too cheap to buy a lap dance from one of the dancers, you can forget it too. Remember that your only pay is your tips and you're going to need to share those with the bartender, the house, the bouncers—it's worse than paying taxes—so you got to make sure you get tipped well."

Now that it was all about to begin for real, I was trembling. I tugged at my costume but there was too little of it. I regarded the other cocktail waitresses, who were confidently approaching their tables. I felt exposed and inadequate.

Misunderstanding my trepidation, Dawn said, "No worries. Once you start doing the Champagne Room, you can bring in more than a thousand a night."

My eyes flew to hers, shocked. Earning money at a rate like that would take care of my problems. I'd be free of the snakeheads. "What's that?"

She gestured toward a beaded alcove I hadn't noticed earlier, with yet another bouncer seated next to the entrance. An older man in a navy suit parted the beads to lead a giggling cocktail waitress inside, his other hand straying to squeeze her butt. The bouncer didn't bat an eye.

I stared. "I thought they weren't allowed to touch us."

Dawn raised an eyebrow. "They don't get to touch us at length, *for free*. Light groping doesn't count. And anything goes in the Champagne Room. Officially, it's not permitted but the bouncers won't tell if you tip them."

Somehow I had believed there would be a bright line in the sand: on the one side, the exotic dancers who did lap dances and were pawed by the men; on the other, the cocktail waitresses who simply served drinks and were off-limits physically. I'd thought if I made my gaze a bit more myopic, I'd be able to pretend I was working in a normal club. To allow a total stranger to grope me for money, to perform sexual services . . . now I understood why the women here needed to drink and do drugs. I'd been drunk before, alone in my bedroom when Wen was away in Beijing, but had never touched any other substances, especially not under the disapproving eyes of his parents. I felt the color high on my cheeks. Even though I was no stranger to sex, I felt like I was swaying on the edge of a cliff, the wind swirling around me. This was territory I'd thought I could navigate with some difficulty, but the landscape was turning out to be even more treacherous than I'd imagined.

I asked, "Do *you* do the Champagne Room?"

Dawn looked away for a moment, then gave a bright trill of a laugh. Her voice was brittle. "If they're paying, why not? I get pinched anywhere I work. At least here, I get paid." Something stark like shame or regret crossed her lovely face, then she said in a half whisper, "Aunt Glory expects it of us, though most of the time, it's the dancers who get asked. If you avoid the Champagne Room for too long, she'll fire you. That's where the serious money is made."

A customer gestured at her and she sashayed over to him.

Nothing at Opium was what it appeared. Aunt Glory had pointed at a deer and called it a horse, and I had foolishly believed her. The urge to flee took hold of me again but I was standing there in my skimpy outfit. And I didn't know where else I could possibly earn enough money in time. I was trying to hold on to the illusion that I could work in a place like this and do it on my own terms, but I already knew, deep inside, that Opium was going to infiltrate my skin, soak into my pores until I wouldn't be able to tell where I ended, and it began. Walk often enough by the river's edge and your shoes will get wet.

The dancer working the pole onstage closest to my tables was wearing a white cowboy hat with iridescent gold piping, a vest complete with fringe and glitter, and matching chaps she ripped off to expose a sparkling golden thong. Men reached out for her with bills in their hands, hoping to get in a grope while tucking the money in her bra strap or garters. She was swinging a lasso, which she deftly wrapped around a delighted, sweating man while she licked her glossy red lips. The crowd hollered and whooped while a few shy ones gawked from a distance. One of the waitresses circled with a tray of shots, which she placed on her neck and breasts for the clients to drink. A dancer was giving a lap dance, undulating in front of a man. The look on her face, though, which he couldn't see, was blank and bored.

I realized I was already being summoned by one of my patrons and hurried off to serve my first table.

He was middle-aged with a potbelly and white-flecked stubble, heavy eyebrows and lips above a flannel workman's shirt. "Hey, you new?"

I forced myself to smile at him. He ordered a rum and Coke and as I was placing it in front of him, I stood too close and he slapped me on the hip, making me jump. I stared at him, utterly horrified even though Dawn had warned me about this.

He paid in cash, leaving me a minuscule tip, and then called out to Dawn, who was laughing flirtatiously with a group of businessmen in her section, "I want you! Can you serve me instead?"

He had not only drawn her attention but Aunt Glory's as well. To my dismay, both she and Lily were standing in the shadows, observing me. Aunt Glory's eyebrows were pulled together in a furious line while Lily smirked. I felt like the entire club was watching my humiliation as Dawn hurried over.

The man glared at me with disdain. "I don't want someone who looks like they think I'm a fucking animal. I'm not the animal, you are, understand?"

My breath caught in my throat, and I jerked my head back. I couldn't do this.

Aunt Glory pulled me aside. She hissed, "Because this is your first day, I'll give you another chance. Screw up the next one and you can change into your slob clothing and go home, understand? You're giving us a bad reputation. Where is the woman I saw the other night when you landed this job?"

Lily followed her away, turning back to shoot me a triumphant look. My face blotched. I wanted to walk out at that very moment, but I would need to pay for my uniform out of my savings. I would finish this one shift, leave, and never come back. I just had to survive tonight.

Dawn, having mollified the man, appeared beside me. She swayed a bit on her feet, and I realized she was feeling the ecstasy she'd taken. She giggled, her eyes glassy. "L-listen, you don't got to change completely. Some men really dig the graceless thing. You're fresh meat. Some will want to s-save you and some will try to use you." She laughed again, tossing her head toward the bouncers, dressed all in black, standing on boxes around the edges of the room. "The big boys will get involved if things get too rough. It's a game, honey. Smile and flirt, jump away if they're too close. You gotta be the fantasy they can't have."

And so that was what I did. I imagined a protective layer that covered every inch as I dove back into the pool of men at my tables. I was still awkward. I wasn't as flirtatious as Dawn. I couldn't always hide my distress, but I pushed the revulsion deep beneath my skin, until I could pretend it didn't exist. I used my good memory to deliver drinks to large, rambunctious groups without a single mistake.

By the end of the night, my feet were killing me, and I was freezing, and I hated all men. If Aunt Glory didn't exactly look approving, at least she was no longer glaring. I clutched my big wad of bills and even after I'd tipped everyone and paid for my uniform, I had hundreds of dollars left that I could keep. I felt the money in my hands in wonder. It would only be for a few months, I told myself. I'd have enough by then. I could quit and no one would ever know. First repay the snakeheads and then build a life with Fiona.

It wasn't as if Wen would find me here.

SEVENTEEN

Rebecca

Brandon comes home so late Rebecca has no idea what time it is anymore. She only wakes up long enough to register the water droplets on his neck. He's always so considerate. He knows how much she hates it when he smells of alcohol and cigarette smoke after a night out. He gives her a kiss on the cheek but doesn't say anything. He's learned through the years not to wake her in the middle of the night, or she'll never be able to fall asleep again. She runs an affectionate hand through his damp hair before drifting off.

In the morning, he's sleeping like the dead. Rebecca considers him in the half-light, the sandy lashes, the hint of stubble on his square jaw. He's home; there was a reasonable explanation for everything; she believes him. She feels so much better today.

She steps into their large walk-in closet, where all their clothing hangs in neat rows, organized by type and color. Shedding her apricot silk pajamas, she changes into a soft Bottega Veneta shirt that zips up the front, gathered at the waist and shoulders. It has the feminine lines of a peasant blouse while the navy makes it more authoritative. As she pulls on a pair of black tailored pants, she wonders if she should ask Lucy about the condom. But it would be so awkward and it's none of her business, though it's still hard to imagine her nanny with a boyfriend. When Rebecca spoke to her about telling Fifi ghost stories, Lucy vehemently denied ever doing such a thing, so she was likely to do the same with the condom.

No, it's fine, Rebecca decides. The matter's been resolved and that's all there is to it. The corner of doubt that kept eating at her has been smoothed down by a good night's sleep and she's grateful to step back into her old life.

After a busy day, she searches for Lucy and Fifi in the throng of shrieking and chattering little girls streaming out of the ballet studio, and finds them with Brandon in the corner of the bright hallway. Fifi is tugging on his jacket and he's ignoring her, which is unusual. He's standing over Lucy in what an impartial observer might call an aggressive way, only Brandon's not aggressive. Rebecca has never fallen for macho men, with all their testosterone and condescension. Suddenly she's racked by self-doubt. Why hadn't he woken her last night? Was it thoughtfulness or was he still angry? He's speaking to Lucy with quick, sharp gestures. His neck and shoulders are tense, his face white, though he appears to be keeping his voice so low, Lucy has to tilt her head to hear him. Is he admonishing her? What has their nanny done? She doesn't seem apologetic. Her lips are set in a stubborn line, cheeks flushed with anger, her jaw set. And no one is paying attention to their daughter.

"Fifi!" Rebecca calls, her voice carrying.

Startled, the three of them rotate to face her, faces blank until her daughter pulls free and runs over. "Mommy, what are you doing here? Did you see me dance?"

A pang of guilt stabs her. She's hardly spent any time with Fifi recently. She bends down so she can catch her child in her arms and feels herself loosen. Her sweet, darling girl. Fifi is flushed from dancing, her new light blue leotard dappled with sweat. Rebecca kisses her dewy cheek. She remembers how Fifi had said "I love you" to Lucy instead of Rebecca. "I'm sorry I missed your class, but I promise I'll come watch you soon."

She straightens and they walk hand in hand over to Brandon and Lucy, who are both silent. Rebecca reaches up to kiss him on the cheek and he doesn't react. She says quietly to him, "What is going on?"

He gives her a tight-lipped smile. "Nothing. Just waiting for you."

"Oh?" She knows what she saw and that doesn't fit his answer at all. Alarm rises within her. Her arrival hasn't eased his tension. In fact, his face is as hard as a slab of marble. He looks like hell. He hasn't shaved and his eyes are hollow, deep, and shadowed. "What's wrong?"

"We'll talk about it later."

Now she's becoming truly worried. "Brandon, please talk to me."

He gives her a little shake of his head. "Let's get whatever you need to do here done first."

Of course, he's right. In front of their nanny and amid a crowd of small leotard-clad girls isn't an appropriate place to have an uncomfortable conversation. Perhaps it hadn't gone well with the Chinese officials yesterday. Is he still upset with her about the condom misunderstanding? Maybe he'd been taking his sour mood out on Lucy.

Rebecca gnaws on a nail before turning to Fifi. "I need to talk to your dance teacher."

"She's in there." Fifi points to the studio.

When the ballet instructor catches sight of Rebecca, she quickly averts her gaze and shrinks back. Rebecca makes a frustrated sound in her throat. They've already had several fruitless discussions about Fifi advancing to the pre-professional level. She should have known better anyway. The same young woman with the huge eyes and prominent cheekbones had taught Fifi's earliest ballet class and when Rebecca insisted then that her daughter was very talented and ready for more advanced material, the teacher had burst into laughter, right in her face. Granted, Fifi had only been two years old at the time, but still.

Rebecca crosses her arms. "I meant I need to talk to your future dance instructor, the one who teaches the pre-professional level."

Fifi's eyes grow big.

Lucy says, "Mrs. Whitney, should I get Fifi changed?"

Rebecca has asked her multiple times to use her first name, to no avail. Perhaps it's for the best. Her mother always says it's better not to blur boundaries with the staff. You don't do anyone any favors that way. "You can dress her later. Right now, everyone come with me."

Surreptitiously, she scans the crowd for Gina and Emmy as she leads the way to the pre-professional class. The studio is already half-filled with kids stretching at the barre. The hunchbacked pianist tucked in the corner cracks her gnarly knuckles before she launches into a gorgeous, romantic piece. Rebecca cocks her head. *Faust*, Valentin's aria. Despite her own lack of talent with musical instruments, she'd spent hours listening to her father play.

The teacher looks to be in her midthirties, like Rebecca. Her short hair has been dyed an eye-catching color, deep red verging on orange that would look garish on anyone else, but the instructor's lithe, muscular body and erect carriage make it sophisticated. Her every move is choreographed, as if she's constantly aware of her sharp collarbones and precise feet. Rebecca pulls her shoulders back while she approaches with Fifi and Lucy in tow. Brandon hangs back at the door.

Before she can speak, the teacher spots them and says, with a hint of an accent, "You would like your daughter to be considered for this class."

Taken aback, Rebecca nods.

"I have already observed Fiona in the primary lessons. She is quite young."

"She's small for her age."

The instructor turns to her child. "First position."

Fifi springs into place, heels together, toes turned out.

The teacher bends down, takes Fifi's ankle in her hand, and raises it in front, testing her flexibility. Then she gently pulls her leg to the side as high as possible while Fifi does a little hop to keep her balance. Releasing her foot, the teacher gives her an unexpectedly warm smile. "Well done."

Rebecca says, "So, do you—"

The teacher lifts an elegant finger, silencing her. "She is well formed. At this age, her physical gifts weigh more than her mental ones but her attitude is also important." She addresses Fifi. "Fiona, do you actually enjoy ballet?"

Fifi is silent, pushes her glasses up with one hand. At Rebecca's insistent expression, she nods. The teacher gives Rebecca a significant look.

Rebecca studies the teacher's defined arms, the years of training behind her controlled grace. To be teaching at Quill, the woman probably danced for New York City Ballet or American Ballet Theatre. She thinks of thousands of hours of practice and rehearsals, the teacher moving in slow spins, amber circles of light across polished hardwood floors, arms lifted despite the strain. Rebecca quotes Yeats. "To be born woman is to know that we must labor to be beautiful."

When the teacher purses her lips thoughtfully, Rebecca continues, "Of course, pleasure is important, but sometimes the work comes first, and passion follows."

The teacher considers, looking sad. "This is true. Very well. Fiona may attend the technical audition for the pre-professional level in two weeks."

"Hooray!" says Fifi, seeing Rebecca's broad smile.

"Oh, what are we celebrating?" Gina's voice. She's standing behind them, with Emmy's navy blazer draped over her arm. Emmy, hair piled in a ballerina bun, is warming up (or showing off, Rebecca thinks) by doing a few pirouettes toward the barre. "So nice to see you all again. I already said hello to your lovely husband."

In the mirror that runs the length of the room, Rebecca can see Brandon's reflection. He seems so far away, like a stranger. His arms are shoved in his pant pockets, his eyebrows drawn.

Fifi speaks up. "I get to do the audition for the pre-prof, pre-professional class! And I have to like ballet more."

"Why, I'm sure you will. I mean, you do!" says Rebecca, smoothing back her daughter's hair. "You *love* ballet! Why don't you go with Lucy and get dressed now?" She turns to her nanny. "Brandon and I are going out to dinner so please take Fifi home after you're done."

Rebecca and Gina hug while Lucy leads Fifi off to the dressing room. The two women join Brandon and step outside the studio to continue chatting as the class begins.

Taking a deep breath, Rebecca says, "I really must apologize again for ruining your lovely blazer. We have the best dry cleaner—"

"All taken care of. These things happen, please don't worry. It's a shame your nanny hurried off, though, because I've been meaning to ask her where I've seen her before. She looks so familiar."

Rebecca flicks a glance at the school insignia on Emmy's blazer. She pretends to be surprised, though she had already checked the student database earlier that day. "Oh, Emmy attends Corbyn? So does Fifi, what a coincidence. You must have seen Lucy dropping her off."

Does Brandon actually roll his eyes? Rebecca is horrified. What if Gina sees?

Gina laughs. "Isn't it absurd how so many of the kids in this area go to the same school? I swear half of the girls in Emmy's ballet class are at Corbyn too."

Rebecca hums in agreement. "Small world. I always bring Fifi on Fridays," she lies. In reality, Lucy always takes Fifi. Another impatient movement from Brandon. She has to get him out of here before he ruins this for her. What the hell does he think he's doing? She keeps her voice smooth. "That's the day I work from home."

"Me too, along with almost everyone else in publishing, right?" Gina pauses. "Funny, I've never seen you there."

Rebecca hastens to change the subject. This is the moment she's been working toward. She ensures her tone is casual. "You know, I often go for a run after I drop off Fifi. Would you like to join me this Friday?"

"Oh, I don't know anything about jogging. And I usually take the dogs for a walk then."

Rebecca gives her an encouraging pat on the arm. "That's not a problem. We can combine walking and running. The dogs are welcome. They'll absolutely love it. All you need is a pair of sneakers and some comfortable clothing."

Gina touches a finger to her cheek, thinking. "Well, Louis is putting on the pounds. We're not going to mention his owner, of course."

Now Rebecca refrains from rolling her own eyes. As if Gina needs to lose an ounce, but no matter. Despite Brandon's black mood, she wants to dance a celebratory jig down the crowded hallway and can barely stop herself. "Great, it's a date."

As soon as Gina's gone, Rebecca rounds on Brandon with a furious hiss. "What the hell is wrong with you? Did you drink too much last night? Whatever it is, you do not get to stand here and possibly ruin my relationship with an extremely important business contact."

Instead of apologizing the way he normally would, he glares at her. "I'm just wondering, my darling wife, if you've ever done anything you'd like to tell me about."

"What?!" Her jaw drops. Could he possibly—no, he's just tired and in a bad mood. "What in the world are you talking about?"

He leans down so they're nose to nose. She almost doesn't recognize him, his expression is so baleful, with an undertone of restrained fury that makes her shiver. In a low, intense voice, he says, "Have you ever had a *magical night* I don't know about, Rebecca?"

She rears back, eyes wide, horrified. His words knock all breath out of her lungs. She's left in a vacuum, gasping. He knows about Frankfurt. How? She's so stunned that she—articulate, highly educated, editor in chief Rebecca—is speechless. Finally, she manages to squeeze out, "Are you getting back at me for the condom? Now you're accusing *me?*"

"No." His expression is flat, though his eyes are burning. "I simply want an answer."

She pulls herself together and summons her outrage. "Why are you asking me this now? How dare you, when I've never given you cause."

He reaches out and grabs her by the shoulders. He gives her a quick, hard shake. "Have you?"

"Is there a problem?" The dance teacher's slightly accented voice.

Rebecca jumps as Brandon releases her.

The ballet teacher has exited the studio and is regarding them with her controlled gaze.

"No, not at all." Rebecca flushes dark red. They'd completely forgotten where they were. To have a scene like that in public, where anyone could have overheard. Thank goodness the hallways are mostly empty now that classes have started again.

Brandon has recovered and bestows a weak version of his usual smile upon the instructor. "Our apologies if we disturbed you."

The teacher gives them a cold stare before stepping back into her studio.

Rebecca and Brandon quickly walk down the hallway. Her head is spinning. First the condom, and now this accusation. She slides a glance at her husband. He looks like he's got a fever, color high on his cheekbones, a dangerous glint in his eyes. She almost stumbles on the threshold of the exit, she's so stunned.

As soon as they're outside, she takes a deep breath and turns to him. "No, I haven't had any magical evenings without you."

He looks long and searchingly into her eyes; his own are bloodshot and puffy. He clenches his jaw, a tic moving rapidly under the skin. "Are you very sure about that?"

Rebecca pulls on all her years of discipline growing up in a family deeply concerned with propriety. Coolly, she says, "Absolutely. Though I would like to know what you're basing your accusation on. I think I have that right." The outrage surges in her like a tsunami, threatening to pull her under. Despite her icy control, her voice rises. "Where the hell is this coming from?"

He looks taken aback. His eyes shift. What is he hiding? His phrasing of *magical night* is too much of a coincidence. She watches him take all his blazing anger and deliberately cover it with a pleasant neutral expression. It's one of the most terrifying things she's ever seen.

He works his jaw as if having trouble speaking. "All right then. Let's forget about the whole thing."

Now that he's on the retreat, Rebecca's own temper flares further. "No, I don't wish to gloss over the accusations that my dear husband hurled at me! I want to know what led you to say those things."

He runs a hand through his hair. She realizes he's shaking, as is she. He says roughly, "One of the visiting Chinese officials last night made me question if anyone could be faithful, that's all. I apologize."

She's still burning with rage, the adrenaline running through her limbs. She wants him to grovel for treating her this way. She knows this can't be the full story. But does she want him to admit the true reason he accused her, whatever that might be? Even though she's dying to know, what would she say then? She feels the ground shift beneath her feet; this is new territory for them. He's not meeting her eyes. His face is closed and distant.

She stares off into the street. "Fine. Let's just go home. I don't feel like eating out anymore. I seem to have lost my appetite."

Brandon hails a cab. They sit in the taxi and stare out of their respective windows. Standing at the doorway of their brownstone, he fumbles for his keys while Rebecca sighs. Of course, he's misplaced them again. She keeps a wary silence and refrains from a comment about absent-minded husbands. She doesn't dare criticize him when her own secrets might be revealed. She fishes her set out of her bag and as soon as she opens the door, he disappears downstairs to his study, saying he needs to type up some interview notes for his new book. Thank goodness they decided to keep that garden apartment for his home office instead of renting it out, especially with Brandon's subjects traipsing in and out of the separate entrance all the time.

Lucy and Fifi are having dinner in the dining room and Lucy half rises out of her chair when she spots Rebecca.

"Mommy, why are you home so early? Are you going to eat with us?" Fifi asks.

"I'm sorry, I have work to do." Rebecca gives her a kiss, then goes upstairs.

Once in her bedroom, she heads into their bathroom, locks the door, and calls Mason.

When he answers, she hisses, "Who did you tell?"

His southern accent seems more pronounced over the phone. "This is Rebecca, I presume? I haven't spoken to a soul, like I promised."

She can barely contain her rage. "Then why is my husband asking me if I've had any *magical nights?*"

A long, low whistle. "That does seem coincidental. But it didn't come from me."

She wishes she could see his face so she could tell if he's lying. "So even though we're both in competition for Isabel Navarro and Brandon suddenly drops this little tidbit on me, you had nothing to do with this? Do you actually expect me to believe that?"

His voice hardens, the edge of anger in it sharp enough to cut. "Let's be honest here. Despite whatever we might have shared in the past, we know where we stand. We're both ambitious as hell and ready to fight tooth and nail for what we want. No one gets into Harvard because they're sweet. And I'm telling you right here, right now, that I intend to land Isabel Navarro, no holds barred. But I don't need to use Frankfurt. You know why? Because I'm going to win and it's going to be much more satisfying to know I did it on my own, just like I've earned everything else in my life."

Before he hangs up on her, he drawls, "I didn't tell your damn husband. Someone else must have done it."

EIGHTEEN

Jasmine

I didn't want to return to Opium but what was the alternative? I sat at my desk, sketching a pigeon perched outside my window. Thoughts of Dawn, Lone Wolf Jack, Lily, and Aunt Glory spun through my mind. I weighed that against being forced to work as a prostitute for the snakeheads. A life far from Fifi. My phone buzzed.

Anthony had given up on words this time. He had texted me a photo. What could this possibly be?

I squinted at the blurry image, impatiently tapping at my phone's screen until it fully loaded. Some GIF to show me he didn't care if we ever saw each other again? Despite his recent texts, I couldn't shake his look of disdain.

When the photo finally came into focus, I gasped. It was a close-up of his wrist, a man's wrist now, but I immediately recognized the bracelet I'd made for him all those years ago. The red thread and knotted beads had faded but the thick braid was still strong. He'd changed the closure. Was that gold? He'd had a jeweler add a clasp so the bracelet could be taken on and off, probably for when he bathed.

Joy rose in my chest, so sharp it felt like pain. I pressed a fist to my mouth. He had kept my gift all these years, through my union with another man, his belief that I'd betrayed our friendship, his anger and frustration, his move away and arrival in this distant country. A part of him had never stopped being my Anthony.

He was a good man. I couldn't afford to have someone like that in my life, though. I needed to be free of entanglements. I needed to be ruthless enough to pursue my goals. What would he think of Opium and all that I was doing? And he didn't even know I had a daughter.

I understood what I had to do.

It rained in the night. Lying in my bed, I closed my eyes, listened to the droplets patter against the roof above my head, melting the last of the spring snow that had accumulated. The steady drumbeat seemed to pound against me, chipping at the walls I'd erected. A wave of feeling swelled, immense, dark, and unknown. I wrestled it back until I was calm again.

In answer to my tentative "When would you like to meet?" Anthony had replied gratifyingly quickly, almost as if he'd been staring at his phone, though I knew better than to believe that. I was supposed to see him at some sort of promenade in Brooklyn, tomorrow. I worried the rain would continue, but the day dawned cool and clear.

It took me a while to puzzle out the subways and I missed the stop, which meant I had to double back. I was late. I tried to text him but had no reception underground and once I emerged onto the quiet, tree-lined streets paved in cobblestones, I was so surprised that I forgot. What a strangely quaint place in this impervious city. I walked down a ramp, the trees beginning to bud above my head, each step bringing me closer to the breathtaking view of the Lower Manhattan skyline, as glorious as a celestial sunrise. It was as if I were entering some magical, liminal pocket of time from which no one emerged unchanged. This. This is the Beautiful Country. This was the dream that had lured so many hapless immigrants to this place: the endless sky filled with soft white clouds, the pristine skyscrapers glinting in the brilliant sunlight, ferries daring to cross the rippling waves; this land of power and possibility, heartbreak and ecstasy.

I scanned the long pedestrian walkway for Anthony. There was no sign of him. Perhaps he'd left. Had I missed my chance? The rows of benches were mostly empty, except for a small group gathered around a musician playing classical guitar. The music drifted over, intense and passionate, coiling itself around me. I scoured the crowd. Surely, he would have waited a bit longer. I wasn't that late. I searched every face, so intently a few people stared back at me—one guy in a baseball cap with piercings through his nose and ears gave me a wink—but no Anthony.

My shoulders slumped with disappointment right as the wind blew a lock of dark hair into the young musician's eyes, and he tossed his head. He was silhouetted, almost too bright to see against the clouds skimming across the sky, but from that quick, impatient shake, I knew. The last time I'd heard Anthony play, he'd been fourteen years old and just learning how to pick out simple melodies. He didn't notice me now. He was preoccupied, eyebrows furrowed, focused on his playing and some ominous internal landscape. His expression was stark, all grim edges and severe lines. Had he changed his mind about seeing me?

Now that I finally had the opportunity to gaze upon him as much as I liked, I realized that Anthony had truly grown up. His features had morphed into sharp angles and a strong jaw, wide cheekbones and determined brows. Not to mention his playing, which hinted at a depth and complexity of feeling that only made him more compelling. A young woman stood in the front, her dangly earrings tangled in her ashy blond hair, all sparkle and flash, leaning forward, hands clasped together, entranced. And she wasn't the only one. His fingers flew across the strings, the impassioned melody wove through the crowd, and all were transfixed. I imagined the trees bending closer, the water pausing its flow to listen. When had Anthony learned to play like this?

Suddenly, like a swift, treacherous kick to my ribs, I remembered how much I had missed him. From the moment Wen appeared in my life, Anthony started withdrawing, as if the two couldn't coexist in the same reality. At first I'd been bewildered, clutching at my last moments

with my best friend. Even though I understood that everyone else expected our friendship to end, I never imagined that we would follow
those rules. I expected us to sneak off the way we always had but he
became ever more irritable and distant. Then came what I thought
was his rejection. I turned my back on him after that, though my ears
still listened for the sound of his footsteps, my eyes anticipated his face
at my door, dragging me off to see some marten tracks he'd found,
chiding me that I'd scare all the warblers away with my chatter and
questions. I'd been busy, of course, with the wedding and moving into
Wen's house, my new role as wife and potential mother, all of which fit
me like a poorly cut robe, much too large and misshapen for the child I
still was. I was playing dress-up and decided to forget Anthony. A few
months after my wedding, his family moved away. I told myself I was
relieved.

I didn't allow myself to think about him after that, not even when
it was late, or Wen started leaving on his trips to Beijing, or when I
staggered to bed after hours of working in Wen's family's restaurant.
But Anthony was a spirit hidden in the corners of rooms and bright
bubbles of laughter. At the marketplace, my head would whip around,
sure I'd glimpsed him scampering around the corner, just beyond
bundles of sugarcane at the periphery of my vision. Was I looking for
him or myself?

Now, I shifted my weight from foot to foot as the music grew darker.
He was striking the strings with barely contained frustration. Taking
in his thunderous expression, I worried I wouldn't be welcome after all.
Perhaps I should tiptoe away. He clearly had another purpose for being
here: he came to play and possibly, incidentally, to meet me. All I could
think about was how joyful the two of us had been, how shockingly
and sublimely innocent, despite my unhappiness at home. This Anthony who told me I had never meant anything to him was like some
distorted reflection created to mock me. I saw the desire in the sparkly
woman's eyes but I would have sold a limb to have my gawky Anthony
back for even one moment. I shivered.

The sleeve of his navy jacket, the same one he'd been wearing in the
studio, pulled up then and there was that bit of red string around his
wrist. My bracelet. I found myself leaning closer, then caught myself.

I was being silly. I should leave. I started edging toward the periphery of the group.

That was when he looked up and saw me. He froze, staring, while his fingers played on. Tension ran through his rigid frame. All expression drained out of his face, leaving it as blank as a mask. I was clutching my coat collar with whitened knuckles, balanced on my toes, poised to turn heel and run, scared I'd made a terrible mistake and somehow completely misinterpreted his messages. His eyes were intent, edged in wistfulness and hope. At that moment, I remembered when I'd seen him like this before: when he was coaxing some snarling, wounded animal to allow him to approach. He wasn't irate, I realized. He was afraid I would vanish on him, exactly as I was planning.

At this, I pried my fingers loose and gave him an awkward wave. "Hi."

For a second he didn't react, and I wondered what I should do now. Then his hands fell away from the strings midnote, and he stood, set his guitar aside, gaze still fixed on mine. A corner of my mouth pulled up in a smile and in answer, his entire face relaxed. The glow in his eyes became so bright, it dazzled me. I took a half step forward and he swooped toward me and suddenly I was in his arms, engulfed in his scent of sandalwood. His jacket was cool against my cheek and his body was warm and solid underneath it. I closed my eyes. It felt like the years were tumbling backward like leaves in a sandstorm, unwinding like a film being played in reverse and we were on the playground again, collapsing, exhausted and satisfied, after a long game of tag. I shuddered, exhaling. For a breathtaking moment, I felt alive, like the young girl I had been, a brief and miraculous reprieve. It dawned on me that I was happy, truly happy, for the first time in a long while.

Behind us, there was a discreet bit of throat clearing along with some whooping and we sprang apart, red-faced and guilty as if we'd been caught in some illicit lovers' embrace. The crowd was gaping at us.

A young guy with a skateboard slung over his shoulder said, "Hey, man, you done playing? You gonna pass the hat?"

Anthony's brows furrowed and he looked with some surprise at the people gathered around. He patted his head, as if feeling for the object in question. In careful English, he said, "I have no hat." He gave the group a formal little bow. "Thank you for your attention."

To me, he said in Chinese, "Why does he want my hat?"

I gave him a baffled look. As every immigrant knew, Americans were unfathomable.

While the crowd slowly dissipated and the sparkly woman gave him one last lingering look, Anthony laid a hand on my cheek. "You came."

Perhaps it was that young woman who seemed to think she had a chance with him, maybe it was his incredulity at my reliability, but I was irritated, and pulled away. "Of course I did. I wouldn't have stood you up. I do the things I say I will."

"I know. I was still worried." A tentative smile played on the periphery of his lips, as if unsure of its welcome. "I always seem to say the wrong thing to you nowadays."

The words slipped out before I could stop them. "Like 'You were only a silly little girl who followed me around'?"

He flinched, then put a hand on my shoulder. "I-I didn't mean it. You know that."

"How could I?" I raised my arms in an exaggerated shrug. "When I was watching you play, I wasn't even sure you still wanted to see me."

His eyebrows shot up. "Of course I do. Why would you think that?"

"I saw your face. You seemed angry. I hope that wasn't because you were waiting for me." I began chewing on my lip. "I understand you felt guilty, and I appreciate your texts. There's been no harm done. Our friendship was a lifetime ago."

"Stop." He threw up his hands. "You have always had the ability to drive me nuts."

"What?!" I crossed my arms, indignant. "*Me* drive *you* nuts! You are the one who—"

He actually clamped a hand over my mouth. I was so incensed that I bit his fingers, not hard enough to draw blood but close. He let go with a yelp, shaking his hand. "Ow! What the hell did you do that for?"

My voice was too high for dignity. "You started it!"

"Because you won't shut up!"

I glared at him. "I am a very quiet and peaceful person."

"Ha!" Then he caught himself and, unexpectedly, began to laugh. After a startled pause, I joined him. Soon we were both guffawing until finally, we could breathe again.

"Come here," he said, still wheezing slightly, settling on the park bench. "Sit down."

When we were seated, me still a wary distance from him, he sighed. Reaching out, he tucked a lock of my hair that had escaped from my barrette behind my ears. "They still stick out."

I gasped. "My ears do not—" I pressed my lips together. Okay, maybe they did jut out the tiniest amount, but I wasn't going to admit that to him. I grabbed a few strands of my hair to cover them again.

"Don't do that. They're adorable." His face was alight with mischief. When I narrowed my eyes at him, he pulled a small plastic package out of his jacket pocket. I recognized the printing before it fully emerged. "I have something for you."

"Shredded dried squid," I squealed. My favorite snack. "I can't believe you remembered. I haven't had this in forever."

He smiled at me shyly. "I remember everything."

I peeked at him from underneath my eyelashes. "I'm touched."

The tops of his cheekbones reddened. He ducked his head and assiduously avoided looking at me, even as I tore the bag open and inhaled the aromatic scent.

I took out a delicate handful of the shredded squid and let it melt on my tongue. I closed my eyes. Chewy, sweet, and spicy and salty all at once. Now Anthony was staring at me. I looked at him, shamefaced, and offered him the bag. "Oh, do you want some?"

He chuckled as he took a pinch. He chewed it slowly, paying more attention to it than it required, and then stared into the distance, the breeze ruffling his hair, as he said with studied nonchalance, "So, are you here for good?"

I stopped mid-swallow. "I want to be. But I don't know if I can stay." I changed the subject. "How long have you been here?"

"My uncle brought me over three years ago. I had a hard time at first because my English wasn't that good, but I'm enrolled in college now. What about you?"

"I've only been here for seven months. What are you studying?" So strange to think of Anthony in college, like a real adult.

"Accounting."

I snorted. "You hate math. And you're terrible at it."

He shrugged, not meeting my eyes. "Ya—I mean, my aunt and uncle think it's a good future for me."

"Of course it is, for some people"—I cocked my head—"who are good at math. Though it's been a long time. Have you gotten better?"

"No." His grin was sheepish and we both chuckled.

"You give too much of yourself to other people." I gave him a gentle punch. "You're too kind. You should think about yourself and what you want."

He rubbed his arm where I'd hit him, pretending it hurt. "I'm also volunteering at an animal shelter. We just got a litter of kittens."

"Really?" I breathed. I adored cats, although I'd never been allowed to keep one. Then, before I could stop myself, I blurted out, "Can I come see them sometime?"

His mahogany eyes shone. "Yes! We could go right now."

That's when I remembered I'd promised myself I'd only see him this once. We would clear the air and go our separate ways. I really shouldn't have come at all. He represented the way my life could have gone, and in the face of Opium and Wen, the illusion was incredibly seductive. I thought about my dreams with Fifi and my new job. He would never understand. Plus, he was connected to Wen and my parents and everyone else I was hiding from. What if they found out where I was? What if they heard I was working at a strip club? In the distance, a siren wailed, a high, pitiful sound.

"I mean, sorry, I am actually really busy today. I do want to see them but maybe later." Much, much later. Like never. I had to leave before he asked any other questions. Like *How did you get here? What are you truly doing here? Where is Wen?* I shifted my legs and swung my bag into my arms. "Well, it's been really nice. I should be going, though. I'm glad we got to clear the air."

He stiffened and nodded without looking at me. Ignoring what I'd said, he asked, "Do you remember the cat I brought to the self-defense studio?"

I stopped. "Of course."

"They'll probably have to euthanize her soon." His voice was low and sad.

"What?"

"There's not enough space or money to keep all the animals they find, so they have to get rid of any that don't get adopted after a certain amount of time. That's why I take them home when I can. So they have a little taste of love first."

I remembered the small cat leaning so trustfully against my knee. "Humans are the worst monsters of all."

He pressed his lips together. "Sometimes life doesn't give us a choice." A heavy silence fell in between us. I was about to try to leave again when he asked, "So, where's your sketchbook?"

"Oh, I don't draw anymore," I said airily. I didn't want him to see my drawings these days. "Such a childish hobby."

He knew I was lying because quicker than thought, he nabbed my bag and opened it, then pulled out my sketchbook. "Given it up, huh?"

I tried to snatch it out of his hands, and we tussled briefly, the pages flying open, before he let me have it. I clutched the closed book to my chest, breathing hard.

He held his hands up in a calming gesture. "I know how important your drawings are to you and I'd never look without your permission. After all, a book is a garden you carry around with you." He'd never peeked before, but I couldn't be sure with this Anthony, this Franken-stein amalgamation of old and new. "Who's the little girl, though? I caught a glimpse."

I froze. "No one," I said, swallowing. "Just a kid I saw in passing on the street."

He nodded. I had always been private about my art. "I can pose for you if you like."

I sniffed, though secretly, I was tempted. People were always changing the angle of their legs, scratching their noses, chewing gum, messing up the line of their jaw. I had to do most of my work from memory. "Why would I want to sketch an ape like you?"

He gave me a smug look. "You want to, admit it."

"Attractive people are the least interesting to draw," I said haugh-tily, then stopped myself from clasping a hand over my mouth when I realized what I'd implied.

"You think I'm handsome?" He seemed far too pleased with him-self.

I huffed. "I didn't say that." Then, grudgingly, "Though I suppose you are, in a very boring kind of way."

A flash of white teeth from him. We both knew I was lying. He was anything but dull. To change the subject, I said, "You are sadly quite uninteresting to look at, but you do play beautifully."

He laughed quietly, then glanced at the guitar leaning against his knee. "Just a way to pass the time."

I nodded, understanding. I felt the same about my artwork. We were immigrants. There was no room in our lives for lofty visions of individual self-fulfillment. To carve out a bit of breathing room in this country's future, already packed with so many others' dreams, that was enough for us. All we wanted was to meet our basic needs: shelter, food, safety, and possibly, someday, something better for our children.

Anthony and I could not afford passion.

There was a pause, then he said, still staring at his dusty sneakers. "Jasmine, could we be friends again?"

My chest clenched with so much emotion, I didn't know how to respond.

"I have other friends, of course." He cast me a sidelong look. "Mostly hairier, stronger friends."

A snort of laughter escaped me.

Glancing at me ruefully, he said, "But none like you. I promised myself I'd be honest if you ever gave me the chance to speak to you again. The truth is, I got here an hour early because I couldn't wait any longer. I was pacing back and forth. I started playing just to occupy myself. I was afraid I'd driven you away with my bad temper. When you were late, I was sure I'd never see you again. That's why I looked so unwelcoming."

A heated sheen covered my eyes. I sniffed, thinking of how lonely I'd felt. "You weren't very nice to me. Even before my wedding banquet, when I really needed you."

It was the first time either one of us had brought up the past, and for a moment, he hesitated and stretched out a palm to me, hovering. Then he grasped my hand firmly with his warm one. "I'm truly sorry. I told you I wasn't hurt. That was the biggest lie I've ever told. I swung between running after you like a puppy and pushing you away. Before your banquet, I'd convinced myself you'd find a way out of it since you were the bravest, cleverest person I knew. And if you did go with him, then you were no true friend of mine anyway. It was immature. I was only a teenager, though. Then afterward, I was upset but I hoped to still be in your life in some small way. That's when you rebuffed me."

I tried to keep my voice steady. "I thought your family told you about my choosing you first and that you'd said no. I believed you were just trying to be nice to me because you felt guilty."

His hand tightened on mine. "I had no idea. I was furious when you told me. I've missed you so much over the years."

I gave him a small smile. "Yes, I'd like to be friends again." Joy blossomed in my chest. I wouldn't be so alone anymore. I could have Anthony in my life again and with time, maybe I could tell him everything: the snakeheads, Opium, Fiona, all my troubles and dreams.

Happiness blazed across his face, lighting up his eyes, then he grew serious. He pressed his lips together. I braced myself. Better to get this over with. I wasn't surprised when he asked, "Where is Wen?"

I was silent a long while. Finally, I said, "In the past."

He gave me a long, searching look. "So, you're free now?"

My voice was filled with regret. "Anthony, I'll never be free."

Bending so close we were eye to eye, he said, "I phoned my parents that night to tell them they had no right to make a decision like that without consulting me. Imagine my surprise when they told me it didn't matter, since you had disappeared without a trace."

NINETEEN

Jasmine

I stood and tried to yank my hand free. Anthony held on. This was a terrible idea. Why had I come to meet him? What had he told his parents? I had water in my brain. I should never have done this. They'd find me, I'd be caught.

"Jasmine, stop. Please don't run away. I didn't tell them I'd seen you. No one knows where you are. They assumed my uncle finally told me." He drew me into his arms and held me until his words sank in. I relaxed back into my body, no longer feeling like I needed to race off into the distance until I disappeared completely. He pulled us both down so we were sitting on the park bench again.

He spoke softly. "They told me Wen was devastated. He doesn't know what happened to you. He thinks you might be dead. I thought you loved him."

I stared into the deep, rippling waters. "I did."

When it was clear I wouldn't add anything else, he said, "After your wedding, I kept hoping. I told myself you'd been forced into the marriage, that you were being obedient to your family. But then, one day, I saw you with Wen at the market. You looked at him like you wanted to grow old with him. That was the worst, knowing that you loved him. He'd replaced me in your life, and it was like I'd never mattered at all."

His voice broke. It was true. I had loved Wen with all my young heart, until I'd realized what sort of man he truly was. I wanted to reach out and wrap my arms around Anthony's shoulders until the rigidity left and he could look at me again. But he was so still, braced against the raw hurt of the memory, and I couldn't tell if he would welcome my touch. "No, Wen could never take your place."

He turned toward me, a small smile peeking through his pained expression. "I missed you terribly. I was acting out. Some nights, I wouldn't come home and passed out drunk in the fields. Gangs started trying to recruit me. That was why my father moved us out of the village. To be away from you, since you didn't seem to want anything to do with me anymore."

I was gaping. "I was upset because I thought you'd rejected me but that wasn't the only reason I stopped talking to you. Wen didn't allow me to have contact with any other men."

Anthony's face hardened, falling into stark lines. For a moment, something primeval and dangerous took over his face. His voice was deceptively soft. "Oh? What else did he do to you, that you felt you had to leave him?"

I hesitated, a flood of words rising to my lips. How many times had I wished for someone to confide in? I looked into Anthony's velvet eyes and realized that despite the fear I'd developed of most men, I had never been afraid of him. Deep down, I never stopped trusting him. "W-Wen was very possessive of me, even though he had mistresses in Beijing." My voice grew stronger as I spoke. "He was enraged if he thought any other man was interested in me. It didn't happen often but when it did, I paid the price."

Although I kept my tone expressionless, he understood, and unlike me, who had hesitated to comfort him, he reached out and wrapped an arm around me. It felt good to lean against his solid shoulder.

In a tight voice, he asked, "Did he hurt you?"

I swallowed. "Sometimes."

I saw his hands curl into fists. He gritted out, "I failed you. I couldn't see beyond my own feelings. I should have been there for you. I could have stopped it somehow."

I looked up and laid my hand against his face, the stubble a surprise to me. I repressed a sudden urge to rub my cheek against his. "You were a child."

His eyes were fierce. "So were you."

I nestled my head back in his shoulder. I couldn't tell him about Fiona. I was barely hanging on to my self-control as it was. "I planned my disappearance in secret for years."

"Didn't you worry about grieving your parents?"

I gave a bitter little laugh. "They didn't care."

"What?" There was kindhearted, oblivious Anthony again. "Of course they do. They love you."

Suddenly I couldn't take his naïveté anymore and pulled back so I could look him straight in the eyes. Now that we were in another country, I blurted out another secret I was never supposed to reveal. "They're not my real parents. Didn't you ever wonder why they treated me the way they did?"

He furrowed his brows. "What in the world are you talking about?"

I threw up my hands. "I can't believe you never figured it out. Everyone else in the village knew, even though no one said anything. My biological parents moved away right after I was born and left me on the side of the road."

I'd known for as long as I could remember that I didn't truly belong to my so-called parents, and naturally, that meant I spent my childhood in a state of longing. For acceptance and love, yes, but also for kinship, to be part of a group, no matter how tattered or disheveled. Even though my adoptive ma and pa (who were actually my aunt and uncle) proclaimed loudly in public how much I resembled them via the dimple that appeared in my left cheek when I smiled or the mole in the crook of my knee, the truth was that I was clearly other. I didn't take after them at all, not even my uncle.

Anthony's jaw fell open and his eyes were as wide as saucers. Now he looked more like the boy I had known. Despite having grown up in the same place, we had occupied two separate realities. "Why?"

"Because my parents wouldn't be allowed to have a son if they kept me. And without a son, there'd be no one to inherit or take care of them in their old age."

"But you know it's not like that here, right? My aunt and uncle are devoted to their daughter."

I gave a rueful smile, thinking of all the photos of the young woman in their office. That must be their daughter. "That's partly why I came to the Beautiful Country."

"But what about Hong?" He was trying to piece it all together. "I always thought he was your twin brother."

"He's actually my cousin and we were born a few months apart. My aunt and uncle pretended we were twins to avoid the penalties even though they hated having an extra mouth to feed. Grandma was the one who took me in. They used to berate her all the time for it."

I couldn't restrain a sob at the mention of Grandma, who tried to protect me as best she could, sneaking me rice, helping me sweep the hog pen when I was too young to do it well enough myself. I used to draw picture after picture of my biological family: my parents and me. I sketched different versions of my mother's hair, my father's nose. I was ashamed of the many letters I wrote to them in my early sketchbooks about how well I was doing in school, how I learned to read Chinese, how fast I could run, so that when I found them again, they would welcome me. In my imagination, my parents truly loved me and it had broken their hearts to leave me. They'd only done it because they had no other choice. I never found an address for those letters.

Anthony drew me into his arms again. I felt his cheek against the top of my head, his strength keeping the gusting wind at bay. There was genuine grief in his voice. "I heard about your grandma passing. I'm so sorry. You must miss her. I loved her too."

I'd never felt as alone as when Grandma died. I saw much public beating of chests on the part of my family but there'd mostly been relief at the troublesome old woman being gone. I'd been the only one who was completely and utterly devastated, and Wen had offered scant comfort. But Anthony had loved her as much as I had. He and Grandma had been two of a kind, both softhearted and crazy about animals. How I'd longed for someone who truly cared—I realized now I'd wanted Anthony—to share my sorrow.

Quietly, he asked, "Have you ever thought about what it might have been like? If it had been me instead of Wen?"

I interlaced our fingers and pushed up his sleeve. He went completely still. I inhaled sharply. There. Finally, my old bracelet wrapped around his wrist. I touched a faded bead, knotted by my hands so many years ago, before I'd been married off, before we'd grown so far apart. In a way, the fable had come true: the bracelet did keep me connected to him. The image became blurry as my eyes misted. "I always imagined that maybe we would have been able to grow up together."

He bumped his forehead against mine. "I would have liked that." His gaze lingered on my mouth.

Unexpected heat flickered through me. I parted my lips, to say what, I didn't know, but then my phone rang, and we both jumped. I lurched to answer it.

I recognized the male voice immediately. It was the snakehead I reported to in Chinatown. "The wedding ring you used in China as partial payment for your debt was registered as stolen and has been recovered by the police. Our colleague barely got away when he tried to sell it. You now owe that amount plus a hefty bonus for our inconvenience." He hung up.

It was like that suspended moment right before a car drove off a bridge, when you could see the upcoming drop, feel the free fall in your stomach, the plummet and ultimate destruction already inevitable. Dread grew in my throat. The sky, which had seemed so welcoming, swirled around me and I was doing a long, deep dive through endless realms of black water. I clutched the park bench to keep myself upright.

If the ring had been found, Wen would suspect I was still alive.

TWENTY

Rebecca

"I've missed you," Rebecca whispers.

They've retreated to opposite ends of the bed even in their sleep and Brandon's lying as far away as possible with his back to her. She moves over to wrap her arm around him, inhaling the warm scent of his cologne. She tucks her cheek against the skin of his neck, feels the faint tickle of his hair. It's early Friday morning.

They had tacitly agreed not to discuss their fight any further. They've been doing their best to maintain a veneer of normalcy, circling one another, two people who've hurt each other, and aren't yet sure if the hurting has stopped or merely been paused. Brandon has returned to his usual self, albeit a bit more distant, though Rebecca thinks she catches a strange gleam in his eye at times, as if beneath the surface he's morphed into an entirely different creature. Their suppressed animosity weighs upon her heart and mind, filling her days and nights with an aching chest and the constant tension of a low-grade headache.

He turns around so that he's facing her now, places his forehead against hers. He bends to kiss her and she's only too happy to lose herself in mindless passion. Yet the brutality in the way he touches her makes her gasp. It's not that he hurts her but there's an edge of barely leashed violence; he grips her hair in his fist, yanks her head back, there's the scrape of teeth against her nipple, he thrusts into her with primal fervor and vehemence. And even though she calls it *making love* in her mind and not the other term, it's as though he's punishing her, or himself.

When they've finished, he gets out of bed almost immediately.

"Where are you going?" She wraps the sheet around her, feeling more bereft than ever. There's nothing like sex to bring people closer or to drive them further apart.

"Early meeting at the university, then I'm interviewing a few people in the garden apartment downstairs. I'll see you tonight." And with a brief kiss on her cheek, he disappears into the shower. He dresses rapidly and leaves with a too-cheery goodbye, and she understands that the secrets between them are breeding like some virus, pretending to be dormant while it burrows into essential organs, swelling its numbers, engorging itself until it's ready to explode.

After he's gone, Rebecca showers, then pulls on her Lululemon tights and a matching fitted T-shirt in lilac. As she's reaching for her running shoes, she realizes she'd forgotten to tell Lucy last night that she would take Fifi to school today herself. She'd better let her nanny know. She can't wait to meet Gina and mentally rehearses the many ways she might charm the agent during their run.

She peeks into Fifi's room and her daughter is fast asleep, clutching her stuffed lion Maya. Fifi sleeps with loose, careless abandon, mouth open, cheeks flushed. They'd added a protector to the edge of her bed to keep her from ending up on the floor every night. Rebecca tiptoes into the room and tenderly wipes the tangled hair from her forehead.

She climbs the stairs to Lucy's room in the attic. She shivers, a draft creeping up her neck. It's been chilly the last few days but why is it so cold up here? Doesn't heat rise? The windows she can see are all closed. She makes a mental note to check if the heating system is working properly. It is an old house after all.

Wetness seeps into her sock. What is that? A puddle. Surely, Calypso hasn't been naughty. She bends down to sniff it and is relieved it's only water. But why would it be damp here? She glances up at the skylight. It is firmly closed, though she can see lingering clouds from the rain she'd heard last night. She thinks about the ghost woman Fifi mentioned and suppresses a shiver. Fortunately, she doesn't believe in any of that haunted nonsense. Lucy must have stepped into the hallway after a shower without fully drying off first. Careless of her; it's not good for the floor.

She knocks softly on Lucy's door. There's no answer. Did she stay at her sister's again last night? Even so, she should be back and getting ready to dress Fifi and take her to school on time. Rebecca raps on the wood again, then cracks open the door.

The inside of the darkened room is, if anything, colder than the hallway. Goose bumps rise on her arms and a prickle goes up her spine. There's a lump in the bed. In the eerie light, the room feels full of wraiths. She can just make out tumbled hair against the pillow.

"Lucy," she says gently.

There's no answer. Lucy is deeply asleep, as if she's exhausted, as if she's dead. Concerned, Rebecca lays a hand on her nanny's head. It's warm, thankfully. Still, Lucy doesn't react. How tired can she be? It's not like they work her that hard, do they?

Rebecca taps her firmly on the shoulder and Lucy sits bolt upright. Both women scream. Lucy's eyes are wide and disoriented. When she focuses on Rebecca, she shrinks back into the pillows, terror written on her face. She mumbles in Chinese, holding up a hand as if averting evil.

"Oh my goodness, you gave me a fright," Rebecca says. "It's only me."

Lucy scans the shadowy room frantically, as if wondering where she is.

"Calm down," Rebecca says slowly and clearly, though she can feel the hair rising on the nape of her neck. "I didn't mean to scare you. I only wanted to tell you that I'll be taking Fifi to school myself this morning."

Lucy is blinking at her, stunned. The room is so dark, Rebecca can barely discern her nanny's features. She wants to snap on the bedside lamp but knows that would be rude. Lucy's hair is tangled, hanging in her face. Why is she always such a mess? Abruptly, all of Rebecca's irritation at her comes to a head, starting with the spilling of the ceviche all over Gina at the party and culminating in the condom incident, which Lucy had indirectly caused.

Her voice is icy by the time she speaks. "However, shouldn't you be up by now?"

Finally, Lucy says, "My alarm not go off. I get Fifi ready."

Rebecca's back is rigid. "Well, maybe you should set an extra one, just in case." She thinks of Fifi throwing herself into Lucy's arms and Brandon's defense of their nanny. Something primitive and animalistic rises in her. She pictures the back of her hand slapping against Lucy's face, and it almost chokes her, how much she wants to do it, how good it might feel. Her knees are shaking as she leaves the room. She's afraid of what she, Rebecca, might do.

While she wakes Fifi and helps her dress in her school uniform and lets her put far too much jam on her toast, Rebecca's mind is whirling. She's overwrought, that's all. She's resentful of Lucy's ability to spend the whole day with Fifi. Rebecca is a wife and a mother and has a career that demands all her free time on top of everything. She has multiple roles, and she wants Fifi to learn that this is possible for her too. Rebecca's not a housewife like her mother. There are so many expectations of what she should be doing, and yet no one judges Brandon for working. When they brought their daughter back from China, he changed the baby's diaper on the plane and the flight attendants had practically swooned. What a wonderful father he was, so clever and capable. Rebecca isn't perfect, she knows she isn't, but she's honestly doing her best.

"Mommy." Fifi tugs on her hand. "The sky's all cloudy."

She jerks back into her body and manages to smile. "Then we'd better take an umbrella, just in case."

While they walk to school together, Fifi bounces next to her, trusting hand in hers. Rebecca breathes in the early morning air, listening to her chatter, and feels a surge of gratitude. Despite the difficulties between her and her husband right now, despite the challenges at work, she is glad for this extra time with her daughter.

As if reading her mind, Fifi asks, "Why don't you take me to school more often?"

A wave of guilt cascades over her moment of cheer. "I wish I could, sweetie." She thinks of how Fifi had asked for Lucy's good-night kiss, not Rebecca's.

Her daughter nods. "It's because you have to work and that's very important."

Is this what Rebecca has conveyed to her? She wants to say that work is indeed important but it's not the end-all of everything. However, Fifi is already singing "You Are My Sunshine" to herself and skipping over the cracks in the sidewalk. Once they reach the school courtyard, Rebecca is surprised by how much smaller everything looks than when she was a student there herself. She still remembers hanging on to her father's hand on the rare occasions he managed to pick her up. He'd always listened to her stories about horses and mean boys with the utmost solemnity. And now he's gone and her mother's grown old and distant, borne away from her like ripples in the ocean. She has a sense of coming full circle, standing here now with her own child.

She waves at a few mothers she knows, parents of Fifi's friends, but honestly, she's not around that much. Lucy takes care of all that and Rebecca doesn't want to be involved in the politics of which girl was or wasn't invited to someone else's party. In fact, Fifi's sixth birthday is coming in about a week and she hasn't even thought about the logistics. Under the cloudy sky, a tall Asian woman wearing sunglasses snaps photos of them and the school. Tourists are everywhere these days.

She hears a high yipping sound and spots Gina stepping into the schoolyard, dragged by two dogs: a small white one with a curly coat that appears to be barking at everything that moves and an apricot one with silky ears. Emmy glides beside her, immaculately coiffed, while Fifi's skirt is already crumpled beneath her blue blazer. Gina is wearing running pants and a fitted sweat-wicking long-sleeve top, looking very trim indeed.

She gives Rebecca a friendly smile while trying to untangle herself from her dogs. "Louis, stop barking," she orders the white one, who totally ignores her.

Rebecca hides a grin. That's the first time she's ever seen anyone not listen to Gina Park.

"And this little gentleman is Graham," says Gina, indicating the apricot dog. "Graham's a cockapoo and Louis is a poochon."

Rebecca, to whom these terms mean nothing, smiles agreeably, but when she bends to pet Louis, he barks again, and she snatches back her hand. She remembers when dogs were simple breeds like corgis, Labradors, and Irish setters and not poo-poo this and doodle-thats.

She politely changes the subject. "Emmy's always so graceful and elegant. I don't know how you do it."

"Oh, that's all her." Gina laughs. "She was born that way. We would have been happy with a boy or a girl, but I have to admit I was secretly hoping for a daughter. Winding up with Emmy was a special gift." Rebecca notices that she doesn't reciprocate with any remark about Fifi looking polished. The agent steps over the leash as Graham circles around her ankles. "Well, you must be very proud of your daughter and her fluency in Chinese. That will be such an asset when she's older."

"What about Emmy? Are you teaching her Korean?"

"Absolutely. When she was younger, we both talked to her mainly in that language and she goes to Korean school on the weekends."

"I didn't know you spoke it." Gina is always so refined, it had never occurred to Rebecca that she had any sort of immigrant background.

"I was born in Seoul."

Rebecca opens her mouth to compliment her on her flawless English but manages to stop herself. For the first time, she realizes how condescending that might be. The dogs have calmed down by now and Fifi and Emmy are huddling with a small group of other kids playing a version of Mother, May I. Emmy is the mother, of course, whom everyone needs to ask for permission to proceed. Each child thinks up an original motion, like cartwheels or leapfrogging, to move forward.

But when it's Fifi's turn, she hesitates, clearly unsure, and a boy calls out, "Do kung fu fighting!"

"But I don't know kung fu," Fifi says. "And I'm not supposed to fight."

Rebecca's mouth falls half-open. She wants to step in, but she doesn't know if she should lecture a bunch of children about the dangers of stereotyping.

"Just because Fifi is Chinese doesn't mean she does kung fu," Gina calls to the kids.

Fifi starts doing some sort of disco boogie as Rebecca turns to Gina.

The agent's eyes are kind. "It isn't easy sometimes, is it? Half the kids think Emmy's Chinese and when she says she's Korean, they're like, 'It's the same thing!'"

"Right before the party," Rebecca says, wondering a bit at herself that she's confiding this, but it feels good to say it to someone who might understand, "Lucy and Fifi were accused of theft in the super-market when I wasn't with them."

Gina's spine straightens and her eyes spark. Rebecca has never seen her mad before. Gina has too much power to be angry; usually the threat of her disfavor is enough to keep everyone in line. "I hope you set them straight."

"Actually, Lucy stood up for her, though I helped." Rebecca blurts, "I worry sometimes that I won't be enough. I'm always afraid I'm fail-ing her."

"Just love her, that's all." Gina lays a gentle hand on her arm.

The bell rings and Fifi runs to Rebecca for a goodbye kiss. "Will you pick me up after school? Please?"

Her heart swells. Fifi's been turning to Lucy because Rebecca hasn't been there enough. Auction or no auction, she needs to start making more time for her little girl. "I'll be here."

As they walk out of the schoolyard, Rebecca is mortified that she confessed her inadequacy. What must Gina think of her? Her mother used to chastise her, "Please stop oversharing. It's neither appropriate nor desired." She sneaks a little glance at Gina but the agent only appears thoughtful. Rebecca tries a few times to utter some graceful or friendly phrase but Louis is running back and forth, tangling his leash with Graham's as they head toward Central Park. How is she ever go-ing to charm Gina this way?

Gina stops yet again to untangle herself. "I really thought it was kind of unfair, the way you were treated by the industry after the

Carey Madison incident. I've always wanted to ask you, did you ever suspect?"

"No." Rebecca betrays no emotion though, inside, she is stunned and pleased that Gina is giving her the chance to defend herself instead of listening to innuendo. Maybe it wasn't such a bad idea to reveal her fear of failure after all. "Carey provided us with falsified documents. We had several fact checkers and copy editors go over that manuscript and none of us found anything. I still blame myself, though. I should have dug deeper. I just didn't expect it."

"That's one of the drawbacks of being an honest person. Some things don't occur to you." Gina bends down to pet Louis, then straightens to face her. "For an editor's reputation to be tarnished by an incident like that is truly a shame."

Rebecca thinks of what Brandon had said to her that night they made love by the fire before their marriage had gone to hell. She decides to be completely truthful. "Listen, I know there are people who look at me and think I'm some society woman who's dabbling in publishing for fun. And the scandal last year didn't help. But I'm an extremely good editor and if Isabel were my author, I would fight with everything I have not only to make her book as good as it could be but to make sure that B&W supports her in every way."

Gina smiles. "I'll make sure you get the manuscript today."

Rebecca stops midstep. Oh, thank goodness. Bands of tension that have been keeping her lungs constricted loosen. She could kiss the agent. She beams. "I'd love that. I'll clear my schedule to read it as soon as possible."

Gina gives a little laugh. "It is a challenge to find enough time to do everything, isn't it? You're very fortunate to have Lucy. You know, I'm realizing I noticed her at the schoolyard because she's so attentive to Fifi. I think it's wonderful that your husband speaks Chinese with your daughter, and you've found a nanny to help with her language skills."

"Yes, I am," says Rebecca, though she's wondering why everyone seems to admire her nanny. Is she truly lucky to have Lucy?

TWENTY-ONE

Jasmine

I startled awake with my jaw clenched so tightly I had a headache. I'd slept terribly. I couldn't stop thinking about that phone call from the snakehead yesterday. I got up for a drink of water but something moved in the dark corners of my room, and I jumped. It was only my reflection in the three-way mirror. I covered it with a blanket, then closed my curtains so I wouldn't see the branches of the tree waving outside my window.

I had to return to Opium now that my debt had increased, and Wen was possibly on my trail. I'd been careful and didn't keep any of the other jewelry he'd given me, but I'd taken a risk with the wedding ring. What if he found me? What if he figured out what I meant to do with our daughter? He'd been in the military. He was dangerous. I shuddered at how enraged he would be if he ever caught up with me.

I'd hurried away from Anthony with a flimsy excuse but not before he'd made me promise to return to the studio this afternoon for a self-defense lesson. I was counting down the hours until the class. It wasn't even that I believed I could learn anything that would save me in a life-or-death situation or that I'd truly be able to incapacitate Lone Wolf Jack, or anyone like him. It was only to have some chance of keeping a dangerous encounter from being utterly impossible.

As I climbed back into bed, I couldn't deny that I also wanted to see Anthony again. Meeting him on the promenade had changed me. I came to America for my daughter, in search of a fresh start, but I hadn't understood how isolated I would feel, unseen among strangers. Back home, so much of my identity was mirrored through other people's eyes. The village I came from, the school I went to, my family name, those all had meaning in China. Here they stood for nothing—all those details disappeared when you were an immigrant, and suddenly all that was left of you was whatever you carried inside.

Anthony made me feel seen and real. He had called me the bravest and cleverest person he knew. I was far from that but, still, it warmed me that he cared about my inner self, not the face I presented to the world. What if his parents had said yes to the matchmaker all those years ago? My heart fluttered and I groaned. I couldn't develop feelings for Anthony. There was no future for us.

I was prepared for the heavy studio door this time, though I had to brace my feet against the floor. I felt a twinge of discomfort when I passed the empty sign-in area where Anthony and I had argued. As I stepped inside the main room, I saw a group of women of all shapes chatting with each other as they stretched. I smiled at their comfortable clothing—quite the difference from Opium. No one took particular notice of me. I scanned the walls. Surprisingly, there were a few photos of people break dancing among the framed certificates. The mat-lined floor had equipment stacked in the corners: punching bags, practice katana blades, rubber guns, a box filled with boxing gloves.

My head turned as the instructors entered the room, all wearing the studio's black kung fu uniforms: Anthony, the young woman Yan, and a tall older Chinese man. Anthony's eyes went directly to me, and his entire face lit up. I smiled back at him.

I joined the other students as the older man spoke in clear, precise Chinese. This must be Anthony's uncle Nick. Every movement he made was controlled and powerful. His round face was smooth, with vivid, mischievous eyes. "Welcome, everyone. Many of you already know this but since this class has rolling admissions and we have a number of newcomers, please bear with me while I get them oriented. The three of us will be your instructors. Some of the more advanced students will be assisting. I'm Nick. I've taught self-defense and martial arts for many years. I'm taking break dancing classes in my free time."

"And he's amazing!" one of the students called out.

Nick laughed. "I'll show you some of my moves if we get the chance. This is my nephew Anthony and Yan. I'll let them quickly introduce themselves."

Although Anthony was supposed to be addressing the entire group, I felt most of his attention on me. "Hi, everyone. I'm Anthony. I've been teaching here for a few years and I'm studying to be an accountant."

"Don't look like no accountant to me," one of the women said, loudly enough that a titter swept the room.

As Anthony blushed, Yan stepped forward. Her features were non-descript. She seemed like the type of person it would be easy to over-look. But she stood steady and strong next to Anthony, her weight distributed solidly between her feet. "My name is Yan. I came here to learn self-defense like all of you, but I did a lot of martial arts back in China."

Nick said, "We are going to teach you to defend yourselves. Re-member that your reaction to a bad situation will not only be about what you're *able* to do; you also need to take into account what you're *willing* to do. We'll start by warming up. Then you'll do some exercises separately and later, we'll have you practice sparring with a partner."

As I huffed through my sit-ups, I was aware of Anthony watch-ing me, as I did him, albeit surreptitiously. During one of the training drills, he, Yan, and Nick were standing close to me. I gave him a quick shake of my head to remind him not to introduce me to his uncle. I didn't want any word possibly getting back to my village. Nick gave me a warm smile of welcome and moved on, while Yan's gaze lingered.

Then we formed lines in front of the instructors. Of course, I was put into Anthony's group.

He gave me a cocky grin. "Go on, try to hit me first."

I would have loved nothing more than to wipe that smirk off his face. I balled up my fists and launched at him. He moved too fast. He caught my wrist and turned me around so he had me in a headlock, my back pressed against his chest. I tried to break free. His hold was so strong I couldn't move an inch. I elbowed him in the gut with my other arm and the jerk didn't even grunt, which only made me more annoyed. Did I ever think he was attractive? I took it all back. He was an ugly, arrogant son of a dog.

"Ready to give up?" The stubble on his jaw was rough against my ear and all at once, I was aware of how closely our bodies were pressed together, how I could feel the heat of him through my clothing. He was all hard muscle and I realized again how confused I was. In my mind, I still thought of him as a boy, but that image flickered back and forth against the reality of the man he'd become. Was he holding me against him on purpose? Could he possibly have feelings for me too?

"Enough." Yan was standing in front of us, her expressive eyes fixed on Anthony's until he released me. Was that hurt I saw on her face? Then she turned to me. "Later on, we're going to teach you how to get out of that situation safely."

Nick had Anthony and Yan demonstrate some basic and advanced moves for the group and I began to understand her reaction. Anthony attempted to attack her while she defended herself, using elbow strikes, kicks, and blocks. Then they moved on to demonstrating weapons. At first I watched them both with awe. She transformed from a plain woman into someone fierce, sexy, and supple, proving herself especially skilled with a practice knife, while Anthony was breathtaking with a staff. They launched into a flurry of moves so flowing and forceful they seemed almost choreographed.

But then I noticed his hand on her wrist, her head against his neck, the familiarity in the way they touched, and it struck me like a fist: they were together.

I struggled to remain calm. Why shouldn't Anthony have a girlfriend? I'd been with Wen, for goodness' sake. Girls had always liked Anthony, followed him around and teased him, but I'd always understood that I claimed first place in his heart as his best friend. I'd only recently started entertaining this ridiculous notion of the two of us together. Still, watching him with Yan and observing the silken intimacy that surrounded the two of them hurt me. It was like a burn: the initial shock, the startled withdrawal of the wounded skin. I knew the pain would only seep further into my flesh later, damaging tissues I didn't even know existed.

For a moment, I wanted, so intensely it took my breath away, to have it be me standing next to him, to close my eyes and pretend we were back home, two innocents catching crabs by the waterfall. If only I might unwind time so all that had come between us was undone and we could return to the days when there was no Wen and Yan, only Anthony and Jasmine.

As everyone was getting ready to leave, I lingered and overheard Yan say to him, "My place tonight as usual?" She flicked a glance at me. She'd wanted me to know.

So it was true. They were a couple. I busied myself gathering my things, pretended I wasn't trying to eavesdrop. As the initial shock faded, I understood what else I was feeling: betrayal. Why hadn't he told me? His girlfriend shouldn't have been a secret and he'd had plenty of opportunities to mention her yesterday. This hurt was too familiar, scorching through the same pathways Wen had burned into my soul— another man who chose not to tell me about the other women in his life. I was so tired of being the last to know. Clearly, we were only friends and I certainly had plenty of secrets I hadn't shared with him, but this omission hurt all the same.

There was a pause, and I could feel the weight of his stare. My heart sank as I heard him say, "Sure."

I thought of Yan and hated her for being so strong and close to Anthony. Some kind of monster was growing in me. I swallowed it down. I refused to do this. I understood I wasn't the only woman in his affections any longer, that in fact, I hadn't been that for some time. I just hadn't known it. I wasn't angry at Yan. I was upset at my-self. I wasn't made to keep a man's love.

In China, I'd seen posters warning girls of the danger of becoming leftover women, women that no one wanted. Leftover like scraps on a table, uneaten food, both a sacrilege and wasteful, something that should have nourished our country squandered and turned into rubbish: unwanted, purposeless, of no use to anyone.

I was a leftover woman, I realized. After everyone else had carved away what they wanted to see in me and taken what they desired, I was all that was left.

TWENTY-TWO

Jasmine

Each time I returned to Opium, I told myself it was only for that night, and yet, the next time I was scheduled, I went again. I did my best to become nothing when I was there: no opinions, no emotion, no shame. I focused only on my body and my body was an excellent liar. It was smooth and pliable and, most of all, it had no voice. The men there liked that. There was no trace of me in it; there was no hint of my past or my plans or anything else. I wished I could tell myself I was working at the club out of curiosity or thrills, but it was only for the money, which was even worse. I chose this. When you sow melons, you reap melons; when you sow beans, you reap beans.

I didn't see nudity any longer. I saw loneliness and desperation. I saw desire and longing. There was escape in many forms: drugs and sex, anything to take your mind off your life for one evening. The naïve and the kind were shafted left and right. I kept my distance from everyone, as much as I could. The staff laughed when they heard yet another man complain that his credit card had been overcharged. One hapless young guy was told they couldn't find his jacket at the coat check unless he paid a fifteen-dollar "search fee." An exotic dancer arranged to give a man a hand job in the Champagne Room for four hundred dollars and he slipped her four twenties instead. The next time another man opened his wallet to pay her twenty dollars for a lap dance, she reached in and plucked out the hundred-dollar bill in the back, then blew him a kiss as she strutted away.

Most of the time, I acted as Dawn had instructed. I smiled and eluded. If the customers touched my skin, I wagged my finger teasingly and removed their hands. I flirted. I ignored anything the clients said that I didn't want to hear. I especially hated the degrading intimate questions, the men who assumed my answers were theirs to demand.

"That's some body you've got. You should strip. Ever think about it?"

"How many men have you slept with?"

Their lies came thick and fast. "Hey, honey, I deal in diamonds, on Wall Street." I didn't even register them as individuals anymore. When they asked for my phone number, I scribbled down a fake one. I drank the cocktails they ordered for me, which Phoenix obligingly mixed with water instead of alcohol, and pretended I was tipsy. I had a finely tuned instinct for when they were likely to make a "friendly" grab and dodged accordingly. Only once did I step over to a table outside of my area by accident and the cocktail waitress there glared at me so darkly that I immediately understood she thought I was trying to poach her client. I was exhausted, not from the work, but from the maintenance of this facade the men were constantly trying to breach. I was disgusted by them, but most of all, I was disgusted by myself. Sometimes, when I couldn't bear it anymore, I'd close my eyes and picture Fiona's face: her slightly wavy hair, her stubborn little chin, and her eloquent eyes. It comforted me. I also wondered how I could ever face her if she learned all I had done.

Dawn had been right. Separately Dawn and I drew attention, but together we attracted a crowd. Aunt Glory asked us to start pooling our tables so we served the same customers. It was a relief in many ways because I could be shy to Dawn's bubbly. The men ate it up. I was better than she was at remembering all the orders, so I took care of most of the practical work. Tips were astronomical and I was stunned by the amount I had in my pocket at the end of a shift. I was intoxicated by the money. Never in my life had I had so much, and not only cash but American dollars. It was freedom; it was power; it was the ability to make my dreams come true and it didn't matter where it came from, or at least, that's what I kept telling myself.

Many of the clients asked to take us into the Champagne Room and they weren't happy when I refused. Dawn, already drunk and glassy-eyed from whatever her drug of choice had been that night, would stumble away with one of them while I stayed outside the beaded curtain with his irritated friend. I still didn't drink and hadn't accepted any of the drugs, though having some sort of mental buffer was increasingly tempting. It seemed ridiculous to attempt to preserve any concept of modesty while working in a strip club but on the other hand, the thought of allowing those men to paw me made my stomach twist.

What would Anthony think? Whenever a shaft of emotion stabbed me, I realized I was still able to feel shame. I continued taking the self-defense lessons, despite the pain of seeing him with Yan. He had taught me how to get out of holds like the one he'd put me in the first day. I kept an amiable distance now that I knew he had a girlfriend. When he brought up getting together, I made excuses. I wanted to see him alone, of course I did, but I desired more than friendship with him, and I couldn't have it. Moreover, there was no room for him in my future with Fiona.

At the end of one long night at Opium, I dragged myself to the ladies' room, exhausted, ready to change out of my uniform. A small group of cocktail waitresses, including Phoenix, the bartender, joined the line behind me.

Lone Wolf Jack was sitting on his stool outside and gave me a long, steady look. "I found a restaurant that makes perfect clay pot rice. The crust is very crispy, and you wouldn't believe the flavor. Want to try it out?"

I blinked at him a moment until I realized he was asking me on a date. In my mind, I quickly riffled through the lines I used to evade the clients until one clicked. "Umm, I'm sorry, I just started seeing someone and he's so possessive."

"That's not a problem."

I didn't answer, only gave him a quick smile and hurried into the ladies' room. Phoenix followed me inside. "You'd better be careful you don't step on Dawn's toes." She must have overheard us.

"He noticed me because I'm new." At least, that's what I was hoping. But I'd seen Dawn giggling with him lately. "What is going on with them? Are they dating?"

"Maybe. Though he might be able to help you out with your little problem."

"I am *not* sexually frustrated," I snapped, then blushed when she burst out laughing. What was this place doing to me? It was all those men offering to service me constantly, that was all, nothing to do with Anthony and the growing desire I'd felt in his arms.

"I meant with your documents. He can arrange anything, you know? For a price." Phoenix waggled her eyebrows at me.

I filed that away in my mind because some high-quality false papers could help me out tremendously. But it didn't quiet the unease I always felt when I saw Lone Wolf Jack's dark, intent expression. One night, I'd seen him and two other bouncers tap one of my customers on the shoulder, a clean-cut man in his early forties who had asked me to go to the Champagne Room with him. The man turned pale. The bouncers escorted him into Aunt Glory's office. I thought I heard a muffled scream, but the music was turned up so loudly I might have imagined it.

I never saw that man again.

The nights sped by. Once, when I returned a sheaf of bills to an exotic dancer who had dropped it, she said, "Oh, so now I gotta be besties with you? Well, I don't think so." As she walked away, she gave me a look over her shoulder that said, *This just means you're stupid.*

Opium was sordid and seedy and corrupt; it was all about sex and ripping each other off, from the coat check gal to Phoenix, who showed up with a huge bruise on her jaw one night, badly covered by makeup, and was sent away forever by Aunt Glory. Aside from Dawn, whom I found red-eyed in the ladies' room, no one seemed to miss her. Now

Aunt Glory made some of the other women fill in at random. Since I didn't have Phoenix to make my drinks anymore, I only pretended to consume them, making sure to splash enough out of my glass to be believable. The beverages took forever and were often improperly made, and the clients complained and blamed the waitresses.

But there was another side to the club. The pimply thirteen-year-old son of one of the cocktail waitresses frequently came for free and sat in the corner eating chicken dumplings and drinking soda while some of the dancers ruffled his hair. One of the dancers was supporting her mom and was always reading her English dictionary during the breaks because she was studying to become a nurse. Not to mention the whip-wielding dominatrix whose phone was filled with photos of her dog, a hideous black and brown rescue mutt with only one eye. Many of the women, like me, didn't have the right documents and couldn't speak English well enough to get any other type of job. Some had been lured here with stories of modeling and acting, only to end up pandering to men who groped them. There was a group of Vietnamese girls who always stuck together, and the grapevine said they were forced to work there by snakeheads.

One of the busboys was in love with a dancer who didn't know he was alive. He visibly died a bit inside every time she went off with a customer. Some of the patrons were more lonely than anything else, looking for connection where there wasn't any. I tried to keep those types of stories at bay too. It was easier to believe that the workers at Opium didn't contain a shred of decency. I didn't want to get close to anyone. However, despite myself, I couldn't help caring about Dawn, who not only regularly saved me from the more difficult clients but also cheerfully babysat for some of the bouncers. When the kids were asleep, she loved to knit or crochet.

One evening, Dawn and Lone Wolf Jack had clearly had one of their fights and she came into work looking hollow and despondent. It was a bad night, filled with rambunctious bachelor parties that tipped badly. After a particularly brutal client grabbed Dawn by the arm so hard he left marks, I said to her, while we were waiting for our drink orders at the bar, "Why are you doing this?"

She looked at me, her eyes wide and liquid.

"What do you really want?" I asked.

"Well, I'd love to open a yarn store one day." Her laughter sounded a little choked. "But what do I truly dream of? You know those families on TV, where they hug the kids and play board games and have pot roast on Sundays? Have you ever had pot roast?"

I shook my head.

"Me neither. That's what I want." She leaned in close, and I realized she was quite drunk. "But I'm never gonna get that."

"Why not?" It was too late for me, but Dawn was smart and kind. I thought of Anthony. "Good men do exist. Real love exists."

Her voice was low. "Perhaps. But not for us. We're meant to fulfill a role, like a part in a movie. True love isn't for women like us."

I glanced at Lone Wolf Jack, who was standing by the entrance of the Champagne Room, his eyes fixed on me instead of her. He licked his lips. I understood now that Dawn had been telling the truth when she warned me about him, even if it had also been to keep me away from him. I'd seen the way she watched him, the way she flinched when he wrapped an arm around another woman's waist. "Nobody is worth your tears and the one who is won't make you cry. You know Lone Wolf Jack's dangerous. Why are you seeing him?"

She shrugged. "I always make the wrong choices with love. I have a little cousin in China who thinks I walk on air, but I got involved with an unsuitable man and had to flee the scandal. I was forced to leave her behind." I could see from the starkness in her wet eyes that she would never forgive herself. "I'm knitting all that stuff so that maybe I'll get to give it to her one day, but she won't fit into it by then."

"What happened with that man?"

Dawn gave a ladylike snort. "He was doing the leg splits without his wife's knowledge so he disappeared as soon as rumors started circulating about us. His wife comes from a powerful family. Which reminds me, you need to be prepared."

She ducked behind the bar, where both of us had stashed our bags. She rummaged through hers, then pulled out a handful of condoms in plastic wrappers and held them out to me.

I felt my cheeks glow red hot. "Dawn, put those away!"

She winked at me, then dropped them into my bag before coming out from behind the bar. "Aunt Glory's not going to wait forever for you to do the Champagne Room, and you need to be careful that you don't go in there with an undercover cop."

"How can I tell?"

"Oh, you'll know," she said, but I wasn't so sure I did. "Anyway, Lone Wolf Jack usually spots them before they can get very far. He takes care of them."

Our drinks were ready. When she stepped forward to take her tray, I said, "Dawn, you never know about love. Watch and the clouds will part to show the moonlight. Maybe one day, after we've stopped doing this . . ."

Her eyes were unbearably sad. "We all say this is temporary. But Jasmine, the truth is, no one ever stops of their own free will. We just get too old and as we age, we get increasingly desperate. We start to go further for less money. That's why I'm here, to get what I can while I've still got it."

"I'm not paying the two of you to chatter." Aunt Glory's cold voice came from behind us. "I'm doing you a favor by allowing you to share your tables. Don't make me regret it."

We jumped apart and Dawn hurried away. Aunt Glory caught me by the wrist. Her lips curled. "I've just had another customer complain that you won't drink champagne with him. He has an AmEx Black Card and now he's upset. You have potential. You could be one of my best girls. But night after night, you're turning down a tremendous amount of money—and not just for yourself but for Opium. Do you think that because I'm a woman, I'm soft?"

I shook my head rapidly.

"It's not easy to be the female owner of a club like this. I have the whole world breathing down my neck: the triads, the snakeheads, the police. There's a target on my back. I need to be twice as ruthless as a man, twice as good, and I'm doing it all for Lily."

I whispered the question I'd wondered. "Why do you make your daughter work as a cleaner then?"

She narrowed her eyes. "To teach her humility but also so everyone will know nothing was given to her. She earned it herself, from the ground up. There's no room for prudes here. Those who eat with one chopstick will stay hungry. Maybe Lily is right that you can't really hack it. If you want to keep your job, you need to show me that you're willing to do whatever it takes to keep the customer happy. Or you're out on the street. Do you hear me?"

I had no choice but to nod. That night, I started drinking my cocktails. I didn't get completely drunk because I didn't want to lose control and tell the men exactly what I thought of them. I only loosened up enough for everything to be a bit more fun, less weighted, a sheer gauze curtain around me that made me feel comforted. I knew I'd taken the first step down a slippery slope, but what else could I do?

I should just give in and do the Champagne Room. It would mean so much more money. I needed to become the architect of my own life, to develop the ability to lay the foundation in advance and wait until the right moment to build. I wasn't married. Wen and I hadn't been legally wed because I'd been too young. I'd already used my body to get what I wanted from him. In case I had to leave Opium in a hurry, I might be able to earn enough now to repay my debts and start to build a future with Fiona. I thought about what Wen might be doing to try to find me and shivered.

When I went home that night, the odd figures hurrying down the deserted sidewalks, heads hunched, gave the city an uneasy, ominous feel. I told myself it was the empty streets littered with trash, the hollow wind sweeping across the concrete, but I knew better. There was a low hum of electricity at the base of my neck, that prickle of awareness that came from someone watching you. I'd felt this before but never this strongly. I walked as quickly as I could toward the subway, doing my best not to whip my head around. My pulse was a wild drum in my ears punctuating the beat of my feet against the concrete. I wondered what I would do if someone jumped me. Thank goodness for those self-defense classes. I might just have a chance.

I was almost flying down the sidewalk now, driven by my fear, when headlights suddenly swerved toward me on the street. I was blinded by the white glare, startled as a hare. I could feel it illuminate my face, my skull, and for a moment, I swayed, feeling as if I might topple directly onto the path of those screeching tires. A horn beeped, long and loud, and I leapt backward, the smell of asphalt filling my nostrils.

After the car roared away, I pressed a hand to my chest.

A yellow cab drove up next to me. A voice in English said, "Lady, are you all right? You need a ride?"

I pulled myself together, got in, and left anyone who might be following behind. For now.

TWENTY-THREE

Rebecca

Rebecca reads Isabel Navarro's novel in one fell swoop that weekend. She settles into her armchair, flips open the first page, and it's like she's diving into a cool blue swimming pool, the water closing over her head so seamlessly that she doesn't even think to stop for air. She feels the tingle of excitement deep in her stomach, the electricity that sweeps through her spine and into her fingertips. She recognizes this feeling: the instinct that's taken her to the top of her profession. By the time she reemerges hours later, blinking owlishly at the fire that's died down low, back in her own body, returning to her own life, she knows without a doubt that come hell or high water, she has to acquire this book.

Since the auction is next week, she'll need to move fast. She prepares the projected sales figures so she can justify the amount she wants to spend. She sends the electronic file of the manuscript to Simone and everyone else who'll need to approve a high advance. But most importantly, she invites Gina and Isabel to lunch at one of the city's finest restaurants, having heard that Isabel has a weakness for black cod with miso.

A few days later, Rebecca arrives at the restaurant early to make sure they have indeed been placed at her favorite spot: the intimate booth in the corner, red velvet benches cozied up to a live-edge elm dining table with a river of smoked resin running through the wood. A sparkling chandelier of shells encases the diners in golden light. She's dressed carefully for this meeting, wanting to seem authoritative yet innovative. Rebecca smooths a hand over her sleek black Yves Saint Laurent textured dress, formfitting, ending above the knee. She's paired it with the matching Mandarin collar jacket and sheer dark stockings.

Gina and Isabel arrive right on time and after the hugging and kissing and everyone's settled in their seats with ice water and perusing the menus, Rebecca takes a moment to take a good look at Isabel, who's wearing red today. She's draped in a crimson top with a matching chiffon scarf tossed over her bare shoulder, and in this restaurant where everyone else is dressed in New York black, she burns like a flame.

They make small talk about the food, industry gossip, and the latest buzzy books they absolutely must read. When she can, Rebecca turns the conversation to Isabel's work.

"I had the opportunity to read your manuscript and I loved it," she says, having decided to play it safe with a generic positive comment. "Beautifully written and such a poignant story."

"I am happy to hear it." Isabel is polite but she's also obviously bored. Her eyes are wandering around the room, her fingertips dancing on the table. She's heard this before.

Rebecca knows it can be dangerous to get too technical too fast, especially about proposed changes to a book. The wrong comment can send a skittish author running in the opposite direction, straight into the arms of a competitive editor, like Mason, for example. Just as on a first date, the key is to play it charming and easy, not too intellectual, not too serious. The time to reveal your cards is after the sale, when the deal's done and the author has committed. However, Isabel seems more engrossed in her baby spinach salad with lobster than with Rebecca, despite Gina's best efforts. If Rebecca doesn't act, she'll lose her anyway.

Rebecca nibbles delicately on a piece of roasted cauliflower with jalapeño salsa. "Ambition, especially in women, has been and is still often considered an unappealing attribute, but I personally admire it greatly, or to be more accurate, I recognize it in myself."

Isabel looks up, a flicker of interest in her eyes.

Rebecca continues. "We know that there is still an anti-powerful-woman bias that lives and thrives, you might say, in a world in which books written by men are statistically more likely to be well reviewed, to win major awards, and to become bestsellers. However, I do believe that there's starting to be a change in awareness, in certain kinds of fundamentals. I'm hopeful that we're at the beginning of more systemic changes in terms of female representation in the corridors of power, especially for women of color, and if you were to choose me as your editor, I would be your fiercest advocate within the publishing house just as I would be your keenest critic on the page."

Gina dabs at her lips with a napkin and gives Rebecca a little smile.

Isabel pushes away her salad. "So the veil drops. I like you much better when you stop trying to be the tasteful, sophisticated woman who always says the polite thing. Underneath is someone sharper and more incisive." She snares a piece of tofu with her fork and dips it into spicy garlic sauce, then looks directly at Rebecca. "Tell me honestly, what do you think of my novel?"

This is it. If she misreads the book or suggests an edit that Isabel balks at, that will be the end. Authors are not obligated to accept the highest bid in an auction with multiple offers. They can go with which-ever publisher they want.

Rebecca cuts a piece of beef tenderloin and swirls it in wasabi pepper sauce as she considers. "There are of course many possible ways to read such a complex and multifaceted novel. On the simplest level, it's a compelling page-turner following a woman of color in the United States and the explosive secret she's hiding. I see it as an interrogation of the way both women and immigrants need to split themselves into different personas and roles. I especially appreci-ated the concept of how a foreigner can only let a slice of themselves be seen in the new culture; the rest is hidden, the submerged part of the iceberg. It's an intricate, tightly woven story about the price of ambition, displacement, and adoption. Its themes of motherhood, identity, romantic love, and race are specific and universal at the same time."

"And how do you think it can be improved?" Isabel is sitting up now, that keen intelligence focused on her.

Rebecca thinks a moment before she speaks. "The novel has tremendous emotional and intellectual resonance. But I'm not sure that the metaphor of woman as commodity completely works in its current incarnation. Although it is a devastating critique of the way women can be treated as fetishized objects, I worry that the ironic distance might not be clearly delineated enough and that some readers might take this motif at face value."

"You mean that instead of understanding that the novel is criticizing this type of social relationship, some might read it as an embodiment of it?"

"Yes, but I believe that can be fixed by a few targeted changes." Rebecca stops, wondering if she's gone too far.

But then Isabel gives her a look of approval. "I need an editor who can help me take my writing and my career to the next level."

Gina says, "And indeed, Rebecca's personal experience with the adoption of a child from a different race and culture would certainly inform her editorial work on this novel."

Rebecca says, "Not only that but believe me, I would make sure this brilliant book of yours receives its due both within and outside the publishing house. Your work reflects the ongoing national conversation about race, feminism, and identity and that would be a part of how we would position it. Plus, I've helped develop an in-depth marketing and publicity plan to highlight your novel. Not that your spectacular career needs any help, of course."

Isabel gives her a wry look. "I'm a woman of color, a lesbian, and a writer. I'm not arrogant enough to believe I don't need support. In fact, I welcome it."

After an in-depth conversation about the manuscript, so pleasurable that they all linger over desserts of dark chocolate fondant and caramel soba-cha brownies, an exhilarated Rebecca gestures for the check. However, when she opens her purse, she bites back a curse. The only thing in it is her phone. She must have left her wallet back at the office.

"Is there a problem?" asks Gina.

"Thanks, not at all," she replies. Thank goodness she's always prepared, she thinks, as she finds the personal credit card she keeps tucked in her phone cover, just in case. She'll get reimbursed later.

She drops it on the bill and hands it to the waiter. She's slightly irritated, then alarmed when he returns after a few minutes to whisper in her ear, "I'm afraid it's been declined, ma'am."

"That's not possible." Even though she rarely uses this card, it's linked to the joint account she shares with Brandon, which has a substantial credit line. "It must be a mistake. Can you please run it again?"

When the man comes back with an apologetic cough and a shake of his head, she stands up. Her cheeks are beginning to burn. Gina and Isabel are looking at her with twin expressions of wariness. "Please excuse me for a moment."

Her stomach begins to clench as she steps up to the bar so she can ring her bank. In the worst-case scenario, Gina could simply put the meal on her own corporate credit card. Rebecca can send over payment later but that's entirely beside the point. In the ridiculously old-school world of publishing, where a handshake can still suffice in lieu of a contract between author and agent, the ritual of lunch is in many ways a courtship. If a hopeful swain demonstrates his ability to support a wife by paying for a meal, then Rebecca will have utterly failed if Gina needs to take over this expense. Her jaw is already painfully tight at the thought of this possible humiliation. It would make her look unprofessional. Inadequate. Unprepared. Not at all the type of editor Isabel Navarro should choose.

Once on the phone, Rebecca demands to know why the card has been declined.

The voice on the line says, "There appears to have been a substantial number of large expenditures in this billing cycle."

"This must be some sort of administrative error. Where were these charges made?" Even as she scoffs, she is thinking of the evening Brandon went out with his Chinese officials. Absent-minded as he is, he often forgets his Columbia credit card and pays with their joint personal one, getting reimbursed later.

The customer service representative names a corporation she's never heard of and Rebecca gasps when she hears the amount charged for one evening. She bites down on her lip hard. She thinks back to what Brandon had said. He was going to wine and dine his guests, possibly take them to a club.

Where in the world had her husband gone?

TWENTY-FOUR

Jasmine

That Tuesday evening at Opium, flashes of blue, green, red, and white light zipped across the floor in coded patterns shifting too quickly to be deciphered. The music pulsed through the walls and bodies, rich and deep, moving from exotic dancer to customer to cocktail waitress to bouncer, a whisper of *sex, sex, sex*. I was feeling unsteady on my feet. My high heels were killing me. Most of my toes were numb; my arms were covered in goose bumps from the air-conditioning. I'd already drunk more than I'd intended and the flitting lights flashed and wove in between the patrons like ghosts, giddy and desperate.

I was hanging on to the back of a chair, gulping, when I overheard Dawn say to another waitress, ". . . speaks Chinese like a native."

My head snapped up. A wave of dizziness rushed over me. I looked in the direction Dawn was indicating and saw a white man with his back to me, sitting in her section, which I shared. A few non-Asians made it through but most of the time, the bouncers kept anyone not well-dressed enough or Asian enough out. The man's light-brown hair shone, and he had his arm around one of his male Chinese friends, laughing. He was wearing a green shirt while the others at his table were all in navy suits. They looked like high officials from China, probably Beijing. I'd seen Wen in that type of starched and pressed outfit.

Now Dawn was speaking to me. I had to shake my head before I could register her words. "... need to cover ... Can you take the table with the white guy?"

I started to stammer a refusal—I felt ill, I had to go home—but the man turned his head. He was in the middle of listening to his friend and his gaze slid over me. Then his eyes ricocheted back, stalled on my face, and widened in surprise. Electricity crackled between us. The room froze all around me. Everything suddenly became crystal clear. His blue eyes, dark and golden like sunlight in water, his high cheekbones, the thick furrowed eyebrows. It was too late.

I stumbled toward his table like I'd been hypnotized. Thoughts raced through my mind. I wanted to run but even I knew this was unavoidable, perhaps had been inevitable from the day I landed in the Beautiful Country. The entire group quieted, chuckling and smirking, as I approached. I was drawn by that one man in the green shirt, the way he tilted his head for me to come closer. He took in my long legs and high heels, my bright lips and mane of hair. He gestured for me to bend down, so close that I could smell his cedar cologne.

Brandon whispered in my ear, "What the hell are you doing here, Lucy?"

Part Three

TWENTY-FIVE

Jasmine

After Rebecca hired me, I tried to tell her my real name: Luli, meaning Dewy Jasmine.

She said, "That's lovely but I think a more American name might help you assimilate. Let's just call you Lucy, shall we? That'll be so much easier for everyone."

Of course, she meant it would be so much easier for her, which was what counted. I addressed her as Mrs. Whitney because I could tell she secretly liked that. It wasn't so much that she wanted to keep me beneath her but that she had an orderly mind and wanted me classified. I was staff and I didn't speak English well, plus I was Chinese. I was so different from her it was like a chicken talking to a duck. However, knowing Rebecca, I believe my tasteless clothing probably caused her the most offense. I deliberately dressed myself in the dowdiest attire I could find. I didn't want to be seen or noticed. I didn't want any questions about my past. I kept my head bowed and my body layered up, so I appeared bulky and not voluptuous, a surprisingly easy task when you were tall and busty. It was better for me that no one asked who I was or what I cared about, not even Brandon, who spoke my language like a native.

I knew I finally had to act after years of stealthy preparation when I read this email from him last year:

> Since Fifi will soon be old enough to start elementary school, we'll be looking for a live-in nanny for her. Rest assured that she is happy and well.

I could escape Wen, flee to the United States, and be close to my daughter. I wanted to look in her eyes and know for myself that she was well treated. I wanted to see someone who belonged to me. I understood the truth then: there was no one for me in this world except for her.

The snakeheads brought me to the Beautiful Country. I prayed every night that the nanny position for Fiona would still be available. It was all worth it the first time I saw her in New York. She was a bit older than the most recent photo I'd seen but the shape of her chin was the same as mine, her habit of chewing on her toy stuffed octopus. I was shaking so hard, I was afraid her parents might notice. I hoped they attributed it to simple nerves, though I felt as if I were trembling in a high gale. A bit longer and I would have let go and fallen into those golden brown eyes. She stared back at me, solemn and shy. I wanted, more than anything I'd ever desired, to reach out and lay a hand on her small black head, to pull her against me and feel her breathing, slight and warm against my chest, as if by taking care of her I could undo time and protect myself at her age. At that moment, I realized I would do anything, even give up my own happiness, for a future with her in it.

I bent down and extended my palm to her. I said in Chinese, "My name is Jasmine. I used to chew on my toys too. I like your octopus. I think he's very special. Will you tell me more about him?"

She smiled, stepped forward, and took my hand.

Brandon paid me in cash. He must have suspected my lack of documentation but decided to ignore it. As the months passed, I loved making meals and snacks for Fiona. I had been a cook in Wen's parents' restaurant and quickly picked up the Western dishes Rebecca liked. When Fiona tasted something delicious, she looked at it intensely as she was eating, just the way I did. For someone who had longed to find a reflection of herself in anyone around them, it felt like finally coming home to find my own daughter. And she was so affectionate, so loving, the feel of her arms around my neck, the brush of her rounded cheek against mine. She was amazed by my drawings. She was the only person I let flip through my sketchbook. She especially enjoyed it when I drew her and her toys. Through her eyes, I caught a glimpse of another version of myself: someone talented, admirable, and worthy of being loved.

Most of the time, I worked hard to keep my thoughts strictly segmented, to forget who she was to me. It would have been too easy otherwise to simply take her and run while we were alone before her parents came home. I knew how disastrous that would be with my debt unpaid and no savings for our future.

Nevertheless, I constantly had to fight my jealousy over Rebecca being her mother. I hid my expression when Fiona called her "Mommy." Fortunately, it was easy to be invisible around Rebecca. She never truly looked at me anyway. She was smart enough to be aware of her privilege, in theory at least, but in practice, she was as blind as anyone else. I wasn't one of them, even if I wanted to be. In English, I was a different person, stuttering, slow, and clumsy. Inarticulate, seemingly unintelligent. Rebecca, for whom appearances meant so much, wasn't able to see past any of that to the woman I was in Chinese. She didn't realize that I could understand so much more than I could express in her language. My features were as impenetrable as a mirror, reflecting back only what she expected to see with her white gaze.

Their house was a shock, their affluence, the luxurious surroundings. I was also stunned by the pure white flowers everywhere, which were extremely unlucky by Chinese standards. The most horrifying of all were the framed photos of Rebecca and Fiona posing with chopsticks. They stuck chopsticks straight up in white rice, as if for a funeral; they put one in Fiona's hair, the other in her mouth; they beat them against the table like drumsticks. Barbaric, unlucky, and offensive. Rebecca would often chuckle when she glanced at those photos. I winced every time I saw them, if only because I knew my daughter had been taught such vulgar manners.

I tiptoed into Rebecca's massive walk-in closet and borrowed her sexy Versace leather minidress, shoes, and cosmetics, which were too light in color for me, to land the job at Opium. I told her and Brandon I was taking English classes, and that I was staying with my sister afterward. I didn't want them to notice how late I returned home each night. Luckily, I was free whenever Fiona was at school or sleeping, and during the weekends as well because Rebecca wanted to have their family time together. There was an apartment building on their corner with a front door that didn't fully close. To minimize the risk of being heard when I came in, I'd often go through that building instead, up to the roof, and walk over until I could climb in through the skylight I'd left cracked open.

I hoped Rebecca wouldn't notice how cold it would get in the attic at times, but she almost never came up there anyway. My room was directly over Fiona's, though, and I worried she might hear my occasional thumping when I had to move the ladder, especially when she began having nightmares about ghosts. I tried to always wipe the floor after I came in with my wet shoes, but it rained so often, and I was so exhausted after my late nights. I only caught a few hours of sleep before I had to get up to tend to Fiona.

I asked Anthony to bring the little three-colored cat that was supposed to be euthanized to the studio and I brought her back with me to the house.

"Look who I found scratching at our back door," I said to Fiona.

She gasped when she saw the cat's limpid green eyes.

"Let her sniff you first," I warned.

When she bent down, the cat bumped her knee with her large pink nose. Fiona scooped her up in her arms and that was the end of it. They named her Calypso.

It wasn't until that evening last week when I was reading Fiona a fairy tale about Beauty and the Beast in front of the fireplace that it all started to slide, like when you're climbing a steep hill and feel your foot slip, right before the downward plunge. My bag toppled over, and a number of things fell out. When Brandon handed me my sketchbook, I saw his eyes flicker over the name and address for Opium, which Dawn had written on the back cover. His expression remained casual, though. I hoped he hadn't noticed and wouldn't recognize the name but clearly, he had. He'd probably already suspected that I couldn't have a sister with the one-child policy.

When Fiona asked me instead of Rebecca for a good-night kiss, I have to admit I was happy. Later, though, I felt ashamed. Rebecca didn't have enough time for Fiona and sometimes treated her like a pet or doll, but underneath that surface, her love was real. I saw it in the way both her and Brandon's faces softened when they looked at my daughter. When Fiona developed a slight case of eczema on the back of her hands, Rebecca brought her to the doctor immediately. I saw her googling home remedies for hours. Once, Fiona had fallen at school and sprained her ankle. Brandon rushed home in a taxi to care for her himself.

I was envious of Rebecca for taking my place. I admired her too. Not for her wealth or beautiful clothing, but for that fierce intelligence that shone through every syllable she uttered, the competence in every gesture of her elegant hands. Her ambition and brilliance, her willingness to fight for herself and the ones she loved. Who could I have become if I'd had her options? Who might I yet be? What type of woman would Fiona grow into? They could offer her the world. And I understood that a part of Rebecca's goal was to pass on her abilities and choices to her adopted daughter, which I deeply respected, even if I didn't trust anyone else to care for Fiona. Perhaps it wasn't fair that I judged Rebecca by a double standard, just because she was a woman.

But none of this mattered. The closer I grew to my daughter, the stronger I felt that she was mine.

"This is a Chinese-speaking club," I answered Brandon softly in Chinese, "so I go by Jasmine here. And I'm working, as you can see."

I couldn't afford to feel any compassion for them, and Brandon, my employer, would now have to let me go immediately. I needed to treat him like a man instead. And so I became my other persona. I ran my fingers through my hair, tossed my head, and gave him a flirtatious look I'd never allowed him to see before. His friends patted him on the back and laughed as his mouth grew slack.

I winked at him. "We can talk at length later. Let me get you all a drink, what would you like?"

When I brought his Scotch, I let my fingers touch his, just for a moment. I laid my hand on his shoulder while I flirted with the others at the table. They teased him for being my favorite. Sex and pride were a powerful combination.

As it grew late and we all became drunker, I asked him, slurring extra on purpose, "Why did you leave China when you care about it so much?"

"Unrequited love." He sighed. He made a sweeping gesture with his hands, almost knocking over his glass. "No matter how much I love the country I wanted to adopt, it will never love me back in the same way. I'll never be truly a part of things. Notwithstanding how good my language skills might be, regardless of the number of years I lived there. It doesn't count that I was born on their soil: I'll never belong because of the color of my skin. It's so tiring, needing to explain your existence as this strange, mutated being, this foreigner who can speak the language, every single time."

And so, I made him an insider that night. We joked and laughed and teased, and in that Asian club, with me draped on his arm, surrounded by Chinese men competing to take selfies with me, Brandon could forget that here too, he was other.

After we'd all sung a few rounds of traditional folk songs, I wrapped my arm around his neck and whispered in his ear, "Please don't tell Rebecca about me."

He blinked slowly, as if he were coming back up to the surface. "I can't keep this type of thing from my wife."

"But she keeps secrets from you." It slipped out but perhaps a part of me meant for it to escape. The truth is, I would have committed almost any crime to be allowed to stay with Fiona and if he told Rebecca about my working at Opium, she would have no mercy. There were many times in my life when I'd done things that skirted the edge of morality, though I could still justify most of them to myself. For me, they remained in that shadowy gray area of purgatory, but what I did next, that was the act that would condemn me to hell. I knew exactly what any decent human being would think of me, and I went ahead anyway.

His eyes were a bright, startled blue. "What do you mean?"

I looked around. The men around us were watching, doing their best to listen in on our conversation. "Not here. Come into the Champagne Room with me." That was the only place we'd be left alone.

Amid the whooping and raucous laughter, I took his hand and led him into the Champagne Room. That moment when we ducked through the beaded curtain—Lone Wolf Jack's jealous eyes on us, a smoldering glare from Lily, Aunt Glory's tiny nod of approval—a high keening set off in the back of my skull. I'd stepped into the flesh-consuming demon's mountain lair, eaten the pomegranate seeds that would trap me there. We settled in one of the velvet couches shrouded with darkness.

"What is it?" He was flexing his hands, his knuckles white. "What has Rebecca done?"

I shook my head. "Not until you promise you won't tell her. I need you to swear you won't do anything to get me fired, whether it's revealing that I work here or what I'm about to tell you." When he looked hesitant, I said urgently, "I'm only here because I owe money to snakeheads. If I don't pay them back, they'll beat me and force me to live in one of their houses. They'll own me. You know what that means." I saw his gaze snag on the couples in the shadows; that was the type of work I'd need to do. "Please. I don't have anyone to take care of me. And Fiona would be devastated if I left."

That decided it. At his slow nod, I took out my phone. Rebecca often gave her cell to Fiona to look through old baby photos. I loved seeing all the years I'd missed too. A text once arrived while I was scrolling: a photo of Rebecca with another man. The message read, "A little souvenir of a magical night in Frankfurt." I felt guilty but I'd always had the ability to file my shame away in the back of my mind and then do what had to be done. I quickly sent it to myself in case I ever needed leverage against her, then deleted any trace of my duplicity. I handed the phone over to Fifi. When she gave it back later, I saw Rebecca's eyes widen. Perhaps even then, I understood that she and I would inevitably collide.

Brandon's reaction was written all over his face. Disbelief, primal fury, and, worst of all, blinding hurt. I wrapped my arms around his shoulders. Tears welled up in his eyes. I held him and comforted him like a child.

"I'm truly sorry," I whispered. "Now, we all have a secret."

TWENTY-SIX

Jasmine

Even through all the champagne, I saw the horror dawning in Brandon's face as he left. He would have told Rebecca, I said to myself. I would have been fired and deported. No one wanted their nanny to be working in a strip club. What choice did I have? Plenty, a small voice whispered in my mind. You chose your own path.

I didn't expect to see him at Fiona's ballet class the next day. His eyes were scorching. He'd had time to understand what I'd done to him; I'd bound him in secrecy with ropes that tightened the more he struggled. Not only had he promised but he couldn't tell Rebecca about me without exposing his own actions at the club. After all, we'd gone into the Champagne Room together and even though we hadn't done anything, would she really believe that? He couldn't confront her about the photo he'd seen and perhaps worst of all, he couldn't ask her for an explanation.

"You put me in an impossible position," he grated out before Rebecca appeared.

I shot a quick glance at Fiona, who was tugging at his shirt. She didn't seem to be listening to us. "You made your own choices every step of the way, as did I."

"I want to tell my wife. I need to know who that man was."

"If you do that, I'll tell her we were intimate," I shot back.

Then suddenly, Rebecca was there. My stomach twisted as I watched his stiff shoulders while he saw her talk to the ballet teacher. Once his wife had arrived, she became the target of his ire. This was my fault. She cast bewildered glances at him as she tried to get Fiona into some other class, the one Gina's child was in. I'd done Rebecca a great injustice.

Whatever the truth might be, my time in their household was running out and I needed to act fast. I had to harden myself. I also had to make as much money as I could, as quickly as possible. One day soon, Brandon would break. He would confront Rebecca and she'd find out about my job at Opium. There was anger and awkwardness between him and me now. The situation was too unstable to last long.

I made another move I'd been planning for a while. I'd understood early on that one of the most profitable jobs at the club was that of bartender. She earned more than the cocktail waitresses, though not as much as the dancers, because she received a share of everyone's tips. She could wear flats and she wasn't expected to do the Champagne Room because her job was too important to be left unattended. She was even able to stand behind the physical barrier of the bar so the men couldn't grope her. At Opium, I tried to learn as much as I could, but I was often too busy with the customers, so it took me a while. I'd been observing Brandon carefully whenever he poured cocktails at home. In my spare time, I'd been watching videos on my phone.

The next time I had a shift at Opium, I suggested to Aunt Glory that I should be the new permanent bartender.

She laughed in my face. "What do you know about mixing drinks?"

"Try me."

"Make me a Zombie."

I went behind the bar and assembled her drink. I added the white rum, spiced rum, orange liqueur, cherry liqueur, absinthe, lime juice, aromatic bitters, grapefruit juice, and sugar in a cocktail shaker with ice, then shook it all well. After I strained the mixture into a tall hurricane glass filled with ice, I poured in the grenadine to color the drink. Finally, I floated the dark rum on top and added a skewer of cherries along with an orange wedge, plus a mint sprig. I'd known she'd choose one of the most complicated cocktails on the menu.

"Not bad." She took a long sip. "Is this to get out of doing the Champagne Room?"

I met her stare. "I thought I proved my willingness last week."

"That you did, sweetie." Her eyes glazed over, thinking of how much I'd earned for the club in that one evening. She pulled me in close. She smelled like sweat and hair wax. "It's almost a pity to take you off the floor."

I could feel the other staff watching us out of the corners of their eyes. Lily glared at me from her table in the corner. I eased my way out of Aunt Glory's hold and looked her in the eyes. "Everyone is complaining about the drinks. I can fix that for you before you start losing customers."

She threw up her hands. "What happened to that shy girl who couldn't even look at me when you applied for this job? All right, fine."

It was a relief to be away from most of the men, though Dawn pouted that she had to work alone again. I only had to fulfill the drink orders, which was easy. I was paid well, and I didn't get pressured or grabbed.

The first night I stood behind the bar, Lily was the one who brought back a drink. "The customer wasn't happy with his Sex on the Beach. Too much beach, not enough sex."

I knew I'd mixed the proportions correctly. "Why are you involved?"

She sneered. "I heard them talking and I volunteered."

I took a deep breath. "Lily, I know you don't like me." I thought about how I'd wronged Rebecca. There was so much animosity that I did deserve, I wanted to try to smooth over the unnecessary hatred in my life.

Her eyebrows shot up.

I continued. "I've been overlooked too. When I'm not in the club, I don't dress in a flashy way, and I can tell people judge me because of how I appear. You and I are not so different." I slid my eyes over to Aunt Glory, who was watching Lily with a tenderness she rarely let her daughter see. "We're both women, and women don't have it easy in this world. Let's not stand on opposite sides of the river."

Lily's face blotched. Suddenly she looked very young and insecure, this cleaning lady in the midst of the overblown hothouse sexuality of the other women at the club.

But then, her lip curled. "That's a nice story. Too bad this isn't some fairy tale."

As she stalked away, I heard my phone buzzing in my bag. I pulled it out, then gasped when I recognized the number. It was a text from Wen.

I'm so relieved to discover you're alive. I look forward to our reunion.

TWENTY-SEVEN

Rebecca

Rebecca will never forget the way Gina avoided meeting her eyes while the agent paid for their lunch. The gracious kisses and hugs as everyone went their own way, the careful avoidance of the topic altogether. The pity on Isabel's face, the absolute last thing any editor wants. Rebecca's stilted promise to repay Gina, which she took care of as soon as she returned to the office. It doesn't matter, though; the damage has been done. Rebecca can only hope the points she'd earned earlier in the lunch might possibly outweigh this embarrassment.

She can barely restrain herself from heading up to Columbia immediately afterward. However, she's already played that game with the condom incident and she's not going to give Brandon or his smug students the satisfaction of another scene acted out in front of them like a soap opera. She's been snarling at poor Oswald all afternoon and she's too upset to go to the gun range. She knows there's a fine line between unwinding there and being out of control. She's firmly on the side of unhinged. She texts Gina with an apology and invites her to Fifi's birthday party at their home on Sunday, which she's just decided to hold. Fifi will be so excited, and Rebecca needs to see the agent again to set things on better footing before the auction next week. She asks Lucy to work an extra day this weekend. They could use the help.

She's lost in thought when she passes one of the glass conference rooms and, to her surprise, notices Mason and Simone are in there, deep in conversation. He's wearing a dark beige suit with a matching shirt that accents his rangy frame. It lends him an elegant sophistication she's never seen before. Is this a social call? No, they look too intense. Plus, he's in a suit—this is business. Rebecca racks her brain but can't come up with any reason they'd be working together. Why does he look so pleased with himself? Mason glances up and sees her. Simone follows the direction of his gaze. All humor leaves her face. She looks grave, thoughtful, and slightly abashed. Rebecca has never seen guilt on her boss's face before. And the gleam of triumph in his expression, that sparkle of joy. She breaks out in a cold sweat.

She plasters a polite smile on her face and walks back to her office, her heart bouncing against her rib cage like a rubber ball. Involuntarily, she raises a nail to her mouth and chews on it while her mind races. They must be considering him for a job. And if it were a simple editor position, Rebecca would be in that room as well. In fact, her boss wouldn't need to be there at all during this preliminary stage.

Simone is considering giving him Rebecca's job.

There's a pounding in her ears. Her throat is dry as she clenches her fists. How could Simone do that to her? When this company has meant absolutely everything to her and her father. Replacing her with Mason, of all people. How dare they treat her this way? She sinks into her desk chair and buries her face in her hands. Once her boss finds out about the debacle at lunch, she's done for.

There's a polite little cough from her doorway. She looks up to find Oswald, who's holding a mug that reads MY WEEKEND IS ALL BOOKED with an illustration of a puppy and a stack of books. She sits up and tries to compose herself. "What is it?"

"I brought this for you." He sets the cup gingerly on her desk, as if the coffee—or she—might explode.

She gives him a wan smile. "Thanks, what's the occasion?"

"You looked like you needed it. Did the lunch go okay?"

She rolls her eyes. "Do you need to ask?" Then she groans. "I messed up."

He hesitates. He's been with her long enough to know how intensely private and closemouthed she is, especially about any failures, and she's not surprised when he doesn't ask what happened. "When things go wrong for me, I comfort myself by remembering that I'm not that important."

"Excuse me?"

He spreads his hands. "I mean, people mess up all the time. They trip when they're accepting the Oscars. They tell the world they're madly in love with someone who then divorces them. You make a mistake and life goes on. You're the one who keeps beating yourself up about it. Most everyone's completely forgotten about you and your screwup by then."

She chuckles a bit. "You know, that actually makes me feel a little better. Thanks." A thought occurs to her. "Hey, you know what? You could try a Siberian cat with your pet allergies. I used to have one. They're supposed to be hypoallergenic."

He nods, then gives her his five-fingered wave and departs.

She doesn't know how she manages to get through the rest of the day, but she does. Once at home, she paces back and forth. It's another one of those nights when Brandon is interviewing someone for his new book and says he'll be late. She doesn't trust herself to get on the phone with him. She thinks of his agile verbal acrobatics. She needs to see his face when they have this conversation. There's no tiptoeing around any longer. She's going to confront him directly and let the cards fall where they may.

She's conducted her research. The name of the corporation on her credit card bill is an Asian strip club called Opium. Obviously, he took his Chinese cohorts there and spent an outrageous amount of money, all without telling her. What else had he done there? She's torn between hurt and outrage and chooses outrage. It's safer. She'd rather feel like she might combust than break down. Was the whole thing about the condom a lie too? *Gullible Rebecca*, as her mother would say.

Lucy looks at her with trepidation as she prepares a dinner of chilled tomato orange soup and grilled lamb chops and feeds Fifi. Rebecca can barely choke any of it down and doesn't bother trying to make conversation. After Lucy bathes Fifi and puts her to bed, she says she's going to retire early, and Rebecca is relieved to have the downstairs to herself. There won't be anyone to witness what promises to be an epic brawl. Every tick of the clock seems to take a year. She tries to edit a manuscript that's due, but the words swim before her eyes.

When she hears Brandon's key in the door, she can't restrain herself any longer and stands waiting for it to swing open, arms folded, lips pressed into a tight line. But when he staggers through the door, she gasps.

His eye is swollen; his cheek is red and scraped, as if he'd fallen onto the sidewalk, a dark purple bruise is growing along his cheekbone, and there's a split in his bottom lip. He stumbles, almost tripping on the carpet runner. Animosity temporarily forgotten, she rushes to support him, grabbing him by the arm and hauling him inside. His skin is clammy with sweat as she leads him to the bench in their entryway.

"Are you all right?" she asks, smoothing back his tangled hair from his forehead.

He looks at her blearily through his puffy eye. "I was jumped by two men."

"Where?! How did this happen?"

He's speaking more slowly than usual, as if it hurts him to move his mouth, which seems likely given the state of his lips. "I was walking to the subway after the interview. It was already dark, and someone jerked me into an alleyway. One of the guys held me while the other one pummeled me. They were wearing ski masks."

Rebecca gives a little cry of distress. "Are you all right? Is anything broken?" She pats him down clumsily, pushing against his ribs.

"Ow, stop that! Are you trying to kill me?" He takes her hand away and then, improbably, chokes out a laugh. After a shocked second, she joins him. Despite everything, guffawing together again feels good. He stops, holding his side. "Oh, that hurts too much." He gives her a wry smile. "I'm fine as long as you don't try to treat me. I think I'm only bruised."

"We need to call the police and get you to the hospital."

"No." His voice is firm.

She gapes at him. "Why not? You have to report this."

He sighs. "I think this was a warning. They didn't hit me for long because someone turned into the alley, so I was lucky. I only have a few minor scrapes and bruises. Before they ran off, they said, 'Stay away.'"

She feels her throat constrict with fear, her breathing high and shallow in her chest. "From what?"

He shakes his head. "I don't know. I don't want to risk getting the police involved and they'll never catch those guys anyway. I couldn't identify them if you put them right in front of me. It's not like the cops are going to give me a bodyguard."

Her precise and logical mind has started working again. "What language did they speak?"

He looks blank for a moment, and she can tell this hadn't occurred to him. He narrows his eyes, thinking back. "Chinese. I think. Honestly, I was so blindsided, I was pretty befuddled. It could have been Korean or Japanese for all I know. But an Asian language, I think."

"One of the few disadvantages of knowing a thousand languages," Rebecca says with a half smile. "Did you see them at all?"

"No. The guy holding me was big, I remember that, but I couldn't make out their hair color, eyes, nothing through the masks. It happened so fast."

"Did they take anything? Your money, watch?"

He feels for his hand and raises his forearm to display the Audemars Piguet she'd given him, unharmed. "I still have my wallet too. I used it to pay for the taxi home."

"So we can safely say it wasn't a robbery, since they left about half a million dollars on your wrist. Why do you think this happened?" She's watching him very intently now.

He shrugs. "I have no idea."

She says carefully, "There were some large charges on our credit card."

A corner of his mouth pulls up in a grotesque semblance of his usual charming smile. "Oh yes, I meant to mention that to you. I forgot my Columbia card at home again when I took those Chinese officials out. I'll get it reimbursed, no worries."

"That's not a problem but I was wondering where you went to rack up those types of expenses."

He gives a slow, disbelieving head shake. "You're going to accuse me of wrongdoing again? After I come home like this?" There's genuine hurt in his expression.

She feels a pang of sympathy for him but if what she suspects is true, he's wounded her more. "My credit card was declined today when I tried to pay for lunch with Gina and Isabel Navarro." Her voice trembles despite her best efforts. "I was so embarrassed."

His eyes fly to hers, his gaze wide and shocked, but there's a spark of anger in there too. "Of course, this is all related to that damn book."

Now she's seething. "I have a right to my career. And to your fidelity."

"As do I to yours," he retorts. "Are you ready for all our secrets to come out?"

For a moment, she can only stare at him, her nostrils flared. She barely recognizes the man she married. Instead of answering, she turns on her heel and stalks up to their bedroom, alone. Her mind is reeling with questions. Who could have attacked him? Could it be someone who didn't want him returning to Opium?

What had her husband done there?

TWENTY-EIGHT

Jasmine

Wen was homing in on me. I was sure of it. On Saturday, I mulled over the dramatic events of the past few nights as I prepared to leave for my self-defense class. An icy calm had descended over me when I received his text message last Wednesday night. This was it. If he'd found my new number, he knew I was in this country. If I was lucky, maybe he wasn't sure yet. I was out of time, though. Brandon came home battered by unknown assailants the next evening. I tried to listen to his conversation with Rebecca but couldn't understand much of what they said. They kept their voices low, and I didn't dare get caught on the stairs. He looked terrible, the bruises stark on his face. Could it involve me? If Wen somehow discovered Brandon had gone into the Champagne Room with me, this would be how he'd react. I shuddered at the thought that Wen might already be so close. I knew him. He would circle me first, try to frighten me, make me docile, then dive in for the killing blow. He liked it when I was scared.

But I was no longer willing to be his victim. At some indefinite point, I'd changed: possibly, it was due to observing Rebecca steer her path through the world with such confidence or how I'd learned to turn an attacker's weight against him in my classes. I was surviving Opium and perhaps most importantly, Anthony had renewed faith in me, and Fiona loved me.

Before I disappeared forever, I needed to say goodbye to Anthony.

I was shoving at the entrance to the self-defense studio later, cursing, when a hand from behind pushed it open for me. I turned around and found myself face-to-face with Yan, Anthony's girlfriend. We were standing so close I could see my reflection in her cool, brown eyes.

She seemed wary, emotionally distant, but not unkind. "I know who you are."

"Who?" I whispered.

"You're the one Anthony could never have, the one he's been waiting to walk through the door. But I'm glad you came back. Because now he knows it was never real." I must have flinched at her words because her face filled with sympathy. "I'm sorry, I didn't mean to hurt you. Of course, he cares about you. But you don't want him, and I do."

There was nothing I could do except nod. I hurried into the training room and braced myself for the sight of him. I'd needed these lessons. It'd been wonderful to feel capable, to develop abilities that had nothing to do with how I looked. The truth was, I loved seeing him every weekend at those classes too, even if we hardly talked after I'd rebuffed his last few attempts to meet up. Yan's presence in his life shouldn't have mattered to our friendship but it did. I ached to know I'd be out of his life after today, but my leaving had always been inevitable.

He was standing with his back to me, facing one of the glass cabinets. I could tell from the way his muscles tensed that he'd seen my reflection. When he turned, he ignored me. Only the closed look on his face conveyed he knew I was there. Every inch of his body appeared ready for battle. I numbly followed the class, tried to pay attention when we learned a new defensive move. I was paired with a disciple who had a fresh, open face and unfortunate ears. He was patient with me, even though he blushed bright pink and stammered whenever he had to touch me. I caught Anthony glaring at us. He appeared to get wound up tighter as the hour progressed. I noticed Yan's attempts to gentle him a few times. His foul mood made everyone give him a wide berth.

He hardly spoke and when demonstrating strikes on the foam dummy, he hit so hard and fast that his uncle Nick stepped in. "Let's not damage our equipment, all right?"

It was as if Anthony knew what I'd decided, which would have been ridiculous, except that he'd always had an extra sense about me. After the lesson ended, I slowly gathered my things, wondering if I should say goodbye or just quietly disappear out of his life. I looked up to find his gaze fixated on me. I couldn't keep the sadness out of my eyes. My heart was throbbing in my chest like a bruise. I wouldn't be seeing him again after this, my Anthony.

He clenched his jaw and before I knew it, he was standing over me. "Can I talk to you?"

I nodded, then followed him down the hallway, conscious of Yan's wary eyes. I remembered the last time we'd been in the office and how he'd asked me to leave.

The room felt smaller than it had then. Anthony seemed to fill it with his presence. He leaned next to the closed door and folded his arms.

"So are you enjoying the classes?" he asked.

Had he really called me in here to ask something so mundane? "Yes," I said honestly. "Everyone's so impressive, especially you . . . and Yan."

"No plans to stop coming, then?" He raised an eyebrow.

My mouth must have fallen open. I closed it and stared at the worn rug. "Of course not."

"Liar. I know you, remember?"

I looked up to find the red bracelet I gave him glistening in the lamplight. He was still wearing it. "Not anymore."

I turned toward the door. I didn't know how to say goodbye to him. I couldn't do it. But as I took a step, my foot caught on the edge of the rug, and I pitched forward. Strong fingers curled around my arm. My momentum launched me against his chest. His hold kept me upright.

"Oh, I'm so sorry," I breathed. I was distracted by my bracelet around his wrist again. Slowly, I brought a finger up and traced it, so familiar and yet so foreign. Anthony went very still. My fingertips felt the braided chain against his warm skin, the small hairs on the back of his forearm. He made a strangled noise.

I was mortified to have touched him like that and snatched my hand away. "I don't know what came over me," I blurted. We were standing much closer than I'd realized. I was pressed against his chest and his eyes were aglow with a warmer mahogany than I'd ever seen.

"I don't mind." His hand came up to hold the side of my throat, the heat of him sinking into me as his thumb rubbed a slow circle in the delicate skin beneath my jaw. With half-lidded eyes, he murmured, "You don't know how many nights I've dreamed of you."

I blinked, not able to process his words, only feeling his fingers, the rumble of his voice. He'd confused me again and I didn't know what to say or do. I should have stepped away. "I've thought of you too."

His eyes flared and he cupped my face with both hands, gentle and yet firm. He leaned forward and brushed his lips against mine. I gasped. He didn't press harder, though. It was only the lightest of touches and then he was pulling away. "I'm crazy about you, Jasmine."

My heavy eyelids opened, and I took a step back, my fingers raised to my throat.

"Wh-what . . . you . . ." I collected myself, then said quietly, "Anthony, I'm a fantasy you formed when you were a child."

Anger sparked in his face, and he spoke with an intensity that ate up all the air in the room. "Don't tell me I'm enchanted by a dream I made up. I've always . . ." He took a deep breath and met my eyes again. "For as long as I can remember. And now, still."

I couldn't keep the hurt from my voice even though I knew I was being irrational. I was the one who left our friendship for another man. "What about Yan?"

His gaze shuttered. "I was trying to move on. But I need to talk to her, and I will. I think she's always known."

I couldn't stop trembling. "I haven't told you everything I've done."

"I know about Opium."

"What?!" I took a startled step backward. I was breathing so fast, I worried I might hyperventilate. How did he find out? Who else knew?

The expression on his face—gaze serious, lips gentle—almost undid me because he looked not horrified, not angry, but sad for me. He reached out and pulled me close again. "It's all right. I didn't tell anyone. I followed you one day after you left here. I meant to try to talk to you, but you were in such a determined, almost grim, hurry that I wanted to know where you were going."

I felt myself flush to the roots of my hairline. I stammered, "So . . . so you know the things I do there." I wanted to sink into the earth and disappear forever.

He placed a hand under my chin and lifted my gaze to his. His eyes were as kind as they'd ever been, only now, they were fierce and heated as well. "You haven't told me your reasons but they must be good ones. I know you, Jasmine. I made the mistake of losing you once. I won't do that again. When you love the house, you must love the crows on the roof as well."

Tears welled in my eyes. He knew and he accepted me. Something unclenched in my stomach. I gave him a rueful smile, then said in a small voice, "Why didn't you tell me how you felt?"

He snorted. "Because you were, and still are, totally oblivious. It's not easy to tell a girl how much you care about her when it's clearly never occurred to her. And then before I knew it, you were engaged to Wen. The truth is I was consumed with jealousy. That you were with him, that he could touch you." He reached out to tuck a stray strand of hair behind my ear. "I decided I needed to tell you now, before you disappeared on me again. Before it's too late."

Then we were both silent and I felt the weight of the unspoken question in the air. The panes of his cheeks were stark and unyielding, but his lips and eyes were soft, revealing how vulnerable he felt. The selfish part of me wanted to hold onto him. He was my Anthony and no one else should have a right to him, but more than I wanted to possess him, I wanted him to be happy. He deserved the truth even though there was still so much I couldn't reveal.

"Anthony," I said haltingly, "I'm broken. I can't have another man in my life. Not even you."

He took my hand and wrapped it in his large, warm ones. He brought it up to his lips in a tender kiss. "Let me help you. Please, let me try."

I choked out the words. "My heart is taken."

He froze, my hand still in his, then he dropped it and stepped back. Through my rapidly blurring eyes, I could see the stricken look on his face. I wanted to soothe it away. I stopped myself. I forced myself to continue. "There isn't room for anyone else. I don't have space for any other dreams."

Fury flooded his face, darkening his brow. He spit out, "After all this time, you still love him. How could you possibly? You told me Wen was in the past."

"Sometimes the past sends shock waves into the future."

He shook his head, a muscle moving in his jaw. "That's not a real answer."

Now I was fuming too. "It's the only one you'll get."

He made a growling sound and pulled at his dark hair. "He manipulated you. He used you. What about the other women?"

I was grabbing my things. I put my hands over my ears. "Stop it!"

He continued relentlessly, "Please tell me this isn't all some ploy to get him back. That you didn't run away from him so he'd follow you and leave his mistresses."

By now I had my bag slung over my shoulder. I paused at the door and turned to him. "Like I said, you don't know me anymore."

His face was hard, his eyes drenched in bitterness. "So be it."

TWENTY-NINE

Rebecca

Despite the undertone of tension that haunts all their interactions these days, Rebecca and Brandon celebrate Fifi's sixth birthday on Sunday in style. His face is healing. They have a tall chocolate cake delivered and Brandon's filling the house with helium balloons while Lucy makes snacks for the party in the kitchen. It's all worth it when Fifi comes down the stairs and gasps, wide-eyed, at her new turquoise bicycle and the birthday decorations.

Rebecca is giving her a big hug when she looks up to see Lucy watching from the doorway. Her nanny wipes furtively under her tinted glasses. Are those tears? There's so much love and tenderness in her expression that a wave of guilt overtakes Rebecca.

"Lucy, would you like to join us? We're going out to brunch at Tavern on the Green before the party this afternoon. It's a lovely place."

Fifi dashes over and takes Lucy's hand. "Please, please, please come!"

Lucy hesitates a moment, her eyes roving over the three of them. Next to Rebecca, Brandon has stiffened. Finally, Lucy places a tender hand against Fifi's cheek. "No, it is your family time."

When Fifi looks downcast, she adds, "But I have present for you."

Lucy pulls a square wrapped package out of her bag and hands it to Fifi, who is dancing from one foot to the other with impatience.

Fifi rips it open to reveal a framed drawing. "It's me! I love it, thank you!"

As Fifi throws herself into Lucy's arms for a hug, Rebecca catches the gift before it can fall on the floor. It's a finely detailed portrait, made with pencil and watercolor paint, in an elegant silver frame. The artist has captured the mischievous quirk of Fifi's mouth and the sweet innocent radiance of her eyes, and yet there's a hint of longing in the slightly furrowed brow. Rebecca knows art well enough to understand that this piece is extraordinary. How in the world could Lucy afford this? And when did Fifi sit for the hours necessary to have it done?

"This must have been expensive," Rebecca says to her nanny, who is beaming. Fifi is still hanging on to Lucy's hand, she notices with a pang.

"She drew it herself," Fifi says. "She's drawn lots of pictures of me, but I love this one the most and I can keep it in my room forever and ever."

Rebecca's mouth falls open while Brandon takes the framed portrait from her loose fingers. He raises an eyebrow at Lucy. "Well, you certainly do have hidden depths, don't you?"

But instead of looking happy at the compliment, all the joy drains from Lucy's expression. "I need check oven."

Before she can run off, Rebecca lays a hand on her arm. "Wait, this portrait is exceptional. Where were you trained?"

Her nanny turns to face her. "I learn myself. It is just a hobby."

"You're incredibly talented. If you'd ever like to develop this further, I know people who could help you."

A slow smile spreads over Lucy's face, infusing it with such a glow that Rebecca blinks, startled. Lucy shakes her head and catches Rebecca in a quick hug before hurrying into the kitchen.

Rebecca stands still for a moment, frozen with surprise.

Fifi says, "Can I try out my new bike?" And the three of them get ready to go to the restaurant.

They have a lovely brunch with as much ice cream as Fifi could desire, then play in the park. It's just like it's always been—Rebecca and Brandon roughhousing with Fifi, running alongside her on her new bike, throwing bread for the pigeons, eating soft chewy pretzels with mustard. The only difference is that all their lightheartedness is saved for their daughter. Whenever their eyes collide, there's a small, cool shock, an infinitesimal pause, before they focus on Fifi again. But all in all, it's a good morning.

On their way home, they stop at Rebecca's mother's penthouse so Fifi can receive her yearly birthday present, a large amount deposited into an account in her name. Despite the generous gift, Rebecca finds herself wondering why her mother couldn't also give her some small toy, a plaything a child could appreciate now.

Fifi squints at the bank statement before saying politely, "Thank you very much for my present, Grandma."

"Of course, dear," her mother says, giving her a cool kiss on the cheek. "You'll never get those grass stains out of her shirt."

Rebecca surprises herself by responding, "It's worth getting a bit dirty to have some fun."

Brandon shoots her a surprised look, then grins at her. Her heart eases. Maybe her marriage is still salvageable.

Gina and Emmy are among the first to arrive at the party, bringing with them a large, boxed set of magic tricks. As Fifi squeals in delight, Rebecca can't detect a trace of awkwardness in Gina's graceful manner. She hopes that's really the case and not simply a sign of the agent's superior social skills.

The only uncomfortable moment is when Rebecca hears Fifi announce proudly to a small group, "This is my mommy."

A girl with her hair in two blond pigtails says in an audible whisper, "Liar. Your mother is the one with the funny clothes." She jerks her head toward Lucy, who has been passing around a tray with frosted cookies.

Lucy freezes. Gina is also listening, and her eyes meet Rebecca's, alarmed.

Fifi answers, "That's Lucy, my nanny. I was 'dopted."

The girl flicks a look at Rebecca. "She doesn't look like your mom. You're just ashamed your real mommy's so strange."

A raw flush creeps up Lucy's face. Rebecca wants to smack the kid and is preparing to intervene, politely of course, when Fifi retorts, "Say that again and I'm going to bite you!"

Everyone gasps.

But then Emmy steps forward and looks down her perfect nose at Miss Blond Pigtails. Emmy is older and taller than the rest of the group and they all cringe. Furthermore, she has a rainbow glitter handbag, the one everyone covets, slung across her midsection. She gives a little sniff, then turns and takes Fifi by the hand. Delighted, Fifi sticks out her tongue at the other girl, who looks suitably cowed, and skips off with Emmy.

Rebecca finds herself blinking back tears. Lucy hurries away, head bowed.

"That was good of Emmy," Rebecca says to Gina, giving a little cough to cover her suddenly hoarse voice.

Gina smiles and squeezes her arm.

The rest of the party continues without a hitch. The girls play pin-the-tail-on-the-donkey, with Fifi getting so hopelessly confused she wanders into the hallway blindfolded and needs to be turned around by Brandon.

Later that evening, Fifi places Lucy's gift on the little table by her bed. As Rebecca is tucking her in, Fifi wraps her arms around her stuffed lion Maya and says out of the blue, "Do you think my real mommy remembers that it's my birthday?"

A sharp, needlelike pain shoots through Rebecca at the words *real mommy* but she tells herself that Fifi just doesn't know the term *birth*. She's thought about this herself. Who is this woman who gave life to her daughter? Will Fifi go looking for her someday or vice versa? The thought of losing Fifi in any way makes Rebecca's stomach squeeze into a tiny, tight ball. "I'm sure she does, sweetie. I'm certain she's thinking about you right now."

Outside in the hallway, Rebecca hears a slight creak. A shadow moves across the threshold. Lucy?

Fifi takes one of Maya's paws and chews on it. "Why did she give me away, then?"

Rebecca's heart breaks a little. Normally, she'd take the paw out of Fifi's mouth—so incredibly unhygienic—but she lets it go this time. Her daughter seems to need the comfort. Without her glasses, Fifi's face looks naked and vulnerable. Rebecca would do anything to keep her as safe and innocent as she is now. "Sweetie, sometimes people don't have a choice and they have to do things they desperately don't want to do. Maybe she was very poor and couldn't take care of you anymore."

Fifi's forehead wrinkles. "Are you always going to be able to take care of me?"

She wraps her arms around her daughter. "Always." She gives Fifi a tender kiss on her round cheek and says, "But more importantly, you're going to be able to take care of yourself. We're going to do everything we can so that when you grow up, you'll have choices."

Fifi nods, then snuggles under the covers. A small voice emerges. "Does she love me?"

Rebecca gives a half laugh, though she can feel the tears underneath. "How could she possibly not? You're the most lovable girl in the world." She lies down on the bed and wraps her arm around Fifi's shoulders until Fifi's drifted off to sleep.

She's the luckiest woman in the world to have her daughter.

THIRTY

Jasmine

"Hey, I need four Tsingtao beers and waters," Dawn called, leaning on the bar. She rolled her eyes. "Cheapskates."

I giggled as I loaded her tray with the frosted bottles. I was going to miss her. I'd tell her at the end of this shift that I wasn't coming back. When I turned to fill a glass, I pulled at the handle and frowned. "That's strange. There's no water."

"What did you say?" She leaned forward to stare at the tap. The color drained out of her face.

"Are you all right?" I asked, alarmed.

She quickly scanned the club. "I heard about this from one of the dancers. It's what happens before a police raid. They don't want us flushing drugs down the toilet so they turn off the water."

My lungs turned to lead. "No, it's probably just a——" I took a deep breath. "Let's check the ladies' room and see if it's working in there."

She nodded, then ducked under the bar to grab our bags. "I don't have a good feeling about this." She handed mine to me. "I knew this would happen one day. The rat and the snake live together here and everyone knows it."

We dashed toward the bathroom. We heard someone burst through the doors. "Police! Search warrant!"

Dawn cried, "I don't have the right papers."

"Me neither. Come on." My mind was racing a million miles a minute. I pulled her toward the cleaning closet I'd walked into by accident my first day. I yanked it open and dragged us both inside. Flicking on the lightbulb, I closed the door behind us. We barely fit. The smell of ammonia and lemons tickled my nostrils.

"Get into your street clothing," I said as I peeled off my uniform and kicked it onto the floor.

I took a quick look at Dawn, who had changed as well. She was still much too vibrant and pretty. We couldn't look like cocktail waitresses or dancers. I grabbed two of the cleaning aprons and tossed one to her. "Cover up your body. Put up your hair."

She nodded, then pulled out a package of makeup wipes from her bag. Thank goodness. Hopefully no one would look at us too carefully.

We both quickly scrubbed at our faces.

"Ready?" I asked, before cracking open the door to pure chaos.

People were shouting and screaming; dancers were being hauled off the stage by the cops. The police were everywhere but they seemed mostly focused on subduing the bouncers and arresting everyone in the Champagne Room—dragging out men in suits with their ties askew and shirts untucked. Lone Wolf Jack stood in the corner in handcuffs. Some of the patrons were arguing with the police while a steady stream pushed their way out the front. The overwhelmed cops at the door held back the cocktail waitresses and dancers but let most of the customers leave. A whole team zeroed in on the offices and there, Aunt Glory was in a heated discussion with a group of officers, Lily by her side.

As Dawn and I made our way toward the exit, Lily spotted our cleaning outfits. Our eyes met across the crowd. She gave me a tiny nod but made no move to expose or join us. I saw her thread her arm through her mother's.

Dawn and I ducked our heads as we approached the door.

One of the exotic dancers brandished her whip as two cops struggled to hold her by her muscular arms. "You got no right to keep me here. I'm gonna—"

The policewoman's face turned toward us, her gaze swept over our bodies, and then we were through. The city swirled around me, a dizzying kaleidoscope of sudden noise and sirens. The wind gusted through my hair and a savage sweep of headlights blinded me. I held up a hand to shield my eyes as everything turned white. It was a wild and acrid landscape, littered with trash, lit by the red and blue flashes of the police cars. Cops were milling all around and a crowd had started to form. We ducked into a nearby alley to catch our breaths.

The streetlight fell across Dawn's face. "Thank you for getting us out of there. I don't know what I would have done if we'd been caught. Someone must have reported the club."

"I'm glad they're shutting that place down."

She nodded. "Maybe this is a sign for us to make a new start."

"Will you be all right?"

She looked hesitant. "Will Lone Wolf Jack and the others come looking for us?"

I knew she meant if she was possibly free of him. "When the tree falls, the monkeys scatter. It'll be a long time before the police let him go."

There was relief in her smile. "Today was a wake-up call."

"Now it's up to you to decide what you'll do with it." A thought occurred to me, and I rubbed my eyes. "If we run into one another in the future, do you think we'll pretend we don't know each other? Because we're too ashamed?"

"I won't pretend," she said softly. "And I'm not ashamed."

I smiled at her even though my vision had gone hazy. "Don't give up on that pot roast, Dawn."

She wrapped her arms around me, engulfing me in her floral perfume. "Stay safe, sister."

I walked alone, my thoughts swirling, until I left the sheltering darkness of the alleyways and entered the bare city streets. There was no place more to hide. Finally, I braced myself and sent the text I'd been dreading.

I know it's the middle of the night but if you could meet me outside the studio, I'd appreciate it.

Anthony might be with Yan. He was certainly asleep. Everyone turned off their—my phone buzzed.

I'll be there.

My body was vibrating with nervousness as I went to Chinatown. Everything was coming to a head, and I couldn't leave things as they were between us. I wanted to see him again, one last time. Every day, I'd caught myself touching my lips, remembering that barely-there kiss. How could it have imprinted on me so deeply? I remembered his voice when he told me he cared about me, the depth of passion in it. Did he really mean it? And what about Yan? She clearly loved him.

It had been raining all day and now the streets were dark and deserted, illuminated only by the small circles of light cast by the streetlamps. Broad and straight, Anthony stood near the doorway.

We stared at each other until finally, I broke the silence. "You came."

He gave me a rueful smile. "For you, I always will."

I stepped close to him. "I don't love Wen anymore."

Regret shadowed his face. "I shouldn't have leapt to conclusions. I was just—"

"I know." I touched his jaw. "I have a daughter."

His face went blank and stunned. Whatever he was expecting, it wasn't this. He moved his lips a few times before he formed the words. "How is this possible?"

My confession had fractured the shell surrounding me and now the weight I'd been holding rushed out like water from a broken dam. "I had her when I was nineteen. I was told the baby died right after birth. Wen made arrangements for her to be adopted by an American couple. I'm sure it was very lucrative for him. He basically sold our daughter. When I found out the couple was looking for a nanny, I paid snakeheads to arrange passage to New York, and her new parents hired me. I'm living with them now."

I hid my face in my hands. I was heaving with sobs like I'd never stop. Anthony took me in his arms, solid and warm. After I quieted, he pulled a tissue from his pocket and offered it to me.

I gave a choked laugh as I wiped my eyes. "I didn't know what Wen had done for a long time, although I'd secretly started taking the pill to make sure I didn't get pregnant again. I couldn't go through another loss. I had several miscarriages before that. I was too young."

He stroked my hair. "So that's why you came here? To talk to that couple and tell them they have your daughter without your permission?"

I inhaled. "I was wild with grief and anger. I came to retrieve my child and at first, I thought they didn't deserve her. But now I'm starting to realize that they really do love her. They can offer her so much more than I can."

"It must be hard to be with them, keeping your identity a secret."

"It was her birthday last Sunday and it shattered me to be there." I stared up at him as my voice broke. "She asked if her birth mother remembered her birthday, if she loved her—and all the while, I was standing outside her bedroom, wishing I could run in and hold her."

"Why don't you just tell them?"

"Talking wouldn't do any good. I've been watching them. They'll never give her up. All of the money and power is on their side."

"The adoption was done without your knowledge or consent." I could see the gears turning in his mind.

I scoffed. "So I make a big commotion, and then what? It's a gray area. Even if I could afford all the lawyers and tests, and let's say I win the case, what do I do then? Take her back to China, where Wen will welcome us with open arms? Somehow, I don't think so."

He leaned in. "What are you planning, Jasmine?"

"I want her back." I closed my eyes as I said the words aloud. My deepest desire. "Fiona loves me and I won't let her go."

He raised a hand to his hair. The moonlight streamed down, coloring his fingers silver, pooling in his dark locks. "That's the reason you need to earn all this money at the club. You're planning to take her and hide."

The night seemed to stand still, listening. "She's mine."

"She's also theirs now."

"They never had a right to her." I clenched my fists. "I never knew my own parents. I grew up lost and alone, wondering if my mother cared for me, wondering why they abandoned me. I won't have that for her. And I need her too. I'll love her forever." My words seemed to echo through the city street. I felt the truth of them reverberate through my being.

"But what can you offer her?" His voice was gentle. "You're going to grab her and run? And leave everything behind? Including me?" He knew I wouldn't let him come with us.

"What about Yan?"

"In the past." He took me by the shoulders. "You know, it's not only that I like you. I like who I am when I'm with you. I changed my major to biology after our talk. I'm going to be a vet. You inspire me, Jasmine."

Despite the way my heart lifted, I hardened myself. I needed to cut him free. I shushed the weak part that wanted to preserve his illusions of me. I'd gone too far and he had the right to his life. Yan would take him back. I kept my voice even. "You don't know the things I've done. The American husband came into Opium, and I made a deal with him."

His eyebrows shot up his forehead and he stiffened as he released me. "Are you involved with him? What did you do?"

"No, I showed him a compromising picture of his wife in return for his promise not to reveal where I was working. I also told him I'd say we'd been together in the Champagne Room if he broke his word."

His rigid frame relaxed a bit and then, "So you did go in the Champagne Room with him? Do you have feelings for him?"

"We didn't do anything. We talked, though I did flirt with him beforehand." At his scowl, I protested, "I had to! That was my job."

He gritted out, "Great, he's probably obsessed with you now."

I gave a wry little laugh. "He hates me."

"I doubt that. First of all, he might be pretending he's mad at you because it's not easy to be involved with you. Secondly, you'd never know if he were fixated on you because you're oblivious."

"I am not! And it is not hard to be with me." I folded my arms and glared at him.

"Don't you think that's quite a coincidence, that he walked in there? You know, it's possible he knew about the irregularities of the adoption all along. Are you sure you didn't fall into his trap instead of him falling into yours?"

"I don't know. The address was written on my sketchbook."

"I'm so sorry you felt you didn't have any other choice." His eyes softened. "I'm sorry for all you've suffered."

I let my hair tumble over my face. "You don't think less of me?"

He bent to press a tender kiss to my forehead. "Never. I know who you are. If you were ever to unleash yourself, your talents would burn brighter than the sun."

I wanted to wrap my arms around him, to hold on tight and never let go. But I'd already chosen my path and there was no room for him on it.

"You've been wronged but how far are you willing to go to right that wrong? How will you support the two of you?"

Dawn's words echoed in my head. *No one ever stops.* "I'll figure it out. I can get us false documents. I'll do whatever it takes."

He pulled me in closer and asked in a hoarse, defeated voice, like he already knew the answer, "Just tell me—what about us?"

I swallowed. "There is no us."

He brought my fingers to his lips and kissed them, his breath warm. Low and intense, he said, "Please, don't do this. Stay. We'll figure it out. We can talk to them, bring her into our lives. Choose me. Give us the future we never had."

"I wish I could, Anthony." His eyes flared when I said his name. But as I pulled away, I whispered, "I can't. I'm not going to drag you down with us. She's the only thing in this world that's ever belonged to me. No matter what happens, regardless of what I have to do, I'm going to get her back."

I turned to walk away but he swung me around and I was in his arms again. I was stiff with shock and then his lips descended and all I could think of was him, his smell of sandalwood, the tenderness and strength of him, the lean muscles beneath my fingertips. We were bewildered and dumbfounded by one another. His hands were entwined in my hair, stroking, letting each strand fall. I was arched over his arm by the sheer force and ferocity of that kiss. He was gripping me as if he'd been hungering for me forever. I too had been starved for him without knowing it; I was stunned by him; my entire body reached for him as the world around us disappeared. We were moving as if time had no meaning, like we had eternity in the palms of our hands, desperate for each other. How could I ever let him go?

That thought snapped me out of the spell and with a small moan, I pushed myself away. "Anthony, I can't," I whispered.

He reached out a hand to grasp me again and I held up a finger, warning him to keep his distance. Then I ran away, the light of the streetlamps blinding me.

THIRTY-ONE

Rebecca

Why are two police cars parked outside her brownstone? Rebecca's footsteps slow. Their lightbars are flashing red, casting long, distorted shadows down the street, and an officer in uniform is walking out of her house toward one of the vehicles. Her skin goes clammy as she starts gulping for air. Has something happened to Fifi or Brandon? She breaks into a sprint, her heavy bag thumping against her side. She's an experienced runner, she knows this, and yet she can't seem to catch her breath. Normally, she's all lean muscles, ready to face any challenge but her legs feel as if they're encased in concrete. She's lurching, arms flailing, hyperventilating, her lungs incapable of expanding.

The policeman—older, burly, clean-shaven, white—regards her warily as she gasps out, "What happened?!"

He says, "Who are you?"

"This is my house." She points to the house. The dark blue door is ajar. "Is anyone hurt?"

"I'll need to see some ID."

She heaves out a sigh. She turns and is about to dash up the stairs into her own home when the policeman grabs her wrist. His tone is even less friendly than before, if that were possible. "Little lady, I need to see ID."

She wrenches away and pulls out her driver's license. "Please don't call me that. It's offensive. Can I go now to find out if my family is all right?"

The policeman's face is impassive, his round, pale eyes blank. "Your last name doesn't match."

By this point, she's ready to punch him. She should have gone flying into the house instead of trying to get answers out of this surly cop. Please, please let everyone be okay. She bites out the words. "Because I kept my maiden name. You'll find that my surname is the one on the property title."

She's craning her neck, notices the curtains to the living room are partly open. She catches a glimpse of Brandon. He's rubbing someone on the arm, a woman. Is that Lucy? He shifts and she sees that it is indeed Lucy, who is hunched over, hugging herself. It looks like he's comforting her. Panic flashes through Rebecca. Her knees go weak. There's no sign of their daughter. Where is she?

The policeman finally escorts her into the house. As she steps through the door, she can hear the thudding of heavy footsteps against her wooden floors and the murmur of voices in English and Chinese. All of the lights are on as brightly as possible and for a moment, she barely recognizes her own home, with all of its comfortable corners harshly exposed. How has her life turned into this disaster? Instead of turning off into the living room, he continues leading her up the stairs. She wants to go to Brandon but what's up there? Is Fifi all right? Her pulse is deafening as she follows.

Then she sees what's lying in Fifi's bedroom. Her stomach is in free fall, the roller coaster out of control, ready to plummet off its rails. She stares at the tiny, crumpled form sprawled inside the door, dark hair disheveled, skull smashed, blood staining the wood.

She screams and then Brandon's there and he's got her in his arms, grounding her until she can finally understand what he's saying. "It's not Fifi. It's not Fifi."

"Wh-what?" she manages. He is turning her toward that horrific little body again and she realizes it's much too small to be their daughter.

Thank goodness. She sags, suddenly boneless. Brandon catches her weight and holds her upright. It's a baby, no, not even. It's a doll. There are shards of porcelain, not skull, lying next to the shattered head.

Now Fifi is running into her, almost knocking her over. "Mama!" She's so upset she starts babbling at her in Chinese. Sometimes she still mixes up the languages. Rebecca catches her daughter in her arms and holds her tight. Fifi is all right. She smooths back the strands of hair from her daughter's hot face and kisses her.

Her heart is still pounding when she draws in a shuddering breath and someone—Lucy—gently takes her child from her. She stands, then bends down to look. It's Henrietta, her beloved doll, only someone's hacked off her long, beautiful hair in irregular chunks. There's something large and silver protruding from her shattered eye: a knife with a wicked serrated blade. Rebecca recognizes the handle. It's one of their own kitchen knives. The intruder has smashed in her skull. It's just a prank, she tells herself. She needs to calm down. She has to figure out what's happening.

She sniffs—what is that smell? Alcohol. Someone has poured red wine all over to make it look like blood. This is a threat, to their daughter, to their little family. What is the meaning of this? And who did it? As she scans the room, she sees that the floor's been strewn with books, toys, and clothing. The intruder's ransacked it. Fifi is clutching both Octie Lee Squiddy and Maya protectively, her eyes wide. Both stuffed animals are unharmed.

Rebecca looks at her childhood toy, remembers all the tea parties they attended, dressing up and snuggling in bed, and sadness fills her like a balloon. She murmurs, "Oh, Henrietta."

Anger begins to rise within her. Who dared to mutilate this symbol of her youth? How did anyone get into their house and past their alarm system? She knows of only one person, aside from herself and Brandon, who had access to the room. A woman with excellent knife skills. She looks at her husband, to see if he's come to the same conclusion, and finds his eyes focused on Lucy. His face is unreadable.

Rebecca stares at her nanny, who's pale and trembling, her gaze fixed on the broken doll, but when she scrutinizes Lucy's face, she realizes that despite the appearance of dread and horror, there's an emotion lacking in her expression: surprise.

Lucy isn't surprised at all.

THIRTY-TWO

Jasmine

Fiona and I had returned to the brownstone. She was eager to show me a new magic trick she'd learned earlier that day from the set Gina and Emmy had given her. She sprinted up to her room. I was shutting the front door behind us when I heard her scream. I raced upstairs and froze when I saw the mutilated limbs on the floor. I grabbed her and yanked her behind me, so that we both stood in the open doorway.

"She's dead!" she wailed in Chinese. "The ghost killed her!"

My mind was spinning. I could barely breathe through my trembling lips and my legs were shaking. I had to be strong for my daughter, though. "Who? What are you talking about?"

"Henrietta," she sobbed.

Then I understood what she had seen right away. It was no child. It was that eerie doll Rebecca cherished. Someone had broken it to frighten us. The rest of Fiona's room had been ransacked as well. Was this a burglary? I quickly checked Rebecca and Brandon's bedroom. It was as pristine as ever. Why break into a child's room? My heart was beating a drumroll of fear in my chest. "There's no ghost, my love.

This is a cruel prank someone is playing but we're not going to let them scare us, are we?"

She stared up at me, her eyes wide, her lips firm as she shook her head.

The violence that had been done to her room was shocking in such a calm, beautiful house. I prayed it was a coincidence and that it had nothing to do with me. Something glittered at the base of the knife that had been jammed through the doll's head. I gasped. Could it be?

But then the security alarm went off and we both jumped. I led her back outside. On the sidewalk, people had slowed and were already gathering to look. Someone started dialing on their phone.

"Wait here." I didn't want her to see that mess again and I wasn't sure if the rest of the house was safe. I was yelling to be heard over the noise of the alarm. "I need to turn that off and I'll be right back."

The wailing was painful. I pressed my hand against my ears as I made my way to the control panel and turned it off.

"Come!" Fiona cried.

I ran outside to find sirens blaring and two police officers jumping out of their car. I wrapped my arms around her but one of them wrenched her away from me. They barked at me in loud voices in English, a cacophony of sound ringing in my ears. I finally understood they thought Fiona and I were trying to break into the house, which was probably what the bystander who phoned them had said.

"I have key," I tried to explain. "I live here."

"Sure you do. We received a report of intruders standing in the doorway," the bulky police officer said, curling his lip. He flicked his eyes over my clothing. "Pretty fancy neighborhood for the two of you, don't you think? Can I see your ID?"

I felt the blood rush from my face. "I don't have any."

What was I going to do if they investigated me further? This was a disaster. I could be deported. I was fighting back tears when I realized that Fiona had pulled out her little emergency flip phone, the one Rebecca had given her just in case, and was babbling in Chinese to someone.

"We need to take you in for questioning," the policeman was saying when she cried, "My daddy's coming!"

At that, the cops exchanged a look. "Well, let's have Daddy join the party."

They tried to question me further, but I clammed up now that I knew Brandon was on his way. They probably thought her father was an accomplice too. They both straightened up when he shot out of the taxi in his blazer and pressed slacks, with his light hair and blue eyes.

I saw their eyebrows rise. "That's your daddy?"

Brandon dashed up the stairs and clasped Fiona in his arms. He looked at me intently over her shoulder. "Are the two of you all right?"

I nodded though I had to lean against the brick facade to remain upright. Within moments of his arrival, the police officers were smiling and preparing to come inside for coffee without even checking his identification.

I snuck away while they were chatting and rushed upstairs. I stepped in Fiona's bedroom, bent over the broken doll, and forced my violently shaking hands to pull the knife out of the doll's eye. A small round object dropped onto the palm of my hand.

My wedding ring.

Part Four

THIRTY-THREE

Rebecca

The next morning, Rebecca wakes with butterflies in her stomach. This is the day of the Isabel Navarro auction. She's postponed everything else in her life: deciphering whatever message the destruction of poor Henrietta was supposed to send, what to do about Lucy, figuring out the mess that is her marriage. It can all wait. She has everything ready. The offer letter has been written and she's managed to get B&W to approve a staggering amount.

"It's not only about the money," Gina said. "Isabel would like to see everything on the table before she makes her decision."

"Please let her know that I love the intricate plotting of the novel but it's what's underneath that counts," she said, trying to do every little thing she can to swing the odds in her favor.

Oswald bounces into her office wearing a suit. It fits him well, even if the jacket, pants, shirt, and tie are all covered with large multicolored dots.

She recoils. "My eyes . . ."

"What? This is my lucky suit." He gives her two thumbs up. "I only break it out when I really need it. Otherwise, its luckiness will wear out."

She chuckles. "Where did you get that monstrosity?"

"On sale," he says happily. "I know how much this auction means to you."

She looks at him, really looks at him. After the scandal, he hadn't considered leaving her for a moment. He's always upbeat despite her difficult moods. He works long, endless hours and takes home extra manuscripts to read in whatever little pockets of spare time he might have, most likely in some decrepit apartment miles from the city. "Oswald, thank you. I don't say it enough but you're a treasure."

He turns a hot pink to match some of his polka dots, then coughs a little. "Oh, by the way, we're looking into the Siberian cat thing. Thanks for the tip." He hurries away before she can reply.

Crossing her fingers for luck, she emails her offer letter to Gina.

The day seems interminable but finally, in the afternoon, she hears the initial results. That rat Mason has managed to edge out her bid by a small margin. With a few phone calls, she could increase hers enough to top his. Of course, he'll be doing the same in hopes of beating her counteroffer. She needs to prepare for this final round.

Isabel doesn't need to choose the highest amount, but most writers do. And after the debacle with the declined credit card, Rebecca understands she can't rely on much goodwill. If she doesn't offer the most money, she can kiss Isabel, her book, and all of Isabel's future work goodbye. Hell, Rebecca might lose even if she is the highest bidder. She knows that in Simone's eyes, this is a competition between her and Mason. If she loses to him, that would be an open invitation for Simone to fire her and hire him in her place. To be dismissed from the very company her father cherished, his pride and joy, would be proof that Rebecca isn't, and will never be, good enough.

She's adjusting her sales projections for the next round when her computer freezes. Biting her nails, she restarts it only to moan in frustration when she sees that all her recent updates disappeared. Her phone rings. It must be Gina, asking what's taking so long. "Gina, I'm almost through the paperwork—"

Lucy, high and quavering. "M-M-Mrs. Wh-Whitney . . . help . . . Fiona."

She sits bolt upright, icy fear clamping her spine. "What is it? Is Fifi hurt? What's happened?"

"C-come . . ." Lucy's voice is fading in and out. There's traffic in the background, the blare of a horn. Are those sirens? She's sobbing so hard, Rebecca can hear her gasping. "Hospital."

A stone crushes her heart. She's clutching the receiver so hard her knuckles are white. "Which one? Which hospital?"

There's a long pause while Lucy apparently tries to read the sign. "M-Mount Sin-n-ai."

Rebecca's already grabbed her bag and is racing out the door.

She's running down the hallway when she almost knocks over Simone, who calls after her, "Where are you going?"

Rebecca doesn't answer. She's already gone.

She feels the pulse of the city speeding through her veins as the taxi zips through traffic. It's like someone's bashed in her skull; white stars explode behind her eyes. She wants to call Brandon, then curses when she realizes she left her phone on her desk. Her cab stops, caught behind an altercation between a delivery van and a BMW, and she almost hops out to start running but she's still too far away. She has to wait, swearing and fuming, until they start moving again.

Please, please, please, she prays. *Let Fifi be all right. I'll give up everything else: my career, my health. Just let her be okay.*

She hadn't realized how deeply Fifi had entwined herself within her heart, so closely there's no distance anymore between Fifi and Rebecca. Without her, Rebecca would lose the most precious piece of herself. It's true, what people say, she realizes with wonder, that your children are parts of your soul walking around outside of you. What happened? Why hadn't Lucy called Brandon instead? It would have been far easier for her to express herself to him in Chinese and at least Rebecca would know instead of this nauseating uncertainty.

But when she bursts into Fifi's hospital room, she finds that her husband is already there.

In fact, he's holding Lucy in his arms, murmuring softly in her ear.

Brandon and Lucy leap apart when they see her. His neck is flushed, his eyes glittering with emotion. Her nanny wipes her eyes with her sleeve. Rebecca stands frozen, the rags of her old life falling at her feet. She knows intimacy when she sees it: the way his hand lingers at Lucy's waist, the angle of her head close to his cheek. How has she been so blind?

The doctor is finishing up with Fifi, who's sitting on the examination table. Her daughter appears incredibly small in that room, but she has all her limbs and she's awake and alert. Rebecca's entire being seems to loosen when she sees that Fifi is all right, if somewhat banged up. She pushes Brandon and Lucy out of her mind for now.

"Mommy!" Fifi wails, holding out one good arm to her.

The female doctor gives her a surprised look. Rebecca clenches her jaw. Clearly, the doctor had assumed Brandon and Lucy were the parents. Fifi's other arm is wrapped in a cast. Her cheeks are scraped, and her lip is swollen. Rebecca gathers her daughter close, careful not to jostle her injuries, and lets her weep great heaving sobs onto her shirt. "I was so scared!"

Rebecca meets her husband's eyes above Fifi's head. He looks wary. Lucy is standing by the window, staring at her, her face wan and pale. Rebecca's chest is burning on the inside, raw and hot.

"She's going to be fine," the doctor says. "She was very lucky. The only injury appears to be the broken arm and some mild abrasions, although you should monitor her to make sure there's no dizziness or other signs of concussion."

Rebecca finally finds her voice. "What happened?"

"She fell into the street and was hit by a bicycle," Brandon says.

"What?!" She wraps her hand protectively around Fifi's hair. Her daughter could have been killed. "How did that happen?"

Lucy speaks up, her voice thick. "It was my fault."

Rebecca feels a surge of fury. She can only focus on Lucy's figure by the window. She'd hired this woman to care for Fifi, to make sure she didn't come to harm, and instead, Lucy may have caused it in some way. She's a usurper, trying to take Rebecca's place with both her child and husband. The light highlights the outline of Lucy's body, making her into a target. Rebecca doesn't even realize she's left Fifi's side, that Brandon has taken her place and is joking about how Octie Lee Squiddy is going to love her cast, that the doctor has slipped away, giving them a moment of privacy. Her mind has gone slippery and dark, like the depths of a lake filled with subterranean monsters. In that moment, she recognizes the primal animal within, one that will wound or kill to keep that which is hers.

She leans in close to Lucy and she's shaking so much, from anger and fear, she clenches her hands into fists. "Tell me what happened."

Lucy's pale face is shuttered despite her declaration of guilt. Behind her large, tinted glasses, her eyelashes are spiked with tears. "It happen after the ballet audition."

Rebecca draws in a breath. She'd completely forgotten. Today was the day of the test for the pre-professional level that she had pushed so hard for, so she could get closer to Gina. A wave of shame washes over her. All of that for her career, which seems so inconsequential now compared to her daughter's well-being.

From the glint in Lucy's eyes, she knows that Rebecca forgot. "Fifi passed. She very happy."

A small voice from behind Rebecca says, "Are you proud of me, Mommy?"

Rebecca turns and scoops Fifi up in a gentle hug. "Absolutely. You must have been wonderful!"

Her daughter grins, wincing when it hurts her wounded lip. "I acted like I loved ballet very much."

Rebecca gives her a kiss, then returns to Lucy. She wants to grab her nanny by the shoulders and shake her until her teeth rattle, but Fifi is there. "What happened after that?"

Lucy's expression is remorseful. "We wait for the bus, like always. It was busy on the street. Fifi so happy, jumping up and down. Bus coming. I not know, maybe Fifi let go my hand but she fall into street. Bicycle hit her. I scream. People pull her away and call ambulance. I am sorry. I should have hold her better."

Rebecca is breathless, picturing this scene, imagining what could have occurred if Fifi had ended up under the bus's wheels. She feels like the air in the room is as thick as fog, ready to swoop into her lungs and smother her. "How did she fall? She isn't a clumsy child and she knows not to step into the street."

Lucy casts her eyes downward, avoiding her searching gaze. "I don't know."

"Did someone push her?"

"I don't know."

Brandon is watching the two of them intently. There have been a number of strange incidents involving their nanny, not the least of which was the smashing of Henrietta. Rebecca shivers. Was that some kind of warning? What's Lucy's role in all of this? At best, negligence at not watching Fifi closely enough, for letting go of a small child's hand in the middle of a crowded street. Could Lucy have hurt Fifi herself? And what has Lucy been doing with Rebecca's husband?

Silence hovers over them.

Rebecca's eyes are dry and burning. Suddenly, she's exhausted and nauseous, so sick and tired of everything. "Come on. Let's go home and we'll figure everything out there."

Her nanny is hanging her head. Once, Rebecca would have assumed it was out of shame or fear. Now she wonders what it is that Lucy is hiding on her face.

THIRTY-FOUR

Jasmine

That night, alone in my bed, I tried to stop shivering. Was Fifi's accident a coincidence? Wen had been inside the house. I was sure of it. I stared at my dark curtains, flinching when the wind through my open window caused them to flutter. It felt like he was everywhere. Would he go so far as to hurt his own daughter? He'd given her away. She meant nothing to him. Or had I been the intended victim? No, if he got his hands on me, I might not survive his punishment. He wanted me terrorized so I'd leave quietly with him whenever he appeared. Except, I'd be gone by then, with Fiona. Any doubts I'd had about taking her were erased now that she might be in danger from him.

I realized one thing, though: Wen must have had help.

He hadn't set off the burglar alarm. In fact, it was on when I opened the door. How could he have gotten into the house and disabled it, then enabled it again before he left? There was no sign of a break-in. I'd immediately pocketed my wedding ring and put the knife back the way it was. The only possibility was Brandon, Wen's old friend. I'd seen in their emails that even their parents had been close. Rebecca had seemed genuinely shocked and horrified over the incident. Her husband was always harder to read, with his attractive surface as impenetrable as any mask.

Anthony had called me a few times since our last meeting. I refused to answer. It would be too easy to allow him to derail my plans. He'd said I might be oblivious to Brandon's true motives. Was it possible that Brandon and Wen were working together somehow? Was Brandon beaten up to throw us off the scent? Or was he being punished for going into the Champagne Room with me? Had I manipulated him at Opium, or had I fallen into his trap? How much had he known about the adoption? And was what he'd said to me today an innocent reassurance to a distraught employee, or did it have a deeper meaning? My head was spinning with wild conjecture.

I'd had Fiona's hand firmly in mine, I was sure of it. The crowd was dense, almost pushing us off the sidewalk while we waited for the bus, and then a quick movement behind us. Her little hand went skidding out of my grasp. The bicycle hitting her. Fiona, sobbing in my arms, as she lay on the concrete. Her glasses had flown off and she looked much younger as she cried. My head exploded; my lungs were on fire. She was my beloved, precious baby. No matter how she fell, I should have been there to catch her, always.

"Help! Call ambulance," I'd shrieked.

I felt so helpless and alone as I rode in the ambulance with her to the hospital. I called Brandon and then Rebecca. I'd never felt so happy to see him as when he arrived, calm and competent, talking to the doctors and soothing Fiona.

After the kind doctor assured us that my daughter was fine, I burst into tears. Brandon wrapped his arms around me.

It was a relief to speak Chinese again. "It was my fault. I should have taken better care of her."

"No," he consoled me, stroking my back. "It was an accident and she's all right."

I choked out the words. "She could have died. I was responsible. Rebecca will want to fire me, and rightly so."

He bent close to my ear and murmured, "I'll help you, no matter what."

THIRTY-FIVE

Rebecca

"We need to talk." Rebecca is no longer worried about decorum or appearing ladylike. Now that Fifi's in bed and Lucy has gone up to her room in the attic, Brandon's going to give her some answers.

He goes still as he leans against the fireplace. "What's this about?"

She gets right to the point. "What were you doing with Lucy today?"

His lips quirk up in the charming smile she hasn't seen in days. "Don't tell me you're jealous, darling. It was nothing. She was upset and I was comforting her, that's all."

She crosses her arms. "It appeared rather intimate." Can she trust him? She doesn't know anymore. She wants to believe him, so much.

He comes over and embraces her. Despite all her doubts, she sinks into him with a little sigh. He feels so familiar and safe, beloved. "You don't need to worry. No one can compare to you."

She rests her head on his shoulder. "It's been so terrible. Do you think that those men who attacked you and whoever trashed Fifi's bedroom had anything to do with the accident today?"

Brandon pulls a hand down his face, his usual handsome features lined and shadowed. "It all seems to be a warning of some kind, but I can't make heads or tails of it. And how in the world did they get past the alarm system?"

Rebecca meets his eyes. "I was thinking the same thing. It has to be Lucy. Either she did it herself or she helped someone else. We should let her go as soon as we can arrange a replacement."

He looks hesitant for a moment, then nods. Her mood lifts at his willingness to fire their nanny. "By the way, I know this is terrible timing, but I invited Wen to dinner tomorrow. You remember, my old friend from China whom I've been interviewing for my book? He's leaving the next day so there isn't another opportunity and I do feel like we owe him for all his help. I'll deal with the food, so no worries."

"Of course," she murmurs. Wen was the one who'd brought Brandon and her together. She really doesn't want a dinner guest, but he has been very helpful to them over the years, and she can't handle any more conflict with her husband.

Brandon goes upstairs, saying he has to get up early tomorrow, and she starts to wonder. One of the editors she'd worked for when she was an assistant had insisted on getting rid of one of their interns, accusing the young woman of sloppy work, but soon afterward, Rebecca heard that they were having a torrid affair and the editor didn't want to get caught with a colleague. She thinks back to how Brandon and Lucy had fit together, like they were familiar with the curves of each other's bodies. Or is she simply being paranoid? She won't get the truth out of either one of them. If there are any answers, she'll have to find them herself.

Rebecca sits in her favorite chair and braces herself to start reading her email on her computer. She's glad she hasn't been able to check her cell phone. She's dreading seeing what sort of damage she's done to her career. She knows she lost the auction and Isabel with it, possibly her job as well. The taste in her mouth is already bitter and she doesn't want to take another swallow from that glass today. A cold, wet grief seeps into her at the thought of losing that bright, brilliant author.

It's not even just about recovering from that scandal or upholding her father's legacy. Rebecca had come close. She'd had a chance, despite that unfortunate lunch. She'd felt that hum of electricity, a resonance similar to when a perfectly pitched violin string vibrates to the tuning fork. She and Isabel had that click that distinguishes the best author–editor relationships, the ones that bring out stunning, magnificent work in both parties. She aches at the loss. For a moment, she sees them floating around her like ghosts, all the tender, blazing words Isabel would have brought to her in the years to come.

When her home phone rings, she's relieved to delay opening her laptop for a bit longer. She checks the caller ID. It's Mason. At least it's not Simone.

She picks up. "Calling to gloat?"

A long moment, then he drawls, "To the contrary. Just wanted to congratulate you."

She snorts. "For what? Losing a manuscript and author that I would have given an arm and a leg to acquire?"

There's a brief pause. "Rebecca, are you serious? What planet have you been on?"

Her spine goes rigid. "My daughter was in the hospital. I left my cell in the office. I didn't participate in the last round of the auction, and you already had the highest bid."

Mason gives a short, hard laugh and even through the phone line, she can hear the bitterness in it. "Isabel chose you."

"Wh-what?" She's flabbergasted. Something sweet and soothing flows through her, like vanilla ice cream on a scorching day.

"Don't rejoice yet." His words are clipped. "I want you to bow out."

"What? You lost, fair and square."

"I admit I underestimated you but I'm not playing by the old rules anymore."

Her head is whirling. Slowly, she absorbs what he's saying. "Exposing what happened at Frankfurt's not going to make you look good either."

"I have a feeling I'll survive. But will you? You'll lose her anyway."

She rubs the heel of her hand against her aching temple. "I can't just give her up, even if I wanted to. What would I tell Simone?"

"Make up some excuse, lie, I don't care." His voice lowers to a growl. "Just get out, Rebecca."

Quietly, she says, "Or what?"

"Or you'll have a very magical day tomorrow."

THIRTY-SIX

Rebecca

Rebecca calls herself and Fifi in sick the next day. Brandon is already gone when she wakes up. She wishes she could shut the door to the rest of the world forever. She understands she's crossed over to the other shore. The landscape of her life has changed for good, all her beloved and familiar landmarks mutated into mirages that flicker above the sand.

After a quiet breakfast, Lucy leaves to run a few errands. Rebecca needs another cup of coffee before she can face the confrontation with her nanny. Could their suspicions about her be true? It seems unbelievable in the warm morning light and Rebecca's intuition tells her that Lucy loves Fifi. Her daughter is lying on the couch with her arm in the cast, leaning against Octie Lee Squiddy's tentacle and watching cartoons while Calypso purrs beside her. Fifi has her stuffed lion tucked under her head like a pillow.

Rebecca is laying out the accoutrements of espresso-making when the open page of the newspaper catches her eye. Brandon must have paged through it before leaving.

Her eyes widen with shock. "Oh no."

She'd been aware of what would happen from the moment she gave Mason her carefully composed and eloquent answer last night: "Fuck you."

But she hadn't expected this. *Publishers Marketplace*, perhaps, maybe a few other trade magazines. Even though the article is short, that the story is big enough to make it into mainstream media bodes ill, though she already knew she was royally screwed. Her choice had been to either let Mason expose her or allow herself to be blackmailed for the rest of her life. She's a woman competing in a man's world, and she can lie down and conform, or she can stand up for herself. If this entire disaster with Lucy has taught her anything, it's that burying her head in the sand won't save her.

A photo, dark and slightly out of focus, but clearly Rebecca, laughing, drunk with alcohol and exhilaration, leaning back against a man's chest. He's clad in a blue button-down oxford, an arm wrapped around her neck, a male hand draped dangerously close to her breast: the hand is broad, with dark hairs running up the forearm—not Brandon's long, tapered fingers, not his tawny hair. Her cheek is snuggled up against his wrist with a lover's intimacy.

Only the bottom half of the man's chiseled jaw and sensual mouth is visible, but people will have no trouble identifying him: Carey Madison, Rebecca's now-disgraced author, originator of the scandal that almost cost her career. It doesn't matter that his full face isn't shown; proof won't be necessary. This won't be fought in court. Merely the appearance of impropriety is enough.

It had been taken late at night, after the bar was mostly empty, leaving only Rebecca, Carey, and Mason, who could hold his liquor extremely well. Somehow he'd stayed sober enough to take this photo and send it to her weeks later with a text she immediately understood was a threat: "A little souvenir of a magical night in Frankfurt."

She quickly scans the article. "A trusted industry source reports a heated affair between Carey Madison and his then-editor, Rebecca Whitney, leading to renewed speculation regarding the extent to which his publisher decided to turn a blind eye to the falsehoods and plagiarism rampant in his bestselling memoir." Mason has won. This will spark a social media storm if it hasn't already. She'll lose Isabel through this moment of foolishness. The author will go to him, and she and Mason will live happily ever after while Rebecca's career and marriage will be destroyed. Simone will fire her and hire him instead. That's a certainty after Rebecca ran out on the auction yesterday and this revelation.

She flips open her laptop and amid the many emails she's missed is a terse message from Simone that they need to talk as soon as possible. There's also a polite note from Gina expressing her regrets that Isabel will be accepting another offer in light of recent developments.

A tear rolls down Rebecca's cheek. "I'm so sorry, Daddy."

Her father would have been very disappointed in her. And what does Brandon think? It says enough that he hadn't come upstairs to wake her so they could talk about this. What could she say to defend herself? She truly hadn't known about the plagiarism but perhaps that was because she'd been too infatuated with Carey. He was so charismatic, with his wicked eyes and self-rolled cigarettes, the kind of man her mother had always warned her about. Brandon had the Whitney stamp of approval and it felt freeing to flirt with a man her mother would have hated.

She was only protecting her interests as an editor, she'd told herself. An editor was supposed to woo her authors. Cheating on her husband was a line she'd never crossed and some part of her thought that meant she never would. Transgression had no place in Rebecca's orderly world. Yet at Frankfurt, she and Carey had been high on the seven-figure deal they'd just closed for German translation rights and after they'd gotten drunk as skunks, they'd kissed. She was deeply ashamed. It hadn't just been a violation of Brandon's trust; it'd also been an abuse of the author–editor relationship. Later, she realized that Carey had likely planned it. Even when she started to have doubts about inaccuracies within the manuscript, he knew she'd be more hesitant to expose him. She'd felt guilty afterward and yet Brandon never seemed to suspect a thing. And it doesn't matter now that she and Carey never actually slept together because it looks like they did.

This mistake is going to cost her everything.

Rebecca whirls and climbs the stairs to Lucy's room. Her professional life has been destroyed and now she has to know the truth about Brandon and their nanny, one way or another. Once she confronts Lucy, Lucy might destroy whatever evidence might be found. She'll start with her nanny and then move on to her husband.

She looks around Lucy's bare room. There isn't much in the way of personal belongings. She represses a twinge of guilt at invading Lucy's privacy in this way. If she's wrong and Lucy is innocent, then at least Rebecca will have some assurance and not just wishful thinking. She checks the bed, which is neatly made, and underneath the mattress. Nothing.

She jumps at movement from across the room, a flash of color, exhales when she sees it's only her own reflection in the mirror on the vanity. On a hunch, she walks over and peeks behind it. She inhales sharply, staggered, even though she had been searching for just such a clue. Several bulging envelopes are stuck to the back of the mirror. She pulls one off, tugging at the thick duct tape, and even before she opens it, she knows what she'll find.

Cash. She riffles through the stack of bills, her mind racing. There is no way Lucy could have saved this much with what they pay her, especially since the bulk of her nanny's payment is in the form of room and board. This must be drug or mafia money.

A storm of insects are chattering in her skull: *This is your fault. You let this woman into your precious safe haven.*

She takes a moment to tape the envelope back the way she found it. She doesn't want to warn Lucy that she's been exposed, not until Rebecca has figured out what she's going to do.

There's a scrap of red fabric lying on the floor. When she shakes it, she finds a skimpy leotard with a Mandarin collar. Where has she seen this before? Then she remembers. When she was researching the corporation charged to her credit card and found that Asian strip club, Opium. This is what the staff wears. The room spins around her like she's caught in a blinding blizzard. She clutches the back of a chair to retain her balance. Her limbs have gone numb. She touches her fingers to her face but can't feel a thing. Only there's a piercing pain in her chest, like she's being ripped open from the inside.

Opium. Brandon. The high charges on the credit card. Lucy's been working there, and she and Brandon are having an affair. What a fool Rebecca's been. She's never looked at her nanny closely enough to realize what a threat she was. Foreign Lucy, with her shirts buttoned all the way up, her baggy pants and awkward demeanor, her accented, limited English. Sophisticated Brandon, what's the attraction? Lucy is hardly what you would call articulate, though a small, uncomfortable part of Rebecca realizes that Lucy may well be quite different in her own language. Part nanny, part cocktail waitress; that's enough to attract many men but she'd never considered Brandon to be common. That her own husband might be involved in whatever nefarious scheme this is with Lucy makes the grief rise up in Rebecca, as acrid and hopeless as when her father died.

She has to know how far this has gone. She has to know what he's doing. She goes downstairs and grabs the spare key to the garden apartment, which she never uses. That's Brandon's territory, where he writes his books and keeps their paperwork. She theoretically had a study there as well, but prefers to do her work curled up in front of the fireplace, so he's taken over that space to interview his subjects.

She takes a deep breath to compose herself as she unlocks the door to the ground-floor apartment below the outdoor steps. Everything is neat and clean, as she'd expect from Brandon, the only mess a pile of books in Japanese and Chinese on the coffee table. She goes to the back, past the small utilitarian kitchen, to his inner office and flicks on the light.

The room is midsize, with a low ceiling, dominated by his large desk and dual monitor system. There, in the corner. The tall black filing cabinet. That's where he keeps their documents and receipts. She pulls out a drawer and starts riffling through the paperwork, uncaring of hiding her tracks. They're going to have a major confrontation after this, so it doesn't matter if he finds out she's searched his things. Everything is different now.

Her mind is testing all the possibilities as she pulls out folder after folder of research notes and insurance papers, not sure what exactly she's looking for but knowing she'll recognize it when she sees it. Could Brandon possibly be involved in the strange things that have been happening recently? How well does she know her own husband?

And then, there it is, in the mass of folders regarding Fifi's adoption.

We regret to inform you that we cannot approve your application due to the applicant's previous drug possession conviction in China.

The shock ripples through Rebecca like an earthquake. She wraps her arms around herself. The momentum of her wrecked life is rushing downhill and although she's trying to hold it back with all her might, the mass crashes right into her. So that was why Brandon never returned to China after his field research; not out of some romantic inclination to stay by her side, as she'd thought. In fact, he'd told her that his work had gone so well, he'd completed it early, and she'd been delighted to have him in New York. He must have been expelled. This is the reason he'd relied on his Chinese contacts like Wen to push the adoption through.

What else has he been hiding? Her parents had warned her about the dangers of being extremely wealthy from the time she started liking boys. It was best to find someone who couldn't benefit from her, her father often said. Otherwise, you never know, her mother always added. But Rebecca had met Brandon with only a backpack full of dingy, worn clothing. He hadn't known about her affluence, or had he?

She sinks to the floor, legs splayed. Piles of paper surround her, a reflection of her wild, scattered thoughts. She presses the back of her hands to her eyes. Lights explode behind her eyelids. She doesn't understand any of this. She needs to confront him and Lucy. She feels like a rubber band pulled so tightly it could snap at any moment. She has to release some of this tension somehow.

She pulls herself together, gets up off the floor, and goes back upstairs to her own territory. Fifi has fallen asleep in front of the television. Even if Rebecca's emotionally compromised, she needs to blow off steam before confronting her husband and nanny or she'll explode. She climbs up to her bedroom and punches in the combination to the small jewelry safe that contains her gun.

It's empty.

THIRTY-SEVEN

Jasmine

I decided Fiona and I had to leave that night.

After the attack on her yesterday, I knew our time was running out. I'd spent a restless night tossing and turning. In the end, there was only one inevitable conclusion. I had to move my timetable forward.

I went out in the morning to buy a large suitcase for our things. It was finally happening. I had enough saved to repay a large portion of my debt and to sustain us for a short while, plus I had the jade pomegranate hairpin as extra insurance. The most important thing was to escape Wen. I didn't allow myself to consider Rebecca and Brandon and their inevitable pain. I'd still have time to get the rest of the money to the snakeheads. I would find work, one way or another. You couldn't catch tiger cubs without entering the tiger's lair.

When I returned to the brownstone, I was relieved to see no sign of Rebecca, even though Fiona was half-asleep on the couch. I gave her a kiss on her forehead before bringing my things upstairs. I quickly grabbed a few items from around the house I thought we might need, including some clothing for Fiona and a few of her favorite toys and books, then packed the money and my meager belongings.

I heard Rebecca enter through the front door and go up to her bedroom. I hoped she would stay there for a while. I had no desire to face her and any awkward questions she might ask. I quietly slipped downstairs, where Fiona had woken up and was sitting on the couch, playing with her stuffed animals.

She looked better today. Her bruises had faded. I hoped her cast and broken arm wouldn't make her too recognizable. We needed to travel far away. I stepped on a plastic fox on the floor, and it emitted a high, eerie wail.

Fiona looked up. "Maya's paw is hurt. Do you want to kiss it?"

"Of course, my sweetie," I said.

"Why did you have a suitcase before?" she asked, her eyes big without her glasses, which had broken in the accident.

I cast a look up the stairs. No sign of Rebecca. It might be better to prepare Fiona. "We're going on a trip together later, just you and me."

"What about Mommy and Daddy?"

I tried to hide my wince. "They're not coming this time." I walked to her and sat down on the side of the sofa. "It'll just be us. Don't you think that will be fun?"

She nodded quickly, then her eyes darted away. "Only for a little while, right? Then Mommy and Daddy will meet us?"

"Maybe," I said but she'd picked up on the hesitancy in my voice.

Her chin, so much like mine, jutted forward. "I want them to come too."

"Don't you want to be with me?" I heard the dismay in my voice. I didn't care, though.

When she shook her head, I felt every shake reverberate through me. I started to tremble. Sweat broke out on my forehead as I wrapped my arms across my stomach. There was a sour taste in my mouth. I should have known this could happen. Fiona loved Rebecca and Brandon, of course she did. I had hoped her affection for me would be enough to overcome any homesickness. All the hugs and kisses and I-love-yous. She was still so young. With time, I thought, she'd forget. Now, looking at the set of her small jaw, I realized too late how wrong

I'd been. It had been my dream for so long that I'd been blinded to the glaringly obvious.

Fiona didn't want to leave with me.

"Lucy?" A voice from the door startled both of us. Fiona leapt up and, to my dismay, ran past me into her mother's arms. I felt like my heart would never stop aching. Rebecca looked drawn and brittle, the skull underneath her skin prominent, her eyes aflame. "Fifi, why don't you go and play in your room?"

We stared at each other while Fiona raced up the stairs.

Rebecca was righteous, burning with rage and betrayal as she glared at me. "Lucy, what were you just doing?" When I didn't answer, she started to pace. The words exploded from her. "We invited you into our home and our family. We treated you as one of our own and yet you've embarrassed me in front of my colleagues. You've been plotting against us from the beginning. You've been working secretly in a strip club. You might be involved with the mafia, which led to Brandon's attack. You smashed up Fifi's room and destroyed Henrietta to frighten us. Worst of all, you caused my daughter to be hurt. Do you have anything to say in your defense?"

My mouth gaped at this mix of truth and lies. I wanted to defend myself. I started to speak but then I realized she must have found out about what happened at Opium. In my mind, I heard the accusation she hadn't voiced, the one at the basis of her pain and fury: *You came here to tear my family apart.*

And because she was absolutely right, there was nothing I could say. While I was struggling for words, a key rattled in the front entrance and the door squeaked open.

I heard Brandon's voice, then the low murmur of someone else. He wasn't alone. With a baleful glance at me, Rebecca stepped into the entryway, out of my sight, to greet them. "What a surprise." Her voice was strained. I could hear the barely banked fury in it, rage directed at me.

"You remember our dinner tonight," Brandon said, sounding wary. "I can't find my key, so I need to grab the extra one. We'll do our interview downstairs and be up later."

I had a pounding headache. I needed quiet to think about how to re-create my dream of a life with Fiona and how to address Rebecca's accusations. I stood to tiptoe out of the living room before Brandon and his guest left and she could confront me again.

An awkward laugh from Rebecca. "Actually, it totally slipped my mind. I'm afraid the timing is—"

I crossed the threshold and stopped short, as if freezing would make me invisible. There he was: the linchpin keeping all of us together, Wen.

He turned his head and his eyes blazed when he saw me. He was unchanged: that sharp intense gaze, the arrogant jaw, the military stance. He released a short, ragged breath, as if he'd been holding it ever since I left him and now, he could finally exhale. In Chinese, he breathed, "Jasmine."

I stepped backward. I felt flushed as if with a high fever, strung tight and vibrating with tension.

He held out his hand to me, palm up. Gently, he said, "I'm not angry. I'm so sorry for everything I did. Please, hear me out."

Out of the corner of my eye, I saw Brandon's head jerk back.

The sight of Wen's familiar face, the way he was looking at me with so much passion and tenderness, made a part of me want to relent like I had so many times before. He'd apologized. He would forgive me. He always did and he always would. All I'd have to do was believe his lies again. And so, I didn't move.

Rebecca's eyes were darting in between us, her brow furrowed. Even though she couldn't understand what we'd just said, she was an astute reader of tone and body language. "How do you know each other?"

Brandon crossed his arms, his face impassive.

"She is my wife," Wen said in English, keeping his eyes on me.

"I was not legally marry to you," I retorted. His eyebrows shot upward. He didn't understand that I was no longer the young girl who'd given him her heart, the one who cowered at his anger, the one who thought she was nothing without him. I saw now that although he'd done his best to control me, I had power over him too. I remembered the obsession in his eyes, the urgency in his hands. "I never go back with you."

Brandon and Rebecca were staring. He recovered first and turned to address Wen. "So you came here for her."

There was dawning sympathy in Rebecca's gaze as she considered me. "If Lucy's your wife, why did she leave you? What did you do to her?"

At Wen's silence, Brandon said, "Let's all go into the living room and talk this out." He led the way and the rest of us followed, though a part of me wanted to bolt out the front door. But Fiona was still in the house.

Once we were there, all the emotion of the past months burst out of me. Finally, Wen was here. I could vent my rage on the person who deserved it. In a low, intense voice, I spat out, "How could you do it?"

Wen drew himself up even straighter. "I had no other choice. You are furious with me, but I *saved* our baby from being killed. You were abandoned to die yourself. This way, she was able to survive and have a brand-new life here with parents who care for her."

"What?" Rebecca interjected, her face as pale as wax. "Who are you talking about?"

I ignored her. "You had choice! Instead, you give her away and not tell me. You say she was dead. We could have keep her and love her." My voice broke. "We could have be together."

Rebecca drew in her breath, a sharp, frightened sound. She staggered back and turned to Brandon, who looked stunned and haggard. So he hadn't known. They were beginning to understand. She was raking over my features. Now, for the first time, she saw me.

Wen bowed his head. "I understand that now. But I serve my country." He met my eyes then. "There are too many mouths to feed. We need to be a strong, powerful nation and the only way is to limit the population. I wanted an heir, a healthy son to continue our family line and to take care of us when we grow old." He took a deep breath. "Please, we will be a unit, just like you and I always wanted. The three of us. The plane tickets are in my pocket. We can go right now. I'll never hurt you again, my love."

Now I understood why he'd been speaking English. He wanted Rebecca and Brandon to hear everything. My breath hitched. He was offering me every daydream I'd had as a young girl, to have a little family with him.

A cry of rage from Brandon. "You're talking about taking *our* daughter?"

Rebecca's eyes were drenched in tears. She didn't seem to have registered Wen's words. She was fixated on me, now that she understood I was Fiona's mother. "Oh Lucy, I'm so sorry for the way I treated you. I didn't know who you were or what you must have been going through. Why didn't you tell us?"

"You would have fight me. You do anything to keep her."

She bit her lip. I could tell she wanted to deny what I'd said but wasn't sure if I was right or not.

"She can't fly without her parents' permission," Brandon said.

Wen smiled. "We *are* her parents and I have her Chinese passport to prove it. I have a friend who is very talented with documents."

Everything clicked into place. "Lone Wolf Jack," I breathed. "You two attack Brandon."

"Imagine my surprise when I saw a photo of you posted on social media by one of my high official friends." Those selfies that had been taken of me by the men Brandon had been courting at Opium. That was how Wen had found me. "I'd known you were alive after Nick mentioned you were taking classes at his studio. He kindly gave me your number. Then after I saw the photo, I got in touch with my contacts at the club. Lone Wolf Jack told me you'd gone into the Champagne Room."

Brandon had been staring at the man he thought was his friend with surprise and dismay but at this, anger hardened his face. "Come and try it again. Two on one, that's an easy win, isn't it?"

I said to Wen, "You report Opium to the police."

He nodded grimly. "No one touches you. I hoped you would wise up after I left you that message in Fiona's room."

"You watched me disarm the alarm," Brandon said. I could see him reasoning it out. "And that's why my keys are missing. I told you about Henrietta when I was interviewing you about Chinese ghost stories."

A chill ran through me. Wen had been so close to us this whole time. From the way Rebecca shuddered, I could tell she was thinking the same thing.

Wen continued. "I wanted to scare you into coming home and leaving the child here, but it'd become clear that you wouldn't leave her no matter what."

I thought about all that had happened. I pressed a hand against my mouth. "Did you push her?"

"No, of course not. That was a coincidence, I swear. She's a part of you, a piece of us. Please, let's start again. You won't need to run and hide. I'll take good care of you both and of your debt to the snakeheads too."

Rebecca said, "There is no way you can just take our child and leave. We need to let the courts sort this out."

Wen laughed, a dark, savage sound. "Your husband has an offense on the record for drug possession in China."

From the look of guilt and shame on Brandon's face, it was clear this was true. Rebecca's expression didn't change. She'd known.

"This is why he needed my assistance to adopt a child," Wen continued.

"You asshole," Brandon gritted out. "We'd been friends since we were little. I asked for your help because of the drug charge but I had no idea what you'd do." He turned to me. "I am so sorry. I would never have agreed if I'd known. I thought Fifi was truly an orphan with no family. And those drugs weren't mine. I still have no idea how they wound up in my jacket."

"He did it," Rebecca said, her clear eyes fixed on Wen. "Right? I bet they were his and he didn't want to get caught himself."

Wen gave her a little nod. "No one will believe you. Brandon, my friend, I trusted you with my own daughter. Furthermore, if this shady adoption comes to light, allegations of child trafficking could be made. I will be safely back in China, and I have many others I could blame. But you, your reputations and your careers will be ruined. What will people think of you? And who knows, the police might even get involved."

Brandon and Rebecca looked serious. His job at Columbia, her career, their glittering friends and parties, their families. Everything they'd built up through talent, hard work, ambition, and privilege. Everyone who'd ever met them would reconstruct everything they thought they'd known about them. Not to mention possible legal trouble if the police took the child trafficking allegations seriously.

There was a glint in Wen's eyes. "We will simply undo a wrong. The girl should never have been adopted. Her true parents will take her home. You will go on with your beautiful American lives and everyone will be satisfied. This is the only path that allows you to preserve appearances."

The old, scared part of me wanted what he was offering. I wouldn't need to toil at clubs like Opium to make ends meet. I could be with my husband and daughter, accepted as an upstanding member of our village. I wouldn't need to be on the run. Fiona and I would be together. With Wen. Yes, I would be with my child, but at what price? I thought about what I'd overheard Rebecca saying to Fiona on her birthday, about giving her choices when she grows up. I remembered Anthony telling me that if I ever unleashed myself, my talent would shine brighter than the sun. Anthony, his warmth, honesty, and generosity. Wen was a meticulous planner. That was one of the things I'd most admired about him. And this new leaf he'd turned over was the next step in his plan. He tried scaring me back into his arms. He tried threatening me with Fiona. Wen had figured out that she was the key to my soul. If he controlled her, he had me. If I accepted his deal, we would never be free again.

Rebecca and Brandon exchanged a look, communicating with each other in that nonverbal way that people who have loved one another for years possess.

He said to her in a low voice, "I'm so sorry for all I did."

"Me too," she said, her eyes bright. "I made so many mistakes."

When she looked at me and gave a slight, firm shake of her head, I understood.

"No one agree," I said. "I rather leave Fiona with Rebecca and Brandon. They love her. She only a hostage for you."

"Go ahead and destroy our reputations," Rebecca said to Wen. "You are not taking our child."

Wen was staring at us, caught off guard. He didn't like being out of control. I held my breath. He was dangerous when he felt cornered.

Brandon stepped forward, his fists clenched. "Now get the hell out of our house."

The men faced off, both of them strong and broad. Wen didn't back away, so Brandon grabbed him by the shirt to physically throw him out the door, but Wen threw a punch that slammed into Brandon's stomach. Recovering lightning fast, Brandon flattened Wen with an uppercut to his jaw. Wen smashed against the wall.

Then the hairs on the back of my neck rose when Wen pulled a dark object out of his pocket. "Don't move."

THIRTY-EIGHT

Rebecca

At the sight of the gun in Wen's hands, Rebecca steadies. The world goes cold, clear, and precise. *Please, let Brandon not do anything stupid.* Lucy is staring at Wen. She's removed her glasses, which now lie on the ground, forgotten, and Rebecca is astonished by the sharp harmony of her features. This is Rebecca's fault. She never imagined Lucy could have any right to Fifi, only that her nanny was trying to steal her husband and ruin her career. Lucy hasn't been challenging Rebecca; she'd been protecting Fifi, her child. How can she blame Lucy for loving her daughter? Rebecca's been all too ready to believe the worst of her Chinese-speaking nanny. How much had Lucy's race and class informed her distrust?

Now Rebecca's entire family is in jeopardy.

Wen is furious. The anger has erupted in red blotches across the surface of his skin. She can read him like a book. He's been thwarted, and like a child he'll smash everything in his vicinity if necessary. If he can't have Lucy, then no one will. He keeps the gun trained on Brandon, who is backing away with his hands in the air. She narrows her eyes. It's a Glock 19, a semiautomatic handgun. There's no manual safety, no need to cock the hammer before he fires. He's holding it easily, like someone who's comfortable with the weapon and knows how to use it.

Wen pulls out a set of handcuffs wrapped in a handkerchief with his other hand. *He's thought about the fingerprints*, she realizes, terror leaping into her throat. *He came prepared to kill.*

He turns to her. "Rebecca, will you be so kind as to come here?"

When Brandon bares his teeth, ready to rush him no matter what, Wen says, "Don't worry. I won't hurt your wife. I just need her to help me."

She steps closer. Wild thoughts of attacking him cross her mind but she doesn't dare take the risk, not with Brandon and Lucy in the room. Wen's eyes don't waver from Brandon as he passes her the handcuffs. "Chain your husband to the radiator and everything will be all right."

He keeps the two of them in front of him, watches as she reluctantly closes the cuffs around Brandon's wrists and the pipe next to the wall. He checks that the handcuffs are tight enough so Brandon can't get loose, then has her precede him as he walks to the door, where Lucy is hunched over, terrified, both hands shoved deep in the pockets of her pants. He addresses her. "Go upstairs and get Fiona."

Lucy raises her head and straightens her shoulders. "No."

Surprise flickers over Wen's face. A cold brutality overtakes his features. As if in slow motion, he hits the small slide release on the side of the pistol, right above the trigger, and releases the slide. Rebecca stops breathing, panic smothering her. The Glock's loaded and ready to shoot.

"May I watch a movie on my iPad?" Fifi's childish voice from upstairs.

They all freeze.

Rebecca calls up, trying to keep her voice steady, "Go ahead, honey." Her eyes meet Lucy's and she understands. Instead of being separated by their differences, they now realize how similar they are: They're both mothers. They'll do anything necessary to protect their daughter.

He points the gun at Lucy. "Tell her to come downstairs."

She snarls, "Never."

He grabs her arm. She pulls back. There's a brief tussle and then he has her in a headlock. Rebecca gives a little cry of horror. But Lucy pivots and does something with her leg and now Wen is crashing onto the floor. Lucy's mouth is wide and she's screaming, but Rebecca can't hear her. It's as if they're all underwater, everything moving at half speed—the frenzied swing of Lucy's hair as she blurs, lurching away. Rebecca, who has spent so much more time aiming down the barrel of a gun than staring into its muzzle, has her eyes fixed on the black, deadly weapon and sees with the accuracy of a sharpshooter where that bullet is headed: right into Lucy's chest.

Rebecca lunges in front of her and the world explodes. Thunder shakes her. Searing pain shatters her body. There's a spray of blood but she feels no fear. Her eyes are wide open, fixed on Lucy, who is unhurt. She snaps her head around to find Wen jumping on Lucy and grappling with her—that gun can fire again and again until everyone Rebecca loves is dead. She sees it go flying, skittering across the floor. Wen scrambles for it. He's bigger and stronger than Lucy. Rebecca is wounded, Brandon chained to the radiator, yelling a stream of obscenities.

Wen has grabbed the gun, he's whirling around. They're all dead.

The world explodes a second time.

The house is utterly silent, as if the blast has sucked all sound from the world. Rebecca tries to get up, to do what, she's not sure. She has some idea of shielding Lucy or Brandon. Her head is spinning. Where is Wen? She's in a half crouch but there's something wrong with her shoulder; she can't seem to move it. She manages to focus on Lucy, who is standing in front of her, dangling Rebecca's gun from her fingertips.

"I take from jewelry safe." Lucy's face is spattered with blood. "Just in case."

Wen is lying on the floor, eyes sightless, a part of his jaw blown off, a lake of blood spreading around his body.

"Who would have thought he'd have so much blood in him?" Rebecca murmurs mindlessly.

She is trying not to breathe through her nostrils. Even so, she can taste the stench in the room. She's so cold, she's convulsing uncontrollably. Brandon. There he is, he's about to yank the radiator out of the wall but he's safe.

Lucy places the gun gingerly on the coffee table, then staggers over to the sink in the kitchen. She vomits, retching. When she returns, Rebecca can see her tears dripping into her parted lips. She bends down over Wen's body. Her shoulders are heaving. She sniffs, then wipes her sleeve over her face. She plucks a set of keys out of Wen's pocket. She goes to Brandon and unlocks him.

He rushes past Lucy to gather Rebecca in his arms. "Oh, my love. You're hurt." There's blind panic in his eyes. He's patting her down with rough hands, checking if she's wounded elsewhere, blood trickling onto the floor. She's starting to feel light-headed, but she knows she can't lose consciousness yet. He chokes out, "It looks like the bullet hit your upper arm, but it's not lodged in you, thank goodness."

Lucy has returned with the first aid kit they keep in the kitchen, and now she's pressing sterile gauze against Rebecca's wound to stanch the bleeding. "Wen make mistake."

"What do you mean?" Rebecca asks, trying not to flinch at the pain.

"He think Brandon is only dangerous one here."

Through the fog that seems to be permeating everything, Rebecca realizes that Lucy's hands are covered in blood, Wen's blood. "You did what you had to."

Lucy's golden brown eyes are haunted. "I loved him. The police arrest me."

"No," Brandon says. "It was self-defense. We'll testify for you."

"But I am foreigner. I not speak English good. I work illegal at strip club, with Chinese mafia. I lie, you not know who I really am. And I kill somebody. Police not treat me like they treat you." She sounds despairing, her voice high and stretched.

Outside, they can hear sirens in the distance. The neighbors must have heard the gunshots. The police will be here any moment.

Rebecca's and Brandon's eyes meet. She thinks about Lucy, this woman who was at first invisible to her, then appeared to be her enemy. Rebecca had never truly seen her because she didn't bother to look. Plus, there were so many things she also chose not to notice in her own daughter, whom she'd sometimes used to impress others. The way the other kids teased Fifi, how she disliked ballet and Rebecca forced her to continue, her questions about her own heritage. Rebecca thinks about how she'd thought she was the great white savior when all along, Fifi has been saving her.

"Give me the gun," she says. When he hands it to her, she wipes off Lucy's fingerprints. At Lucy's astonished stare, she says, "I did it. It's my weapon. You weren't even here. You had nothing to do with it."

Lucy's mouth is open. "But you-you, maybe they say you murder him. Your name, your reputation."

Rebecca's lips twitch in a rueful smile. "My life has gone to hell for any number of reasons at this point. It's not going to matter much if suspected murder is added to them."

Brandon stares at her. "Are you sure about this?"

She nods. "Don't worry about me. I'm a white, well-educated woman attacked in my own home, defending my husband and child. No jury in the world is going to convict me. But I wonder if you should disappear for a while, Lucy. If they find any DNA of yours on him, they will investigate. They'll question you and almost certainly discover your connection to him. We can help you—"

"Mommy!" There's a scream from the doorway. Fifi. She dashes over to Rebecca. "You're bleeding!"

"It's all right, sweetie," Rebecca says. Fifi burrows into her side and she cradles her with her uninjured arm.

Lucy is watching the two of them. "I go back to China."

Rebecca's chest winds up as tight as a spring. "But what about—"

"She does not belong to me. She belong to herself. And the life I want for her, to be safe and loved, I cannot give. If I take her now, I make her lose her mother and father. I just kill her birth father. I can only bring her pain now." Lucy's voice is hoarse, her eyes wet and luminous as stars. She pulls out a glittering jade hairpin from her pocket and places it into Rebecca's palm. "This is for her. I come back when she is ready. I trust you. Take care of her for me."

Choking back tears, Rebecca promises, "We will." Fifi is looking back and forth between them, confused.

Lucy gathers Fifi in her arms and places her cheek against the top of her daughter's hair. When she looks at Rebecca, reflected in her eyes is her grief at all the years of Fifi's life that she'll miss. "Sunday is Mother's Day. Give her a kiss for me."

THIRTY-NINE

Jasmine

When Anthony strode onto the Brooklyn Promenade the next day, his eyes passed right over me. I walked toward him. It wasn't until I was within a few meters that his gaze snagged on me. I wasn't wearing anything nearly as provocative as my costume from Opium, but I was in a jade shirt and a pair of formfitting jeans. My hair was loose down my back, hanging in waves to my waist. I'd unpinned my bangs and wore light makeup that brought out the radiance in my eyes.

"You-you look different," he stuttered.

Suddenly, I was insecure again. I bit my lip. "In a good way?"

"Absolutely." He stretched out a hand as if he wanted to take mine in his but then stopped himself. He looked at me searchingly and there was so much sadness lining his face, it broke my heart. "Do you really need to leave?"

I nodded, then reached out and hooked my arm through his. "A part of me will always be here. And I'm glad you'll be able to finish college in a few years. Let's talk."

I led him to an empty bench and started to tell him everything. His mouth was agape, and his eyebrows had long disappeared. When I reached the part where Wen fired the gun and I shot him, my voice faltered.

Anthony gathered me in his arms. "I wish I'd been there."

I leaned my head against his solid shoulder, inhaling the clean sandalwood scent of him.

"I'm so sorry you had to go through that alone."

"I thought I was going to die. And I'd wondered before, what would I hang on to at that moment? If I had to leave this life, what is it that the deepest part of me would grieve the most?"

He'd drawn back and was staring at me with an intensity that made me blush. My hands twisted in my shirt. "Fiona, of course, but also you. I wished I'd had more time with you."

He was holding so still, as if willing me to keep talking, so I did. "You have to understand, Wen was the first man in my life. I thought I loved him, that he loved me. I didn't know any better. But what he felt for me wasn't love. It was obsession. I was an object to him, a possession to give him face." I felt my shoulders loosen as I finally said the words. "And after I broke away from him, I told myself that every man was like that. I thought the way I looked was the only thing that mattered, for good or for bad. Instead of developing myself with art or English or cooking lessons, I used my appearance to make fast money. What I didn't understand was that I was the one who was incapable of love. Until I saw you again and you changed everything for me. Even though I didn't want to admit it, you've always cared for me because of who I am, not because of what I could do for you or what I looked like."

He wasn't breathing. His arms were braced around me, every muscle tense. His gaze was trained on me with fierce concentration. "What are you saying, Jasmine?"

Finally, I said it. "I love you, Anthony. Though I understand that maybe—"

His hold on me tightened until I couldn't escape even if I wanted to, and then he was kissing me, long and devouring and deep. I made a small noise and he growled in response, shifting my head so that he could plunder my lips. There was no more holding back, no more hesitancy.

He trailed a line of kisses behind my ear, down my throat, and then he pulled back to gaze into my eyes. "You smell like meadows. I've been in love with you forever. I've just been waiting for you to catch up."

The golden sky stretched above us on the promenade, wide and open as a beckoning hand. I was there to say goodbye to him and yet, the expansive heavens made me feel as if anything were possible, even for us, two immigrants. It seemed as if the doors to the Beautiful Country had cracked open, as if we too might partake of this land of plenty. I was blinking back tears when I realized that he'd put a velvet pouch in my palm, the sort that jewelers use. I slowly undid the zipper and gasped.

Inside was a finely braided bracelet of red thread, the twin of the one I'd made for him, down to the colorful knots of string in green, yellow, turquoise, and orange set off by dark gold strands.

"But . . . but you were so clumsy," I said, my voice thick.

"I grew up," he said simply. He took my hand and tied the bracelet around my wrist. It fit perfectly.

I gazed at our intertwined fingers, our matching bracelets. "I still have to go."

"I know." His voice was hoarse. "What will you do?"

I breathed in deeply. "I'm going to find out who I can be. Discover my passions, embrace all of them. But I'll miss you and Fiona, every moment. I'll be back someday and next time, I'll do it legally."

He tilted my chin up. "I can apply for citizenship in a few years. I've waited for you this long. I'll wait for you forever."

I framed his face in my hands. "I choose you."

Fiona

May 8, 2022, Mother's Day

It's a beautiful day. Fiona looks down the tree-lined street. The house looks similar to the one she grew up in, the garden apartment downstairs, the steps leading up to the main entrance. She turned twenty-one a few days ago.

She rubs the bridge of her nose nervously, even though she exchanged her glasses for contact lenses years ago. She only vaguely remembers the day that man threatened them and was killed by her mother. The incident turned her mom into a heroine. Everyone admired the woman who shot the intruder with her own hands, despite being wounded herself.

Nevertheless, her mother had been fired from her previous position. She started her own independent editorial company. Fiona's father is a tenured professor of Chinese at Columbia, and her parents still take long walks through Central Park, arms entwined around each other's waists like young lovers. After that day, however, her mom never kept a gun in the house again. Fiona's in college now, doing a dual major in

East Asian studies and visual arts. She's not sure yet what she'll do with her life, but she's got plenty of choices.

She's always wondered about her biological parents. Her mother said she needed to be older before she heard the full story, though she knew her mom shared photos of her and other tidbits with her birth mother.

Now she understands that her birth mother was her nanny from when she was five years old. She remembers and loves Jasmine, who made the most beautiful drawings, and inspired Fiona's own love of art. They'd exchanged sketches, cards, and letters for years. She didn't know until a few days ago that Jasmine was the one who shot her biological father, though. She didn't realize that Jasmine had originally wanted to take her away from her parents. After Jasmine left, Fiona didn't have to take ballet anymore. Instead, she was enrolled in Chinese dance, which she loved. Sometimes she heard her mother arguing with her grandmother when her grandmother became too critical. Her parents also started calling her Fiona and not Fifi, and her mother began taking Chinese lessons, for which her mom had no talent whatsoever, but she persevered. They traveled all over Asia.

But no matter how hard her parents try, they aren't Chinese and never will be. Not being the same race as her parents hasn't been easy but they'd listened when she came home with stories of being teased. She appreciates the serious and sustained effort her parents have made to raise her with pride in her race and culture. Being Chinese is an essential and positive part of who she is—and yet there was no checklist her parents could tick off that would ever alleviate the grief she felt at being abandoned by her birth parents. She had wondered for a long time: Did her birth mother love her? Why had she been given away? Now she knows. And she's here. She touches the jade pomegranate hairpin in her hair, which Jasmine had left for her.

She climbs the stairs slowly. The door is made of wood, inset with glass panels. She cups her hands around her eyes and peers inside. There's framed artwork all along the hallway: drawings, paintings. There appear to be a series of self-portraits of a beautiful woman. A worn classical guitar leans against the railing of the stairs.

There's movement. Fiona almost draws back, except she's too curious. A man enters, laughing, followed by a woman cradling a baby. Fiona's breath hitches. It's Jasmine. After all these years, she recognizes her former nanny, her birth mother, immediately. Jasmine's face is glowing with happiness. She gives the baby a tender kiss on its head while the man looks at them both with devotion.

Fiona feels tears prick her eyes. She raises her hand and rings the doorbell.

ACKNOWLEDGMENTS

First, I have to thank the two women without whom this book would not have been possible. I will always be grateful to my brilliant agent, Suzanne Gluck at William Morris Endeavor, who plucked me out of the slush pile all those years ago, and has guided my career with her unerring intelligence ever since. Jessica Williams, my editor at William Morrow/HarperCollins, is my light in the darkness and has helped me shape my work with her phenomenal insight.

I'm so fortunate to be supported by a magnificent team of agents at William Morris Endeavor, including my fantastic film agent Anna DeRoy, legal genius Lara Bahr, and queen of foreign rights Tracy Fisher and her entire team, especially Fiona Baird and James Munro, who also helped me iron out the Frankfurt plot. Nina Iandolo and Andrea Blatt, thank you for being treasures. Alysyn Reinhardt, my speaking agent at Penguin Random House Speakers Bureau, is so good at her job that she makes everything seem effortless.

Everyone at William Morrow, I can't believe how lucky I am to be a part of the family. You're so passionate and enthusiastic about your authors and their books, moving mountains to help us thrive. I'm indebted to our publisher, Liate Stehlik, who leads with grace and clarity, our dazzling associate publisher, Jennifer Hart, our superb head of marketing and publicity Kelly Rudolph, our fantastic associate director of publicity and my brilliant publicist Eliza Rosenberry, the endlessly creative Sharyn Rosenblum and Holly Rice, marketing geniuses Rachel Berquist and Tavia Kowalchuk, and the rest of the incredible publicity and marketing departments. Julia Elliott, thank you for being absolutely wonderful and all that you have done for me. I have to smile every time I think of the phenomenal library and academic marketing team: Virginia Stanley, Lainey Mays, Grace Caternolo, and Kim Racon. You all rock. Andy LeCount and Mary Beth Thomas, who spearhead our brilliant sales force, we authors owe you and your hardworking teams, and you can count on me for free food anytime. All my gratitude to my copyeditors, the production department, Kyle O'Brien for the lovely interior design, Ploy Siripant for the breathtaking cover, and everyone else at HarperCollins who helped bring this book into the world.

In the writing of this novel, I have to thank Angie Kim, who read every word almost as soon as it was written. Angie, it was such a joy to write our books at the same time and I'll always be grateful for your insight, advice, and support. Danielle Trussoni is an inspiration to me in every way and I'm so glad for our friendship. Wendy Walker is not only a fantastic friend but such a smart reader. Ruth Ellenson, I don't know what I'd do without you. I've been through thick and thin with the brilliant Julia Phillips. Helen Wan, who else could I ask for advice about Netflix galas? Janelle Brown, James Han Mattson, and Tim Weed, thank you for your insightful feedback on my work. Kimberly Belle, here's to more drinks in Amsterdam. There's a special place in my heart for Caroline Leavitt, thank you for listening to me. Jillian Cantor, Melanie Benjamin, Chloe Benjamin, Meg Waite Clayton, Patricia Park, Lan Samantha Chang: I love you and you're amazing. Cathy Yardley, you are brilliant and scary (in a good way). Thanks also to Gretchen Stelter and Andrea Robinson.

I owe a great debt to the glorious Marilyn Ducksworth, who has been my dear friend and adviser from the very beginning of my career.

Here's to Miwa Messer, force of nature, who has been championing great books for years at Barnes & Noble. The magnificent Zibby Owens does so much for authors on every front, from publishing to *Good Morning America*. Robin Kall, your enthusiasm and love for books and authors in Reading with Robin is incredible. Carol Fitzgerald of *BookReporter*, thank you for your tireless and insightful work on the behalf of authors. Jenna Bush Hager, your Read with Jenna picks have changed not only my life but that of so many authors. We are eternally grateful.

I never could have written this novel without interviewing so many wonderful people who inspired me with their stories. You taught me about rural China, strip clubs, animal shelters, designer clothing, language prodigies, guns, editors, martial arts, self-defense, legal rights, Chinese dance, elementary schools, and so much more. I'm extremely grateful to Janie Chang, Jason Criss, Gale Criss, Eton Kwok, Jaime Kwok, Elise Crull, John Dubrule, Janice Fung, Gwendolyn Starda, Lao Hu, Jack Shamburger, Chun Pong Tung, Debra Voulgaris, and Bella Wexler. Anna Lora-Wainwright, thank you for your phenomenal field research. Tonio Andrade, language genius supreme, you enlightened me. Annissa and John Armstrong, your insights were so helpful. Lauren Levato Coyne, your art is an inspiration. Rachel Kahan, I loved our in-depth talks that taught me so much. Emily Nolan, you are my fashion guru and thank you for dressing my characters. Jennifer Kular and the Well Travelled Kitchen, you are the thoughtful creator of all the delicious food in the novel. I appreciate very much the help of Sanneke van Vliet and Marja van Vliet-Barnhoorn.

Special thanks to Kim Palmer Mitchell for her contribution to We Need Diverse Books. Also all my gratitude to lovely Jeanna Park and her dogs. I'm indebted to all the fine folks at Ragdale and to the London Writers' Salon for their support (see you at Writers' Hour).

And finally, here's to my dear friends: JP and Katrina Middelburg, who have always been there for me; David Lau and Rob Wu, who literally took me to the races; Lillie Gertenaar, part beauty technician, part therapist; and my oldest friends, Suzanne Campbell, Sari Wilson, Alex Kahn, and Julie Voshell. Love to the entire Kwok family and to the cats for sitting on me while I'm writing: Sushi, Couscous, Mona, Lisa, and our three-colored Calypso, who plays a role in this novel. Most of all, I'm grateful to my two sons, Stefan and Milan, for bringing so much joy to my life. I'm so proud of you and I love you.

Jean Kwok is the *New York Times* and internationally bestselling author of *Searching for Sylvie Lee*, *Girl in Translation*, and *Mambo in Chinatown*. Her work has been published in twenty countries and is taught in universities, colleges, and high schools across the world. She has been selected for numerous honors, including the American Library Association Alex Award, the Chinese American Librarians Association Best Book Award, and the *Sunday Times* EFG Short Story Award international short list. She is fluent in Chinese, Dutch, and English, and divides her time between the Netherlands and New York City.